echoes of man

navi' robins

Echoes of Man

© 2024 by Navi' Robins

NorthShore Publishing House, Inc.

ISBN:

Book cover design by: Navi' Robins www.navirobins.net

Interior design by: Navi' Robins www.navirobins.net

Building a better world comes with a harsh truth: it must rise from the ashes and bones of the old one.

Prologue:

The Last Breath of Mankind

The world's end came not with the blinding flash of bombs, but with a whisper—a slow, insidious death that slipped through the cracks of humanity's defenses, wrapping its unseen tendrils around the throat of civilization. It strangled slowly, methodically, until every last man lay cold and silent, eyes wide with the stunned realization of his own extinction.

In the year 2174, the clash of steel or the thunderous roar of artillery did not mark the final days of World War III. No mushroom clouds were blossoming in the distance, and no shattered cities crumbling into dust. Instead, it came with a breath—a quiet, suffocating exhale that swept across continents like a shadow. The rattle of dying breaths filled the air, unnoticed at first, but soon, it was the only sound left.

There were no screams. No panicked cries for help. The virus moved too quickly for that. It was a silent killer, slipping into the bloodstreams of men and boys, slipping into their homes, their barracks, and their battlefields. And then, one by one, it stole their voices.

It began as a cough—a single, sharp exhale of discomfort. Within hours, the fever set in, burning like wildfire through veins. But death was swift, too swift to allow time for grief. In cities and villages, in war zones and shelters, men simply fell where they stood, collapsed into the dust, their bodies littering the ground like discarded shells of a species that had run its course.

For months, the world reeled in disbelief, nations frantically scrambling to comprehend the nightmare unfolding before their eyes. Hospitals overflowed, battlefields became eerie graveyards as soldiers dropped mid-march, and governments, powerless and terrified, fell to their knees as they watched their male population die in waves. There was no explanation, no warning—just empty streets and lifeless bodies. Fathers, sons, brothers, lovers. Gone.

The virus had no name at first. It didn't need one. It was a force of nature, primal and unstoppable. Only when the scientific community finally dissected the truth did the name emerge, cold and clinical in its finality: The Y Chromosome Virus—an assassin designed by nature to target only one thing. The Y chromosome.

No bombs, no radiation. Just an invisible specter, woven into the very fabric of the world's DNA, lurking in the shadows of human biology for God knows how long, waiting for its moment. And within six months of its first appearance, it had wiped out half of humanity—every last man and boy on Earth. Extinct, like a species that had outlived its usefulness.

In the aftermath, as the last breath of mankind faded from the earth, the cities of the world stood still. Places like New Lagos—once a roaring, bustling metropolis filled with life and sound—became mausoleums. Skyscrapers, once shimmering beacons of human ambition, now loomed like silent tombstones over empty streets. The air seemed thicker, the sky lower, as if the planet itself was mourning.

In those desperate days, women wandered the streets in dazed confusion, eyes hollow and tear streaked as they clutched the bodies of their husbands, brothers, and sons, cradling them as though their warmth might still return. But the men were cold. Their flesh had lost the memory of life.

And so, the world that had once belonged to men fell into the hands of women—those who had been spared, untouched by the virus that had erased the Y chromosome from the face of the earth. They stood on the precipice of a new reality, staring into the abyss left behind. And they knew one truth, clear and unshakable: life had to go on.

The Council of Mothers emerged from the ruins of civilization, a coalition of scientists, leaders, and survivors, who knew that the world must continue. The old systems of governance, the old ways of war, were obsolete. In their place rose a new order—a world without men, where life would be sustained through science.

The vast stores of frozen male sperm, preserved in cryogenic vaults long before the fall, became the last lifeline of a species teetering on the edge of extinction. Laboratories became the new temples, where artificial insemination and genetic manipulation took the place of natural conception. The children born in these sterile chambers were daughters, always daughters—engineered to be stronger, smarter, and more resilient than their forebears. They quickly and ruthlessly eliminated any sign of the Y chromosome reemerging. The flaws of the past, the violence, the hunger, were systematically erased from the gene pool.

A new world had risen from the ashes of the old, and in this matriarchy, peace and order reigned. The cities thrummed with the quiet hum of efficiency. The streets, once stained with war and blood, were clean, orderly, and controlled.

But beneath the surface of this utopia, something darker stirred.

Whispers emerged from the edges of society, rumors that spread like wildfire through the ranks of the Council's scientists. Genetic anomalies in some of the most recent births. Children born not perfect and strong, but sickly, malformed creatures that should not have been. Quietly, these whispers were silenced. Births that went wrong were erased from records; mothers were reassigned to distant colonies.

But the anomalies did not stop. And then came the first death.

In a sterile, gleaming birthing chamber in New Lagos, a mother died—torn apart by the child she had carried. The attending physicians never spoke of what they saw. The screams, the blood, the thing that crawled from the birthing pod with wide, black eyes and hunger in its bones. But word spread, as it always does, and soon, the Council of Mothers could no longer ignore the truth.

The virus—the Y Chromosome Virus that had wiped out the men—was not dead.

It had mutated. It had learned. And now, it was infecting the very DNA stored in the vaults, corrupting the genetic material that had once been the key to humanity's survival. The children born from these vaults were no longer human. They were something else. Something darker. Something ravenous.

As the Council scrambled to contain the outbreak, to maintain the fragile order they had built, another realization came—one that would shatter their carefully constructed world.

The only cure for the mutation, the only way to stop the virus, lay in the DNA of the one thing they no longer had access to: a living man.

The Matriarchy had spared no effort in its campaign to eradicate men from existence. Following the spread of the Y Chromosome virus and the rise of The Matriarchy, squads of elite hunters were dispatched across continents, each meticulously trained to track and eliminate any males born after the virus went dormant. With unyielding resolve, they scoured cities, razed hidden shelters, and purged underground colonies where men had sought refuge.

No place was safe; dense forests, desolate wastelands, and mountain hideouts were all combed with ruthless precision. Every remnant of a world where men had once ruled was systematically erased, their existence reduced to scattered bones buried beneath layers of earth. Those who survived the virus were either executed or driven so far into hiding that they became myths in their own time, their presence nothing more than fleeting whispers among the Sisterhood. The few remaining males became experts in concealment, slipping into the shadows, crafting new lives in isolation, cut off from any society.

Generations passed, and the presence of men became as repulsed as the history of the world men once ruled. The Matriarchy believed the world was finally cleansed, that their brutal efficiency had extinguished every trace of men. Men became a legend, a cautionary tale, a relic of a distant past that no longer belonged to this new, unbroken world.

But somewhere, in the wilderness beyond the controlled borders of the cities, there was a secret. A boy, now grown into a man, hidden from the world that had forgotten him. The son of a woman who had fled New Lagos, unable to allow the life growing inside her to be terminated, her child born in the shadow of extinction.

Now, that man was their last hope.

And the hunt was on.

Chapter 1:

The City of Goddesses

The sun, a soft orb of golden light, crept over the horizon, casting a radiant glow over the domed city of New Lagos. Its warm rays kissed the towering spires of glass and steel, illuminating the harmonious world below. The magnificent dome, a shimmering shield of translucent energy, glistened in the dawn, protecting its inhabitants from the unrelenting wilderness that lay beyond its borders. Inside, the city was a paradise—a testament to the power of women who had rebuilt the world in their own image, a world without men.

In the centuries since the fall of man, life has transcended the need for struggle. There were no jobs in this new world, only passions. Women pursued what their hearts desired—art, science, exploration, healing—freed from the shackles of survival and scarcity. The streets below were filled with vibrant greenery and gardens, with no need for cars or pollution. The air was crisp and pure, carrying with it the scent of blooming flowers. There were no hideous skyscrapers that loomed oppressively over the earth, phalluses that invaded the sky as worship of men's unrelenting egos; instead, there were tall reflective structures, sleek and curved, appearing to grow out of the ground as if they were part of nature itself.

There was no poverty here, no corporate greed or towering oligarchies. Women were their own deities, their own rulers. So, religion was obsolete and as useless as the ways of the old world. There was no money because there was no need for it. Resources flowed abundantly, and everything one could ever want was given freely. The daughters of this new utopia had millions of mothers—there were no orphans, no lost children. Each woman was a sister, and each child belonged to every woman. They lived and died knowing they were deeply, inherently loved.

And fear? Rejection? Those were relics of a brutal past. The very fabric of the world had been rewoven, erasing the scars of a time when oppression had been justified under the guise of progress. These women knew nothing of wars or conflicts, of political squabbles that tore nations apart. They were stronger, smarter, and more beautiful than any generation that came before them. Their beauty was not measured by any shallow, external standards but was something inherent—an unspoken confidence, an inner fire, and a grace that could stop the wind.

In the heart of the city, high above the gleaming spires and bustling streets, Mara stirred from her sleep. The first rays of dawn filtered through the floor-to-ceiling windows of her high-rise, casting a soft glow across her dark, flawless skin. She did not wake with grogginess or hesitation; such vulnerabilities had been engineered out of her long ago. Her mind was a fortress, unbreakable and unyielding, her body a weapon honed to perfection.

As she rose, her bare feet met the cool marble floor with silent precision, and she inhaled deeply, savoring the crisp, purified air that filled her lungs. Mara's presence alone commanded attention—a woman in her mid-thirties, though in truth, her age was unmarked by time. In this world, the effects of age were muted; genetic advancements allowed women to live for centuries, youth preserved until they were well into their two hundredth year.

Mara's beauty was both striking and disarming. Her skin, a deep ebony that seemed to drink in the light, was flawless, her high cheekbones sculpted as if by the hands of an artist. Her long, thick braids fell past her shoulders, framing a face that was both hauntingly beautiful and unsettlingly fierce. Her brown eyes, sharp and piercing, held an intensity that few could meet without faltering. A body genetically crafted for combat. Her musculature was both lean and powerful, with curves that softened her otherwise imposing presence.

She moved with an effortless grace that belied her strength, each step as calculated as a predator stalking its prey. Every detail of her was a testament to the Matriarchy's genetic engineering—a blend of beauty and lethality designed to captivate and intimidate in equal measure. Mara had long learned that her beauty was as much a tool as her physical prowess, a weapon that could disarm even the most resilient opponents.

As she gazed out at the sprawling city below, her senses sharpened, fully awake and attuned to the rhythms of life around her. This was her domain, a place where she was both protector and weapon, her every breath a reminder of the power she held and the vigilance required to wield it.

In one fluid motion, she stretched, her muscles taut and defined, her limbs extending into impossible shapes. It was her morning ritual—one that connected her to the ancient traditions of women who had long since passed. Her poses— each a testament to her strength—were impossible for any normal human. She bent at angles that defied the laws of physics, her body balanced delicately on the tips of her fingers, her legs stretched in perfect arcs above her head. She held these stances as effortlessly as if she were breathing. This was her concentration, her devotion—her version of prayer.

In a single breath, she shifted from her concentration routine into her martial arts practice. Her movements became a dance, elegant yet deadly, her body slicing through the air with the grace of a ballerina and the precision of a surgeon. Each strike, each kick, was performed with lethal intent, though her face remained serene, calm, as if she were simply moving through water. And then, with a fluid motion, she unsheathed her sword—the curved, gleaming blade of a Phantom Hunter. She moved like the wind, her body spinning, flipping, leaping with unnatural agility, the sword a natural extension of her.

As she finished her morning practice, she stood tall; the sword held steady in her hand. There was no rush. Life here had no deadlines, no rush hours. The city outside her window was alive with serenity.

Across the city, far from the high-rise towers, near the edge of a crystal-clear lake that shimmered under the morning sun, Imani sat in serene concentration, sipping from a glass of cool water as she studied the holo-screen before her. She was a vision of understated power, her brown skin catching the soft sunlight, lending her an almost ethereal glow. Her hair, an exquisite afro, framed her face like a crown, each curl carefully tended, perfectly reflecting her meticulous nature.

Imani's eyes, a striking shade of hazel, seemed almost alive with intensity as they scanned the data streaming across the screen. Her mind processed the intricate patterns faster than any supercomputer, piecing together genetic sequences with a speed and accuracy that was nothing short of astonishing. This ability—this brilliant, rapid cognition—was the result of the council's genetic program, a design to create minds that could keep pace with the endless flow of information and the challenges of a world built on scientific prowess.

To Imani, this was more than work; it was an art. She studied each DNA strand with fascination, her attention absorbed in the elegant glow of sequenced patterns flashing on the screen. She knew the intricacies of each genetic code intimately, understanding every nuance, every possibility within the strands. This was her passion, the essence of her purpose, something far removed from the mundanity of labor in the old world. Here, in this society, her work was a form of creation, a means to push the boundaries of human potential.

As she studied the data stream on the screen, her gaze occasionally drifting to its tranquil waters, Imani appeared a figure of calm control. But beneath that composed exterior lay a mind relentlessly ticking, advancing the Matriarchy's genetic pursuits. Her existence was a testament to the power of evolution—not just in biology, but in the very fabric of their society. And for Imani, every strand of DNA was a step toward unlocking a new future, one meticulously engineered to perfection.

Her home, a Lakehouse that mirrored the serenity of the waters surrounding it, was quiet, save for the soft chirping of birds that had made their nests in the nearby trees. There was no urgency to her actions, no weight of expectation bearing down on her. She had chosen this life, this path, because it fulfilled her. She did not have to worry about survival or the politics of the old world. Every woman here was free to pursue her curiosity, her creativity, her desires.

When she finished reviewing the data, Imani rose, stepping outside onto the glass-like surface of the dock that led out onto the lake. The water was still, reflecting the sky above like a perfect mirror. She inhaled deeply, savoring the fresh, cool air before heading to the nearby station to board the maglev train into the city. As she walked, she passed women of all shapes, sizes, and colors, each more beautiful than the last. They greeted each other with reverence.

"I see you, sister," Imani said with a gentle nod.

"And I see you, sister," the women responded, their voices filled with warmth and love.

It was the greeting of this new world, a way of acknowledging not just the presence of another, but the connection between them all. The bond that made every woman a sister, every child a daughter, every life sacred.

Back in her high-rise, Mara sheathed her sword, her body alive with energy, her mind sharper than ever. She stood before the window, the vast cityscape of New Lagos stretching out beneath her. There were no traffic jams, no hurried commuters. The city breathed with peace and purpose. No one here ever rushed. No one ever worried. The world moved at the pace of its goddesses, and each woman was a deity in her own right.

Fully dressed in her Phantom Hunter armor, Mara left her home. The armor gleamed in the morning light, molded perfectly to her body, every inch designed for beauty and lethality. She moved confidently, her sword now sheathed at her side, her steps sure and steady as she descended into the streets below. There was no need for anxiety. There was no rush. Life flowed as it should, unburdened by the constraints of the past.

Mara walked through the towering halls of New Lagos with deliberate, measured steps, the gleaming floor reflecting the graceful sway of her Phantom Hunter armor. Ahead loomed the imposing double doors of the Council of Mothers' Chamber, heavy with the weight of untold power and decisions that had shaped the world for over two centuries. But as she passed the training courtyard, the sound of steel clashing and voices calling in unison caught her ear.

She paused at the edge of the open space, her keen gaze falling on the group of new recruits, young women in the early stages of becoming the next generation of Phantom Hunters. Their bodies, lithe and disciplined, moved like shadows as they fought, each swing of their blades crisp, precise, and devastating. Mara folded her arms across her chest, her expression one of silent pride as she watched them train, her heart swelling with a reverence she couldn't quite put into words.

"A Huntress must move like the wind, unseen and unstoppable," barked the head trainer, a woman with a scar cutting across her cheek and eyes like tempered steel. "You do not fight for glory. You do not fight for yourself. You fight for the Matriarchy. For the Council. For your sisters."

The recruits stopped in unison; their weapons held with rigid discipline as the trainer approached the center of the formation. Mara recognized the fierce gleam in their eyes—the same fire she had carried when she first joined their ranks.

"You think being a Phantom Hunter is about brute strength? About killing with precision? No. The Council of Mothers chose us to be their shield and spear because we are more than warriors—we are symbols of the future. The old world was dominated by males. Weakness. Ego. Chaos. But we," she gestured to the recruits and beyond to the larger society they fought to protect, "we are order. We are balance. And above all, we are loyalty."

The trainer's voice lowered as the recruits knelt in reverence, resting their blades across their palms.

"The Council chose the black lotus to symbolize the Matriarchy for a reason," the trainer continued, her voice quiet but filled with conviction. "The lotus blooms in the darkest of waters. It rises through the filth and decay, untouched and pure, thriving in environments where nothing else can. It is both beautiful and deadly—just like us."

The recruits listened in silence, the gravity of her words settling over them like a shroud.

"The black lotus endures where all else withers. The Council believes that if this world is to be reborn and made perfect, we must bloom through the ashes. That is why you train. That is why you kill. You are not simply soldiers—you are the flowers that grow in the ruins of male's failures."

Mara felt a shiver run through her, the words settling deep in her bones. It was a reminder of why she had taken up the blade. She wasn't just a killer. She was part of something greater, something eternal—a force woven into the very fabric of The Matriarchy.

The recruits shifted slightly, preparing to recite the Phantom Hunter's Mantra. Their voices rose in perfect harmony, clear and unwavering:

> *"We are the shadows that keep the light pure.*
> *We are the hunters, swift and silent.*
> *We carry no fear, for fear is a chain.*
> *We carry no hatred, for hatred is a flaw.*
> *We carry only loyalty, for loyalty is strength.*
> *Our hearts belong to our sisters.*
> *Our blades belong to The Matriarchy.*
> *We are the Phantom Hunters—beautiful, deadly, and eternal."*

Mara inhaled deeply as the mantra washed over her, each word resonating deep within her soul. These young women, barely more than girls, would soon join her ranks. Their journey had only just begun, but she saw in them the same fire, the same unyielding purpose that burned within her.

"Rise, sisters," the trainer commanded, and the recruits sprang to their feet with a fluid grace, blades flashing as they fell back into formation.

For a moment, Mara allowed herself to stand there, lost in the pride and reverence that filled her chest. Watching these young recruits reminded her of everything The Matriarchy had fought for.

With a deep breath, Mara tore herself away from the courtyard. The double doors of the Council's Chamber loomed ahead, and beyond them, Seraphine awaited with promises wrapped in threats.

The Matriarchy had built a world of perfect order, and yet beneath the surface, the waters grew darker, and the roots of the black lotus sank deeper into treacherous ground.

Mara steeled herself, one hand brushing the hilt of her sword. She had sworn an oath to The Matriarchy, but the lines between loyalty and truth were beginning to blur. And as she walked toward the chamber doors, a single thought bloomed in her mind like the black lotus itself:

The flower may be beautiful, but it is the roots that determine how far the poison spreads. And sometimes, even a flower must be uprooted.

With that, Mara made her way toward the Council of Mothers' chamber. There was an edge to the air, a shift in the energy of the city. The world outside may have seemed perfect, but Mara had seen beyond the veil. She knew that this utopia was fragile, and danger lurked at its edges.

The massive doors of the Council chamber loomed ahead of her, intricately carved with symbols of the Matriarchy's long reign. They opened silently as she approached, and inside, the cool, illuminated room waited. A voice echoed through the vast space, chilling and commanding.

"Mara," Seraphine's voice rang out, smooth as silk but laced with the weight of the world. "I have a very important mission for you."

The doors slid shut behind Mara, sealing her in the chamber with the Council's gaze heavy upon her.

"And failure," Seraphine added, her voice low and deadly, "could mean the end of our world. The end of the Matriarchy."

Chapter 2:

The World Reborn

The city of New Lagos gleamed in the early morning light, a sprawling metropolis carved from glass and steel that reached toward the heavens like the fingers of a forgotten titan, grasping for redemption. The skyline was a shimmering tapestry, each tower reflecting the sunrise, casting long, ethereal shadows that painted the streets below in strokes of gold and amber. A steady hum filled the air—the rhythmic pulse of drones zipping through the sky, automated transporters gliding smoothly along suspended tracks, and the quiet thrum of the bio-grid that sustained life within this meticulously engineered utopia.

Dr. Imani Kasali stood in the sterile, polished corridors of the Biocenter of Creation, the heart of New Lagos's genetic research. She gazed out through the floor-to-ceiling windows, watching the city stir from its slumber. Her brown skin, glowing in the pale sunlight, contrasted sharply with her crisp white lab coat, which fluttered ever so slightly in the artificially cooled air. Her hair, thick and dark, was pulled back into a tight afro puff, emphasizing her sharp features and the quiet intensity in her eyes.

She watched from the window as the women below moved with practiced efficiency, their strides long and purposeful, faces serene beneath the sun's soft embrace. These women—citizens of the matriarchal utopia—were the perfected results of over two centuries of meticulous genetic engineering. They were strong, beautiful, and intelligent, embodying the ideal of progress that the Council of Mothers had envisioned after the fall of men.

For the citizens of New Lagos, life was simple, and harmonious even. There were no wars, no poverty, no violence—just the hum of progress, a symphony conducted by science. Women had flourished in the absence of men, taking control of their future and shaping a society that was flawless in its execution. But beneath this veneer of perfection, beneath the gleaming towers and serene streets, something was lurking, a darkness that gnawed at the edges of their world.

Two hours later…

In the sterile, silvery glow of the lab, Imani watched as Dr. Selene Amari deftly adjusted a set of genetic samples under the microscope, her expression focused, intense, and indecipherable. Selene's presence was captivating, and not only because of her reputation. She was a woman of undeniable beauty, her Italian heritage reflected in her high cheekbones, warm olive skin, and piercing dark eyes that held a depth beyond her apparent age. Her long, dark hair cascaded down her back in loose waves, an elegant contrast to the cold, sterile environment of the lab. Though well over a century old, Selene's features bore no trace of time's passage—a result of the genetic advancements her family had pioneered. Her presence commanded respect, her determination and intellect as sharp as the instruments she worked with.

Imani had admired Selene since she was a girl, drawn to the strength and genius that seemed to run through the Amari line. The Matriarchy itself owed its very existence to this lineage—a legacy carved by Dr. Lyra Amari, Selene's grandmother, whose groundbreaking work had altered the course of human evolution and shaped the world in ways no one could have imagined. But Lyra's story was shadowed by mystery; her death, under suspicion of betrayal, haunted Selene and had made her cautious, wary of the council's motives.

Selene's grandmother had raised her and Seraphine together like sisters, instilling in them the resilience and tenacity required to lead. But after her grandmother's exile, Selene's trust in the council had fractured. She had seen firsthand how loyalty could be questioned, how brilliance could be silenced if it threatened the delicate balance of power within the Matriarchy. This knowledge lingered beneath her careful demeanor, shaping her actions with a guarded resolve.

Yet, Imani could sense an uncharacteristic edge to Selene, something coiled and wary, as if each word carried a potential threat.

"The latest subject," Imani began, breaking the tense silence, "Aurora… it was as if her body was consumed from within. The mutations—they were catastrophic, aggressive. The infection overtook her completely, faster than anything we've ever recorded." Her voice grew quieter, almost hesitant.

"And now there are whispers of a new strain emerging… How could this be happening?"

Selene's gaze flicked up from the microscope, sharp and unyielding. She leaned back, folding her arms across her chest as though bracing herself for the gravity of her own words. "Imani, listen carefully." Her voice was steady, yet it held a note of apprehension. "Dr. Lyra Amari shaped the world we stand in today, creating order from the ashes after the virus eradicated males. Our society has thrived on the basis of predictability. We mastered control, made every aspect of our world orderly, structured, and logical."

Selene paused, her expression darkening as she chose her next words. "In the old world, even amidst the chaos of war, the virus had a rhythm—a purpose, even. Its spread, its toll, even its lethality followed a certain pattern. But this mutation… it defies that rhythm. It's unpredictable, erratic, moving beyond what we understood."

Imani's brow furrowed, her mind racing as Selene's words sank in. "What are you saying?"

Selene's voice dropped, her gaze piercing. "The more I investigate, the more I see something different in this mutation. It's as if… as if something else is driving it. Something we didn't account for. And if that's true, then everything we've relied on—the predictability, the control— may no longer be enough to contain it."

Imani's eyes widened, her respect tempered now with a growing dread. "Something else?"

Selene lowered her voice. "Something we weren't supposed to find, at least not us. Imani, you need to tread carefully. This latest incident—Aurora's infection and the speed of her death—it's being quietly contained. People are keeping things silent. There's a reason why you're being assigned to investigate."

Imani shifted uneasily. "But you... you're saying this mutation could be... intentional? Sabotage?"

A shadow flickered across Selene's face. "Intentionality is always a risk when politics are involved. People will stop at nothing to maintain the status quo, to keep their power secure. You already know that." She glanced around the empty lab, then looked at Imani, her voice barely above a whisper. "This particular strain... it seems almost... weaponized. But there's little time to speculate. If there is a design behind it, a careful orchestration, then understand—our very foundation could be threatened."

Imani leaned closer, a surge of both curiosity and apprehension building in her chest. "Selene, what are you saying? Are you suggesting that someone in the Council, one of our own sisters, is behind these mutations?"

Selene's face softened, a rare crack in her steely demeanor. "I'm not 'suggesting' anything. I'm telling you that knowledge has always been dangerous, Imani. My great grandmother Dr. Lyra Amari proved that when she crafted a world without males. She didn't just reshape the species; she challenged everything we had come to believe. And even now, those same challenges exist."

Imani clenched her fists, her gaze narrowing. "So I should just back off? Pretend I didn't see what I saw?"

Selene let out a slow sigh, her eyes reflecting a strange mix of pride and concern. "Imani, I know you're brave, more than most. But bravery without caution is simply reckless. Whoever may be behind these events… they won't want anyone uncovering the truth. You're not just investigating Aurora's death anymore. You're digging up secrets some would kill to keep buried."

"Secrets? You mean… there's more?"

Selene nodded, her voice growing even softer. "Aurora's death was not just an isolated incident. There are more reports—cases we were asked to dismiss, anomalies swept under the proverbial rug. And these mutations, they have a certain… deliberation to them. Aurora's death wasn't just an accident. The infection, the mutations—it's all too… precise."

Imani's breath hitched, her heart racing. "You mean… Aurora was targeted?"

Selene's jaw tightened. "I can't say for certain, but that's my suspicion. And the worst part, Imani, is that we might be too late. The wheels are already in motion."

Imani's voice turned steely. "Then I can't back down, can I?"

Selene's expression softened, a mixture of admiration and fear flashing across her face. "No, I don't suppose you can. But I'm asking you, as someone who knows the cost of truth— watch your step. Knowledge may be power, but in this world, it's also a weapon. And you, my sister, are stepping into a minefield."

Imani took a deep breath, her mind spinning with the weight of Selene's words. "If I uncover something… if I find something no one wants me to find, what then?"

Selene placed a gentle hand on her shoulder, her gaze intense. "Then come to me. No one else. And remember— when things get out of The Council's control…trust will be a rare commodity under this dome."

Imani swallowed, nodding slowly. "Thank you, Dr. Amari. For everything."

Selene's eyes lingered on Imani for a moment, a flicker of something maternal, protective. Then, as if a switch had been flipped, her expression hardened. She turned away, grabbing a datapad from the counter and pressing it into Imani's hand.

"This is all I have on Aurora's case. But remember, if you find something—something dangerous, something the Council won't like… bring it to me first."

Imani looked down at the datapad, feeling its weight as if it were a live wire sparking with danger. She looked back at Selene, and for a moment, they shared an unspoken understanding—a connection forged from trust and the grim knowledge that even in the Matriarchy, secrets could be deadly.

Selene took a step back, her gaze intense. "Good luck, Imani. And remember… tread lightly."

With that, Selene turned and walked out of the lab, leaving Imani alone, the datapad heavy in her grasp and the weight of her next steps looming over her like a storm.

Imani's hand trembled slightly as she clutched her datapad, the screen displaying a set of reports that had consumed her thoughts for days. The quiet hum of the Biocenter felt deafening now, the sterile air pressing down on her chest like a weight. Her heart pounded in time with the flicker of the datapad's screen, as if her body was bracing itself for the truth she had been trying to ignore.

Aurora. She thought she had been the first, but she was wrong.

A mother selected for her flawless genetic profile, chosen by the Council for her impeccable lineage and health. Aurora was supposed to give birth to perfection—a child engineered to be the next step in the evolution of their society. But what emerged from Chamber 12-C at 03:47 that morning was far from the ideal they had been promised.

SUBJECT BIRTHED WITH SEVERE GENETIC ANOMALIES. PHYSICAL DEVIATIONS OBSERVED. TERMINATION INITIATED POST-BIRTH. MOTHER DECEASED DUE TO CATASTROPHIC TRAUMA.

The cold, clinical language on the datapad did nothing to capture the horror of what had truly unfolded in the birth chamber. Imani's fingers trembled slightly as she accessed the video footage from Chamber 12-C. The sterile report had not prepared her for this—the vivid clarity of the scene that now played across the screen, so real it felt as though she were standing in that room, bearing witness to the nightmare.

The creature that had clawed its way out of Aurora's womb was not a child; it was a monstrosity, something twisted and unnatural. Its body was grotesquely misshapen, limbs bending at unnatural angles, each movement a disturbing mimicry of life. Its translucent skin seemed to pulse, revealing an intricate web of veins beneath, and its eyes—black, soulless orbs—glared up at the world with a hunger so intense it made Imani's blood run cold. The artificial lights above reflected off its slick, glistening skin, casting it in a ghostly glow that only added to the horror.

Imani watched, frozen, as the creature tore itself free from Aurora, rending through her flesh with a brutal, feral strength that defied explanation. The mother's body convulsed under the assault, her final screams caught somewhere between agony and terror. Blood pooled around her, a dark crimson halo spreading across the sterile white of the birthing bed, while the thing—barely formed yet horrifically alive—gnawed its way through her remains, its jagged teeth sinking into the flesh of the woman who had borne it.

The medical team scrambled, their faces pale with panic, hands fumbling for syringes and sedatives, trying desperately to contain the abomination before them. But it moved too quickly, darting across the table with a speed that belied its grotesque form. Its limbs flailed, lashing out with claws sharp and unyielding, slashing through protective gear and leaving deep, bloody trails on anyone who dared get too close. The footage was punctuated by frantic shouts, a doctor's panicked call for restraint protocols, and the shrill, terrified screams of a nurse whose arm was caught in the creature's grip.

Imani's stomach twisted as she witnessed what happened next. Aurora's body, now still and lifeless, began to twitch. At first, it was a slight, almost imperceptible movement—just a finger, then a spasm through her limbs. But soon her body reanimated, rising in a grotesque parody of life, her once gentle face contorted, her eyes vacant and clouded. She moved like a puppet, as if controlled by something dark and primal, her body now a vessel for something beyond death.

Imani's throat went dry, her heartbeat thundering in her ears as she continued to watch the monstrous scene. Aurora—no longer the woman she had been—lunged forward, her mouth twisted into a snarl, joining the creature in its feral assault. A mother and child bound in a nightmare of blood and violence. The medical team's panic reached a fever pitch, their shouts and screams blending into a cacophony of horror that echoed through the footage.

Imani swallowed hard, struggling to calm her breathing as she processed what she had just seen. The datapad's cold glow reflected in her wide, dark eyes, which now flickered with the weight of the unspeakable knowledge she held. She had witnessed mutations before, rare anomalies in the engineered children, but this... this was beyond mutation. This was a manifestation of something far darker—a force they had never accounted for, one that had corrupted life itself.

Forcing herself to look away from the screen, Imani let the reality of what she'd seen sink in. This was no mere aberration. It was a threat—a monstrous evolution that defied everything they thought they controlled. And it was only the beginning.

"Dr. Kasali?"

The voice broke through her thoughts, calm but laced with authority. Imani turned to see Councilor Zuri standing in the doorway, her silhouette framed by the stark light of the corridor. Zuri was an imposing figure, tall and statuesque, her silver hair pulled back in a tight braid that accentuated the severe beauty of her features. Her dark skin gleamed under the sterile lights, and her sharp, calculating eyes never missed a detail. She was a woman who commanded attention with every step, and even now, in the lab, she carried an air of quiet power.

Imani cleared her throat, forcing herself to focus. "Councilor Zuri. I wasn't expecting you this morning."

Zuri's expression was unreadable as she stepped into the room, her movements graceful yet deliberate. "There are matters we must discuss," she said, her voice low and clipped. "The Council has been made aware of... developments. And we need answers."

Imani discreetly slipped the datapad into her lab coat pocket, Selene's words resonating heavily in her mind.

"Trust will be a rare commodity under this dome."

She had known this moment would come, just not this soon. The Council wouldn't be able to keep the truth hidden for much longer—the anomalies were spreading, and the carefully constructed facade of perfection that The Matriarchy thrived on was beginning to crack.

Zuri's fingers grazed the control panel on the wall, activating a large monitor. Data filled the screen—genetic scans, birth records, termination reports. The facts were laid out with cold precision, detailing the growing number of aberrations, like the one born in Chamber 12-C. More mothers were dying. More children were being born... wrong.

"The anomalies have appeared in three additional birthing centers," Zuri says, her voice taut with restrained fury. "The Council cannot afford for this to continue. We've lost control of our own creation."

Imani's stomach churned. "It's the virus," she said quietly, her voice barely above a whisper. "The Y Chromosome Virus. It's mutated…again."

Zuri's eyes flashed with disbelief. "Impossible. The virus was eradicated over two centuries ago. It wiped out every man on Earth. How could it possibly return? And why is it infecting women?"

Imani exhaled slowly, steeling herself for the storm she knew was coming. "The virus didn't die with the men. It was preserved—hidden within the sperm samples we've been using to continue reproduction. It's been dormant in the genetic material for generations, but now… now it's reactivating. It's mutating in ways we never anticipated. The children born from infected samples—they're no longer human."

Zuri's expression hardened, the gravity of the situation settling in as she scanned the chilling data on the screen. "And these… creatures?" she asked, her voice as cold and clinical as the reports. "They're infectious?"

"From what we've observed, yes," Imani replied, her voice wavering despite her attempt to maintain composure. "Anyone bitten or scratched by these… Ferals… is infected, and the transformation is almost instant. They turn in less than a minute."

Zuri's eyes flashed with shock, her voice rising. "How is that even possible? How can the virus spread like this?"

"It's the mutation," Imani said, her voice shaking despite her best efforts. "The virus has fundamentally corrupted their DNA. And it's not just limited to men anymore. It's turning on women now, attacking them from within. These… Ferals aren't just mutations—they're something else. And the infection is spreading faster every day. We're running out of time."

For a long moment, Zuri remained silent, her sharp gaze riveted to the data on the screen, each line deepening the severity etched on her face. The silence between them was thick, oppressive, as the horror of what was happening sank in.

Finally, Zuri straightened, her voice steely with resolve. "We cannot let this spread. The Council's authority, the survival of our society—everything depends on our control. We need a solution, and we need it immediately."

Imani hesitated, her mind racing. There was one possibility, but it was a path fraught with risk, a truth the Council would never want to confront.

"There might be a way to stop this," Imani said slowly, her voice threaded with urgency. "The virus was originally designed to target the Y chromosome—it wiped out nearly all the male population. But with the mutation now infecting women, there's a chance that the cure lies within the Y chromosome itself. If we could find a male… a living male… we could potentially use his DNA to develop an antidote."

Zuri's face tightened as she absorbed the gravity of Imani's words. Her eyes widened, shock and disbelief flashing across her face. "A male? Imani, any males left in hiding would never help The Matriarchy. We've hunted them to the brink of extinction…again. The efficiency of the Phantom Hunters has forced them to live in the shadows for centuries."

Imani held Zuri's gaze, her own expression etched with urgency and a trace of desperation. "I know," she said quietly.

"But there is one—a man who's been hidden from the Council's knowledge, kept alive all these years. I know his exact location. His DNA could be our only chance to counter the mutation."

Zuri's face tightened, her shock giving way to anger as she absorbed Imani's revelation. Her voice was low and biting, each word dripping with barely controlled fury. "A male? You know the exact location of a male, and you kept this from the Council?" Her gaze was sharp, piercing.

"Imani, do you have any idea what this means? After everything we've done to eradicate them, after centuries of hunting and sacrifice, you withheld this knowledge?"

Imani stood firm, her jaw set, her voice steady despite the intensity in Zuri's tone. "I understand the consequences, Zuri. But maybe it's the will of the universe that I kept this secret. If I'd told the Council, he would already be dead—like all the others. And then where would we be? Facing an unstoppable mutation with no chance at a cure."

"What would possess you to keep a male safe?"

Imani lowered her head, a shadow of shame crossing her face as she spoke softly, "The male belongs to Zara."

Zuri's eyes narrowed, anger flickering in her gaze, tempered only slightly by a hint of reluctant empathy. "Your mentor, Zara… I know what she meant to you. I know you cared about her. But I also know what she did." Her tone softened, though the frustration remained.

"You entered into a blood oath with her to keep her son a secret. Imani, you were young. I understand that loyalty. But this is bigger than that now. We're talking about the survival of the Matriarchy, of everything we've worked to create. Keeping his existence from us—if the Council finds out…" She shook her head. "There will be repercussions, and I can't do anything to stop it. And frankly, I won't try."

Imani swallowed, her gaze faltering for a moment. "Zara was like family to me, Zuri. When she found out she was carrying a male… she was terrified. She knew what the Council would do if they found out. She made me swear to keep him hidden, to keep him safe." Her voice wavered, the memories weighing heavily on her. "I couldn't betray her. She disappeared because she feared for her and her son's lives. I did what I thought was right."

Zuri's expression remained hard, though a flicker of understanding crossed her face. "I know she was like family. But that was years ago, Imani. We're talking about a decision that affects all of us. I may understand why you did it, but the Council… they won't be so forgiving. They may see your loyalty to Zara as treason."

Imani clenched her fists, meeting Zuri's cold gaze. "I know. But if we don't find him, if we let this mutation spread unchecked, the consequences will be far worse than whatever judgment the Council has for me."

Zuri's face remained impassive, though a hint of disgust lingered in her eyes. "This… male may be our only hope, but don't mistake my acceptance for approval. I don't believe in the need for males in our world. They're relics of a brutal past, and I have no sympathy for them." Her tone hardened. "When this is over, I won't protect you from what's coming. You made your choice, Imani, and you'll have to answer for it."

Imani's voice dropped to a whisper. "I understand. And I'm prepared for the consequences. But right now, that male is our last chance. Whether we like it or not."

A tense silence hung between them, the weight of Zuri's words and Imani's resolve filling the space. Finally, Zuri gave a sharp nod, her voice a cold command.

"Then find him. Whatever it takes. Pray he's willing to save the very society that would hunt him down without hesitation."

Chapter 3:

The Hunt Begins

The night wrapped New Lagos in an oppressive, heavy silence. The towering structures of glass and steel that gleamed under the sun had now faded into the ink-black sky, their gleaming edges swallowed by the darkness like sentinels of a lost era. The air felt alive, charged with something unseen, uneasy, as though the city itself sensed what was coming. The faint hum of the bio-powered grid pulsed through the streets, a reminder that beneath the perfection of the matriarchy lay a machine sustaining it all—an invisible web of control, much like the Council of Mothers that ruled it with calculated precision.

Yet, tonight, there was something else in the air. Something darker.

Dr. Imani Kasali hurried through the stark, gleaming halls of the Biocenter of Creation, her heart racing, her pulse loud in her ears. Each footstep echoed off the sterile floors as if the building itself was holding its breath, waiting for something terrible to happen. Her mind replayed the day's events in a broken loop she couldn't escape—Aurora's horrific death, the birth of that thing that should never have existed, and Zuri's cold, steely orders still ringing in her ears:

" Find him. Whatever it takes."

New Lagos, the epitome of engineered perfection, was teetering on the edge of a knife. The city's future—its very existence—depended on the success of its carefully crafted genetic programs. For two centuries, women had thrived, building a utopia free from war, free from chaos. But now, the virus had returned, hidden deep within the DNA they had so meticulously preserved. And the Council knew the facade of control was beginning to crumble.

As Imani moved deeper into the heart of the Biocenter, past the towering vats of preserved genetic material, past the sterile chambers where the next generation of daughters waited to be born, a sense of dread settled over her like a shroud. Each new birth brought more deviations, more monsters. The remaining clean samples were rapidly deteriorating, and every new anomaly pushed the city closer to collapse.

Imani reached her private lab, a secluded chamber far from prying eyes. The door slid open with a soft hiss, revealing a space bathed in the dim glow of holographic screens and softly pulsing bio-machines. This was where she had kept her most dangerous secrets. This was where the truth had been buried for decades.

Her hands trembled as she keyed in her genetic code to access a hidden compartment. The wall slid open, revealing an old, weathered datapad, its surface cracked and worn from years of hiding. She hesitated for a moment, feeling the weight of what it contained. Then, with a deep breath, she activated the device, its screen flickering to life.

The encrypted files glowed faintly in the dim light, and she scrolled through them, searching for the one she had been avoiding for years. And there it was—a single file marked Project Echo. She selected it, and the screen filled with data: genetic sequences, birth records, medical logs—all centered on one individual. At the top of the screen, a name burned into her memory appeared: Dorian.

Imani inhaled deeply. She had never met him, never laid eyes on the boy who was now a man, but she had overseen his creation, monitored his development from a distance, ensuring that his existence remained a secret. Twenty years had passed since Zara had fled the city with him.

Zara, one of Imani's mentors, had been a brilliant geneticist—perhaps too brilliant. She had been the first to sound the alarm that the virus could resurface in the carefully preserved sperm samples, long after the Council had declared it eradicated. When she realized she was pregnant with a son— Zara knew that she and her baby would never be safe within the city's walls. So, she disappeared, vanishing into the wilderness beyond New Lagos, taking the growing male inside of her womb with her.

The Council had sent its enforcers after her. And not just any enforcers. They had sent the Phantom Hunters.

The Phantom Hunters were more than mere soldiers. They were a living myth, feared across the entire planet. In the early days of the matriarchy, they had been used to hunt down and eliminate any woman who dared defy the Council's strict laws—especially women who gave birth to male children and tried to flee the cities. The Hunters were relentless, efficient, and utterly without mercy. Each member of the elite unit had been handpicked for their ruthlessness and loyalty, molded into weapons that could slip into any environment, track any target, and neutralize any threat. Their success rate was legendary; the Phantom Hunters rarely missed their mark.

And among them, one name stood alone: Mara.

Mara was known throughout New Lagos as the most dangerous of the Phantom Hunters, her reputation that of a ghost who could move unseen, strike without warning, and leave no trace of her existence. She had a body built for combat, tall and muscular, with skin the color of polished obsidian. Her hair, long and jet black, was always tightly braided against her scalp, a symbol of her discipline and lethal precision. Her dark eyes, sharp and calculating, missed nothing. Stories of her ruthlessness in hunting down fugitives had become almost legend. Mothers would whisper her name to their daughters to frighten them into obedience.

Her presence was the last thing Imani wanted.

Imani quickly accessed the old coordinates Zara had sent just before she vanished. She could feel time slipping through her fingers like sand. Dorian was out there—somewhere in the wilderness that had reclaimed much of the world. If the Council found him first, they wouldn't hesitate to weaponise him, to turn him into the solution to their problem. He was the key to stopping the virus from mutating further, from turning their perfect children into twisted abominations. But she had to get to him before the Council did.

The door to the lab slid open just as Imani secured the datapad inside her coat.

A shadow moved in the doorway.

Imani held her breath as she turned, her heart hammering against her ribs. There, standing in the shadows, was Mara. The infamous Hunter moved with the silent grace of a predator, her eyes cold and calculating as they locked onto Imani. She wore the black combat gear of the Phantom Hunters, a sleek suit of armored fabric that clung to her powerful frame like a second skin. Her hand rested casually on the hilt of the blade sheathed at her side—a blade that had seen the blood of many.

"I knew you'd come here," Mara said, her voice low and dangerous, a hint of amusement flickering in her eyes. She stepped forward, her boots making no sound on the sterile floor. "What's on the datapad?"

Imani swallowed hard, the datapad burning a hole in her coat. She had underestimated the Council's reach. "I don't have time for this, Mara," she said, struggling to keep her voice steady. "You don't understand what's happening."

Mara's lips curled into a thin, humorless smile. "You think I don't know? I've seen the births. I've seen what's happening to those children. But it's not my job to understand." Her gaze shifted to the datapad hidden beneath Imani's coat, and her eyes darkened. "It's my job to make sure the Council remains in control."

Imani's throat went dry. Mara had never cared about politics, about the nuances of power within the Council. She was a weapon, pure and simple, loyal only to the mission.

"I'm not letting the Council turn him into a tool," Imani said, her voice trembling now. "Dorian is the key to saving us, but if they get to him, they'll use him until there's nothing left. He's a person, Mara. Not a solution. Not a weapon."

Mara's eyes lifted, locking onto Imani's with a cold, predatory gleam.

"Wait, so, you and the male are on a first name basis now? What makes you think I care about the humanity of a male?" she hissed. "If the Council wants to dissect that insect down to the last hair follicle, so be it. I'd gladly help them peel the skin from his bones—without a moment's hesitation." Her lips twisted into a chilling smile. "It's been far too long since a male's testicles has tasted the edge of my blade. She's thirsty, Imani. And it seems you're standing in the way of her quenching her thirst."

Imani's mind raced, weighing her options. She knew Mara's reputation. No one who had crossed Mara had ever lived to tell the tale. But Imani had something Mara didn't: knowledge.

"You're more than just a hunter," Imani said, her voice soft yet unwavering. "You were born from the bloodline of the most brilliant mind to ever live. That intellect flows through your veins, driving you to seek knowledge and uncover truths others shy away from. You're someone who wants answers. And the truth is, the Council is hiding something—something they don't want you to find."

Mara's expression flickered, just for a moment. "What are you talking about?"

Imani took a step closer, her voice dropping to a whisper, her tone thick with urgency. "Aurora wasn't the first death, as the Council would have us believe. She's one of many, part of a growing list of victims they've kept hidden from us." She paused, her gaze intense. "And it's not just the children who are infected. The mothers… they're turning too. Not into corpses, but into something far worse—neither fully dead nor truly alive. They rise with an insatiable hunger for flesh."

Imani's voice trembled as she continued, the horror of the truth sinking in. "The virus didn't die with the men. It's been mutating in the genetic samples we've used to create life, corrupting every generation. The Council knew this would happen—they've known for years. But they kept it from us, hoping to control it, to keep it hidden. These children… these things being born… it's only going to get worse."

Mara's eyes narrowed, her hand hovering near her blade. "You expect me to believe that?"

Imani's heart pounded. "If you let me go, I'll show you the truth. I'll tell you everything. You're not a mindless weapon, Mara. You're better than that. Help me, and together, we can stop this."

The silence between them stretched, thick with tension.

Finally, Mara's lips parted, and she nodded, almost imperceptibly. "You have one week. After that…"

Imani let out a shaky breath, nodding in return. Without another word, she turned and fled into the night, her pulse racing as she slipped into the labyrinthine underbelly of the city.

Behind her, the towers of New Lagos gleamed in the darkness, unaware of the storm that was about to be unleashed.

The hunt had begun.

Chapter 4:

The Wilderness Beyond

The wilderness outside New Lagos was nothing short of a savage kingdom, untouched by the sterile perfection of the city. Out here, the wild had reclaimed the world, its rules etched in ancient, primal language. Towering trees stretched like dark titans, their thick branches intertwined in a suffocating embrace allowing only slivers of pale light emanating from the city to pierce the dense canopy, casting eerie, shifting shadows on the forest floor. The undergrowth was dense, thick with ferns and thorny vines that clung to Imani's legs as she pushed forward.

Every breath she took was labored, the air thick with moisture and the smell of decay. It was nothing like the controlled, filtered oxygen of New Lagos, where each breath was a sterile inhale, purged of imperfection. Out here, each breath felt alive, carrying with it the weight of untold years and untamed life.

Imani's heart pounded in her chest, a steady rhythm that matched the rapid beat of her thoughts. Her boots sank into the damp earth with every step, the soft squelch of the mud beneath her feet the only sound that broke the oppressive silence. She had never ventured this far beyond the city's towering walls before, where nature reigned with ruthless authority. Few ever did. The wilderness was a place of exile, a land that time and civilization had forgotten, where even the Council's reach was limited.

Her datapad beeped softly, pulling her attention to the coordinates flashing on the screen. The glowing path guided her deeper into the unknown, farther from the pristine safety of New Lagos.

Find him.

That thought beat in her head like a drum, pulsing through her blood.

Dorian.

Somewhere in this vast wilderness, he was hiding, a ghost in a forgotten world.

But doubts gnawed at her mind. What if he was already dead? What if she had come all this way, only to find a grave, another skeleton swallowed by the wilderness?

The forest seemed to close in around her, the trees growing thicker and more twisted the deeper she ventured. Moss covered their trunks like a velvet cloak, and vines reached out like gnarled fingers, brushing against her skin. Every now and then, the forest would whisper to her—the rustle of leaves above, the snap of a branch behind her—but she couldn't tell if it was the wind, or something watching her from the shadows.

A chill crawled up her spine, the weight of the wild pressing down on her. She had forgotten what it felt like to be vulnerable. New Lagos had dulled her senses, softened her to the harsh reality that lay beyond its walls. But out here, there was no hiding, no controlled environment to protect her. Out here, she was prey.

Imani's hand instinctively moved to the blade strapped to her thigh, her fingers grazing the hilt. She had trained for this once, years ago, when she had been one of the top recruits in the Phantom Hunter program. The Council's elite enforcers, trained to hunt down women who broke the law by giving birth to male children and fleeing the city. It was a brutal training, designed to strip away weakness and fear, to forge them into lethal instruments of justice.

But Imani had never graduated. She had been injured during one of the final tests—a fracture to her leg that took her out of the running. She had watched from the sidelines as her peers, women like Mara, had gone on to become full-fledged Phantom Hunters. And though she had chosen a different path, immersing herself in the world of genetics, she had never forgotten her training. Those skills were buried deep inside her, dormant but ready, and now, out here in the wilderness, they stirred.

Guilt gnawed at her heart as she pushed forward. She had broken her blood oath to Zara, an oath that bound her to loyalty and secrecy. Zara, Dorian's mother, had been her mentor during her transition from hunter to geneticist. Zara had been Imani's inspiration during her studies, and she learned so much from her, resulting in her graduating at the top of her class. And when Zara had disappeared into the wilderness, pregnant with a male child, Imani had kept her secret. That secret had been a weight on her soul for years, but now it threatened to crush her.

Suddenly, a low growl rumbled through the air, cutting through her thoughts. Imani froze, her heart racing as she turned, scanning the forest for the source of the sound. There, emerging from the shadows, was a massive black bear, its eyes gleaming with a feral hunger.

It was unlike anything Imani had ever seen. The bear was huge, its muscles rippling beneath its dark fur, its claws digging into the earth as it advanced. Its lips curled back, revealing jagged teeth stained with the blood of past kills. This was not the domesticated world of New Lagos. This was the wilderness—brutal and unforgiving.

Imani held her breath as the bear let out a deafening roar, charging toward her with terrifying speed. Instinct kicked in, the years of Phantom Hunter training flooding her veins with adrenaline. She rolled to the side, just barely avoiding the bear's massive paw as it swiped at her, the air around it thick with the force of the blow.

She drew her blade, the familiar weight comforting in her hand, and circled the bear, her eyes locked on its movements. It charged again, and this time, she was ready. She ducked beneath its attack, driving her blade deep into its side, the steel sinking into muscle and bone. The bear let out a furious roar as its blood sprayed across the forest floor.

But it wasn't enough. The bear turned on her again, faster than she had anticipated. It swiped at her, its claws catching her shoulder and sending her sprawling to the ground. Pain shot through her arm, but Imani gritted her teeth while rolling back to her feet. She had to stay focused. She had to survive.

The bear lunged once more, but this time, Imani was quicker. She sidestepped its attack and drove her blade into its throat, twisting the steel with all her strength. The bear let out a final, pained growl before collapsing to the ground, its massive body still.

Imani stood there, her chest heaving, her body trembling with the rush of adrenaline. The forest was silent again, the only sound was the ragged rhythm of her breathing. She wiped the blade on her sleeve, blood still clinging to her skin.

This was the wilderness—a place that cared nothing for perfection or control. Out here, it was kill or be killed.

Imani took a deep breath and continued forward, the datapad guiding her deeper into the forest. She had no time to waste. She had to find Dorian. She couldn't let the Council get to him first.

Imani stumbled through the underbrush, her hands trembling as she pushed aside the thick branches that snagged at her clothing. She was no longer the immaculate scientist, the sterile figure of control, wrapped in the comfort of New Lagos's climate-controlled bubble. No, now she was just another body, flesh and bone, struggling to survive in a wilderness that felt hostile at every turn.

The sun had dipped below the horizon hours ago, and the cold was beginning to bite. She wrapped her arms around herself, shivering as the icy fingers of the night air wormed their way through the thin fabric of her shirt. Her body wasn't used to this—this raw, untamed world. Her muscles ached, her skin was scratched and bruised, and her stomach growled with a hunger that gnawed at her insides. She had packed her supplies poorly, the seven days given to her by Mara forced her to rush her preparations and now she felt the burn of hunger. She couldn't eat everything at once. She needed to be smart, otherwise, she would succumb to the wilderness and there was too much at stake.

Her hands trembled as she tried to light a fire. She struck the flint again and again, but the spark kept dying in the wind. Frustration welled up inside her. In New Lagos, warmth was a tap away, food a button press. Out here, everything was hard, every moment a struggle.

"Come on," she muttered under her breath, teeth chattering as another gust of wind blew out the tiny flame she had managed to coax from the flint. "Just once... just give me something."

Finally, a flicker caught. She cupped her hands around the fragile flame, shielding it from the wind, blowing gently until it took hold of the dry tinder. The fire was small and pitiful, but it was warmth, and for that, she was grateful. She sat back, exhausted, her body aching from the relentless pace she had pushed herself to maintain. She only had seven days and a lot of ground to cover.

The wilderness was not what she had expected. It was far more unforgiving. The nights were colder than she could have imagined. In the sterile, artificially balanced world of New Lagos, she had never felt the real sting of nature. There was always a constant, predictable comfort in the city's temperature. But out here? The cold crept into her bones, numbing her fingers, and her toes. She had tried to keep moving at night to stay warm, but exhaustion eventually claimed her each night, forcing her to stop and huddle by her meager fires.

On the second night, she hadn't been careful. In her desperate need for heat, she had let the fire burn too high. The bright glow had attracted a pair of glowing eyes in the distance. A wild animal—a predator. She could see its outline, stalking her from the tree line, its muscles coiled, ready to spring. Heart pounding, she had grabbed her weapon—her Hunter sword. A keepsake from her time in the Phantom Hunter training program.

The Phantom Hunter's curved sword was a deadly masterpiece of craftsmanship, forged with an elegance that belied its lethal purpose. The blade itself was a shimmering crescent, its edge honed to an almost supernatural sharpness. Made from an alloy unknown to most, it glinted with an eerie, silver hue, reflecting light in a way that made it seem as though the blade was alive, pulsing with a cold, inner energy. The curvature of the sword was perfect for swift, fluid strikes—designed to slice through flesh, bone, and armor with effortless grace.

The spine of the blade was etched with intricate, razor-thin engravings—symbols of the old world, a language forgotten by most but sacred to the elite hunters. These runes shimmered faintly in low light, giving the sword a mystical, almost hypnotic quality. It wasn't just a weapon; it was an extension of the hunter who wielded it.

The hilt was wrapped in a dark, leather-like material, supple and worn from use, molded perfectly to the grip of its owner. A guardless design ensured the hunter's movements were unhindered, allowing for swift changes in direction, the blade's curve adding momentum to each stroke. The pommel was capped with a small, weighty orb of black iron—perfectly balanced to offset the lethal arc of the blade, ensuring that every swing was precise and deadly.

When unsheathed, the sword seemed to hum with anticipation, the slightest movement whispering through the air with a quiet menace. In battle, it became a blur of steel—its graceful arc carving through enemies with a lethal elegance that only the most skilled Phantom Hunters could command.

Now, with her hand at the ready, her heart thundered in her chest as she stood there, her breath coming in ragged gasps. She remembered the countless stories told to children in New Lagos about the horrors of the wild. Wild animals were something the domes had made irrelevant. But out here, in the thick, suffocating dark of the forest, they were very real.

The creature had crept closer, its snarling breath visible in the cold air, and Imani knew she was seconds away from becoming prey. But at the last second, something had startled it—and it darted away, leaving her trembling by the dying embers of her fire, terrified and alone.

The following night, she was careful with the flames, keeping them low, just enough to stay warm but not enough to attract attention. Every sound made her jump—the rustling of leaves, the snap of a twig. She couldn't rest, not really. Her body craved sleep, but fear kept her awake, her senses heightened as if the darkness was alive, waiting to devour her.

She found no comfort in the daylight either. The sun brought little warmth and no sense of safety. She had seen wild animals during the day, lurking in the distance, searching, their hunger driving them to stalk through the undergrowth. She would crouch low, hiding behind bushes or up in trees, heart pounding as she watched them pass, praying they wouldn't smell her, wouldn't see her. She had survived so far by sheer luck, but luck wouldn't hold out forever.

By the third day, her body was nearing its limit. Hunger clawed at her stomach, and her legs felt like lead. She was so cold, so tired, that every step felt like dragging herself through quicksand. Her mind wandered, a fog creeping over her thoughts as exhaustion set in. The world blurred around her as she stumbled forward, barely aware of where she was going. If not for the guidance of the datapad illuminating her path, she would have been swallowed by the vast wilderness, lost to its endless shadows. Her mind clung to a single, unyielding purpose—finding Dorian.

He was out here somewhere. She knew it. If she didn't find him, she wouldn't make it much longer. Her survival depended on him.

Her thoughts drifted back to Mara, to that haunting moment when she had emerged from the shadows like a specter. The cold, suffocating grip of fear tightened around Imani's chest as she remembered Mara clutching her sword, her fingers at the ready, determined to fulfill the Council's orders. The weight of that blade had never felt heavier. Mara's words had been a chilling warning, her voice sharp and devoid of mercy. She had given Imani a strict, unforgiving timeframe—a mere sliver of time in which to find Dorian. Not a second more. Imani knew that no Phantom Hunter, least of all Mara, would offer her the luxury of an extension. They were precise, lethal, and driven by an unyielding sense of duty. There would be no leniency.

It felt as though the world was closing in on her, suffocating her under the weight of the wilderness. Every step forward felt like an act of defiance, a battle against the forest itself.

And then, in the distance, the trees began to thin as she pressed on, and soon, she found herself standing at the edge of a small clearing. At its center was a shack—barely more than a crude structure made of wood and scrap metal. It was old and weathered, its roof sagging under the weight of time. A small garden overrun with wild plants sprawled out near the entrance, and a pile of tools sat haphazardly by the door.

Imani's pulse quickened. This had to be it. This had to be where Dorian was hiding.

She approached cautiously, her eyes scanning the clearing for any sign of life. The air was still, the wind carrying only the faint rustle of leaves. She reached the door, her hand trembling as she grasped the worn handle. She hesitated, fingers hovering over the hilt of her blade, her heart pounding in her chest.

What if he wasn't here? What if—

The door creaked open.

Imani stepped inside, instinctively holding her breath. The shack was small and cramped, its interior bathed in dim light filtering through cracks in the walls. The air was thick with the scent of wood and earth. And there, in the far corner, sat Dorian.

He was larger than she had expected, his caramel-colored skin catching the light. His dreadlocks hung around his face, framing his chiseled features. His muscles were defined, every inch of him honed by survival in the wilderness. He was scarred, his body a testament to the years he had spent in exile.

Her breath hitched as she saw him for the first time. He was nothing like the men in the old history books—nothing like the frail memories of the past. This was a warrior. A man who had lived through more than she could imagine.

"Dorian? My name is Imani, I knew your mother Zara." she whispered, her voice trembling.

For a moment, he didn't move. His head remained bowed, his body still, but then, slowly, he lifted his gaze, his dark eyes locking onto hers.

Imani froze.

His eyes—deep, dark, and filled with something she couldn't quite name—bore into her with an intensity that made her shiver. There was a hardness there, a coldness that she wasn't used to. But there was also something else—something haunted, something lost.

"You shouldn't have come here," he said, his voice low and rough, like gravel scraping against stone.

Imani swallowed, her heart pounding in her chest. "I didn't have a choice," she replied, her voice barely above a whisper. "The Council… they know. They know about you, and they are coming for you."

"Now, how could they possibly find that out?"

"I had to tell them!"

"So much for blood oaths of secrecy, huh? I don't expect anything different from a woman, anyway. None of you can be trusted."

That's rich coming from a male, Imani thought, as she fought to keep her composure as Dorian's insolence aggravated her to madness.

"It's the virus, Dorian. It's mutating. And the Council knows you're the only one who can stop it."

Dorian's jaw clenched, his muscles tensing. "I'm not stopping anything."

Imani stepped forward, urgency tightening her chest. "You don't understand. The virus is spreading. It's infecting the children—turning them into monsters. If we don't use your DNA to create a cure, everything we've built will collapse."

Dorian stood, unfolding his muscular frame as he stepped out of the shadows. He towered over her, his presence commanding, his eyes hard as steel. He stared down at her, his expression unreadable, but the tension between them was palpable. Imani could feel it—the weight of the history that hung between them.

"You think I care about your society?" Dorian's voice was cold, cutting. "About your Council? If they had their way, this conversation wouldn't even be happening. I'd have been dust long ago—a forgotten memory. A ghost. Isn't that why you call your hunters 'Phantom Hunters'? Because they erase men as if we never existed. Your Council hunts men for sport, yet you have the nerve to ask me to save them?"

Imani felt the guilt twist in her stomach, but she couldn't let it stop her. "This isn't just about the Council," she said, her voice softening. "This is about everyone. The virus will destroy us all if we don't stop it."

Dorian's gaze darkened, his eyes narrowing. "And you think I can stop it? That I'm some kind of savior? What makes you think men should clean up the mess women made?"

"What do you expect women to do in the presence of males?" Imani's voice trembled, a mix of frustration and desperation lacing her words. "Look at history—how males treated us, how they ruled. For centuries, you've shown us the same, undeniable truth: males can't be trusted. They ruled this world once, and they nearly destroyed it, driving it to the brink of extinction."

She took a breath, steadying herself as she met Dorian's gaze. "But I don't see you as just another male, Dorian. I know what the Council believes, what they teach about males. But I also believe that you can be different, that you can help us change the future. If you help us stop this virus, if you show us that males can be more than history has painted them, it could start something none of us thought possible. You could prove that males can change."

Imani's voice softened, a flicker of hope crossing her face. "This is a chance to show the Matriarchy a new truth. To show them that trust is possible. And it starts with you."

Dorian's laugh was low and laced with bitterness. "And you think women are any better? You think power hasn't corrupted them, too?" He stepped closer, his gaze searing into hers. "It's not gender that corrupts, Imani. It's power itself. The Council isn't rotting from the inside just because they're women—it's because they're human. And humans, no matter who they are, always seem to be corrupted by power."

He paused, letting his words sink in, before continuing, his voice simmering with anger. "You all handed them that power, never questioning, never holding them accountable for their mistakes. You've followed orders blindly just because it was women giving the orders, even when it meant killing other women, all in service to that authority. So, it's not just the Council that's to blame—it's every single one of you who upheld it without question."

Imani stood her ground, her heart racing. "Maybe that's true. But you're the only one who can stop this. The virus is out of control. Children are being born... inhuman. If we don't use your DNA to find a cure, there won't be a future left for anyone."

Dorian's jaw tightened. "And what happens to me after I help? What's waiting for me in that city? Torture? Death?"

Imani inhaled deeply. She hadn't considered that. "I don't know," she admitted, her voice soft. "But I can protect you. If you come with me, we can find a way."

Dorian shook his head, his muscles tensing, but there was something in his eyes, something that told her he wanted to believe her. For the first time, she saw a flicker of vulnerability, a crack in the armor he had built around himself.

And with that vulnerability came something else. Something she hadn't expected. A tension that wasn't just born of mistrust, but of something more primal. Something deeper. Her body responded instinctively, heat rushing through her veins at the sight of him—this imposing male standing before her, powerful and defiant.

"I don't need your protection," Dorian said sharply, his voice edged with defiance. "My mother was a Phantom Hunter before she changed her passion to genetics—she taught me everything about your ways, every tactic, every trick. I can protect myself just fine."

He cast a bitter glance around, his expression hardening. "What I needed…died out here, in this wasteland. You have no idea who you're really up against. You don't know what the Council truly is."

"The Council may not be perfect, but without them, humans would have been extinct hundreds of years ago!"

"And yet, here we are in a world free of male dominance and humanity is right back where we were two hundred years ago. On the brink of extinction. So, tell me, Phantom Hunter, why should I save a world that hasn't learned its lesson?

"I am not a Phantom Hunter."

Dorian's eyes narrowed as he spoke, his tone challenging. "That blade at your side says otherwise. You fought like a Phantom Hunter when you killed that bear. You moved like one through the wilderness—every step, every instinct. Your mannerisms, your skill, everything mirrors a Phantom Hunter. So tell me, how can you move and fight like a Phantom Hunter… yet claim you're not one?"

Imani's eyes widened, shock washing over her face. "You… you saw me fight the bear? You've been watching me this whole time? You allowed me to suffer for days in this…place and didn't help me?"

Dorian's gaze stayed fixed on her, dark and unwavering. "Help you?" he scoffed. "I didn't know if you were coming to kill me or warn me. But I knew who you were the moment I saw you. My mother showed me images of you; she spoke of you often. I've kept an eye on New Lagos my whole life, watching from the shadows, waiting for my chance to slip into that city and put an end to Seraphine. She murdered my mother, more than likely using Phantom Hunters to track her down."

Imani felt the words hit her like a physical blow, her heart sinking. "Your mother... she's dead?" Her voice trembled, the realization settling heavily. "Zara was like a mother to me, Dorian. I can't believe..."

A flicker of sorrow crossed Dorian's face, though he quickly masked it.

Imani took a shaky breath, pieces falling into place. "It was you, wasn't it? The second night out, something scared off the animal stalking me. I thought... I thought it was just luck. But you were there. You probably saved my life."

Dorian said nothing, watching her intently, letting her process the weight of his revelation.

Imani swallowed, struggling to steady herself. "I never graduated from the Phantom Hunter program. I was injured—badly. I thought my path was over, but Zara took me under her wing. She taught me everything she knew about genetics, things I would never have learned otherwise. She was a mentor to me, and more than that... she was family." Her voice grew softer. "I knew about you. When I found out she was carrying a male, she made me swear a blood oath to keep your existence hidden. I would have died to keep that oath."

Imani's voice faltered, her expression torn as she met Dorian's eyes. "But now, with the virus mutating, with people turning into Ferals... I couldn't keep silent anymore. I had no choice, Dorian. If there was any other way, I would've kept your secret safe."

"You may not have graduated, but you enlisted. Dedicating yourself to eradicating any remnants of men that may have survived the virus.

"Did you hear anything I just said? I am not like those women. I could have told the Council years ago about you, but I didn't and had the virus not mutated, I would have taken you and your mother's secret to the grave. I don't want to be around a male as much as you don't want to be around a woman, but I can assure you that if one of these creatures escapes our labs, being hunted by Phantom Hunters is going to be the least of your worries. Soon, this little piece of heaven you got here will be overrun by something much worse."

"Wait a minute, are you keeping these things alive?!"

"No! We are terminating them immediately, but they are extremely difficult to kill and I anticipate one day someone is going to make a mistake and allow one of those things to escape. After that, game over.

Dorian stared up at the shack's ceiling, his jaw clenched tight, the weight of unspoken words pressing down on him. Imani could see the struggle in his eyes, the tension in his body as though he was wrestling with a secret that begged to be released. His muscles tightened, his fists flexing as if the truth were a tangible thing he could physically hold back. Whatever it was, it gnawed at him, threatening to shatter the silence between them.

She could sense it wasn't just his disdain for the Matriarchy or the Council that held him back—there was something deeper, something more intimate driving him. His reluctance wasn't born from a desire to help her or the cause she represented. No, it was far more personal than that. And though he hated the thought of aligning himself with the Council, with women like Imani, something—someone—hung in the balance, someone who meant more to him than his own pride or even his hatred.

Finally, he exhaled sharply, his gaze shifting from the ceiling to meet Imani's. The fire in his eyes flickered with a fierce determination, a silent admission of his decision. He wasn't helping out of care or compassion; he was doing it because he had no choice. There was more at stake than his grudges. And in that moment, Imani saw the depth of his resolve, the lengths he would go to for whatever—or whoever—he was protecting.

"We leave at dawn," he said at last, his voice low and steady, his gaze locked on hers. "But there are conditions. You'll follow my lead—at all times. My mother taught me how to slip into that city unnoticed, and that's the only way I'll do this. I'm not walking through New Lagos like a prisoner, paraded before your Council like a rabid dog. I won't allow myself to be captured." Then his eyes darkened, his tone sharp and unyielding. "If I sense this mission is a trap—if I even think for a second, you're leading me into a betrayal—I'll kill you where you stand. No hesitation. Are we clear?"

Imani nodded, her pulse quickening. She needed him. But as she looked into his eyes, she realized with a sinking feeling that she didn't trust him and the idea of taking orders from a male made her skin crawl. He was a male. An extinct remnant of humanity who no longer had a purpose. To need a male at this stage of human evolution almost felt like an insult. Like a failure of The Matriarchy. She wished there was another way besides being around a male…

But she had no choice.

Chapter 5:

Into the Lion's Den

The barrier loomed on the horizon like a vast, invisible wall, shimmering faintly under the pale light of the rising sun. It stretched endlessly in both directions, a seamless dome of bio-energy encasing New Lagos, the Matriarchy's jewel of technology. From this distance, it looked almost delicate, its surface crackling with faint streaks of blue and violet that rippled like water. But Imani knew better. The barrier was far from fragile—it was a fortress, impenetrable to all but those with clearance.

The hum of its power was a constant, vibrating through the air, and the closer they drew to it, the more intense the sensation became. The very atmosphere felt charged, as if the world beyond recoiled from the invisible force field that kept the wilderness at bay. It was a reminder of the control the Council of Mothers had over everything within the dome's reach.

Imani's breath caught as she stood beside Dorian, her pulse quickening as she stared at the shimmering dome. Up close, the barrier was mesmerizing—a fusion of cutting-edge quantum tech and ancient energy manipulation. Invisible nano grids powered its surface, designed to recognize and repel any living organic matter not authorized to cross. It wasn't just a wall; it was alive, constantly scanning for threats, shifting its energy fields to adapt to any potential breach.

"We're close," Dorian muttered, his voice barely louder than the rustling of the river behind them. His eyes, dark and intense, were locked on the barrier, and his body tensed like a predator about to strike. There was an edge to him now, sharper and more dangerous than anything Imani had seen in the wilderness. The lines of strain etched into his face made him look like a man who had spent his life running, always one step ahead of the death that pursued him.

For a moment, Imani just watched him, her thoughts tangled with emotions she couldn't quite identify. This was the male she had been sent to find, the last hope for their world. And yet, as she stood beside him, she couldn't shake the growing unease gnawing at her gut. Dorian was more than just a male; he was a symbol, a ghost from a time long buried. And she wasn't sure she could trust him.

"How do we get through without alerting the hunters?" Imani asked, her voice steadier than she felt. Her gaze flicked nervously toward the barrier. Beyond it lay New Lagos—a city she had called home her entire life, but that now seemed as alien as the wilderness they had traversed. Getting through the barrier undetected would be near impossible, even with his knowledge.

Dorian turned to her, his eyes narrowing as he studied her face. There was something unreadable in his gaze, something that sent a strange shiver through Imani's spine.

"We follow the river downstream," he said, his voice low and controlled. "There's an old access tunnel near the northern sector. It was used for maintenance before they automated everything. It's abandoned now, but it'll get us past the primary grid."

Imani nodded, her mind racing with the magnitude of what they were about to attempt. The tension between them was thick, an invisible thread pulled tight by the weight of their shared mission. She could feel it—the unspoken understanding that once they crossed that barrier, they would no longer be fugitives in the wilderness. They would be intruders in a city that no longer had a place for Dorian. And they would be hunted.

"Lead the way," she said, her voice barely above a whisper, her throat tightening.

Dorian's face remained unreadable, a mask of calm that gave nothing away. But there was something in the way his gaze lingered on her that sent a thrill of unease through Imani, making her heart pound. Without a word, he turned and led her down the riverbank, his movements fluid and precise. He moved like a shadow through the underbrush, his steps silent, his eyes constantly scanning their surroundings, every sense attuned to danger. It was eerily reminiscent of a Phantom Hunter.

Imani's pulse quickened, the unsettling realization creeping over her—she was watching a man move with the lethal grace of a highly trained assassin. Her adrenaline surged, instincts sharpening as the uneasy truth settled in: Dorian wasn't just a useless male; he was more skilled than she'd dared to imagine.

Imani followed closely, her breath shallow as they navigated the dense foliage. Every sound seemed amplified in the silence—the crack of a branch, the whisper of leaves in the wind. Above them, the faint hum of drones patrolling the skies sent waves of unease through her. She could feel the Council's reach even out here, beyond the city's dome. It was like a cold hand brushing the back of her neck, a constant reminder of the eyes watching, waiting for them to make a mistake.

Suddenly, Dorian froze, holding up a hand. Imani stopped, her heart hammering in her chest as her gaze followed his to the horizon. In the distance, just beyond the barrier, she saw them—hunters.

They moved with deadly precision, their black armor gleaming in the dim morning light. Their faces were obscured by helmets, but Imani knew who they were. The Phantom Hunters. They moved in formation, pulse rifles slung across their backs, their steps silent and lethal.

Imani's blood turned to ice. She had been trained alongside these women once, in the early days of her life, when she had aspired to be one of them. They had been the Council's sword, the enforcers of the new order. And now, they were hunting her.

"There are five of them," Dorian whispered, his voice a low growl. "They're heading toward the northern sector. If we engage them, we're dead."

Imani swallowed hard, her throat dry. "What do we do?"

Dorian's eyes shifted toward her, shadowed and impenetrable. "We wait. Let them pass."

They crouched low in the underbrush, the minutes stretching on like hours. Imani could hear her own breathing, quick and shallow, her heart racing as the Phantom Hunters drew closer. She could feel Dorian's presence beside her, a coiled spring of tension, his body inches from hers. The air between them felt charged, as if the energy of the barrier itself pulsed through the space, vibrating with something unspoken.

As the hunters passed, Imani's breath stalled in her throat. One of them paused, her helmeted head turning slightly, as if she sensed something. Imani held her breath, willing herself to disappear into the foliage, her pulse thundering in her ears. The hunter stood still for a moment longer, then continued on, disappearing into the forest beyond.

Dorian exhaled slowly, the tension in his shoulders easing slightly. "Now," he said, his voice low. "We move."

They moved quickly, following the river downstream, their footsteps light but urgent. The barrier loomed closer with each step, its surface shimmering in the morning light. Imani could feel the hum of its power now, vibrating through her bones, a constant reminder of the technological masterpiece that separated them from New Lagos.

Dorian led her to the mouth of a narrow tunnel, barely visible beneath a tangle of vines and overgrown brush. The entrance was rusted, the metal corroded by years of exposure to the elements, but it was intact.

"This is it," he murmured, crouching beside the entrance as he pulled away the vines. "The tunnel runs under the barrier. It'll take us into the old infrastructure grid."

Imani nodded, her pulse racing. The tunnel was dark, the air thick and stale. She felt the weight of the earth pressing down on them as they stepped inside, the walls narrow and claustrophobic.

"Stay close," Dorian said, his voice a low rumble in the confined space.

Imani followed him into the darkness, her hand brushing the cold, damp walls as they moved through the tunnel. Her heart pounded in her chest, the tension between them palpable. She couldn't shake the feeling that something was about to go horribly wrong.

As they emerged on the other side, Dorian paused, his eyes scanning the area. They had made it past the barrier, but the real danger lay ahead. The city's lower levels were riddled with old security systems and drones—relics of a time when New Lagos had been a fortress against the outside world.

"We need to move fast," Dorian said, his voice tight. "The drones patrol this area, but they're automated. If we're quick, we can avoid them."

Imani nodded, swallowing her fear as they descended deeper into the labyrinthine tunnels, the walls closing in with an oppressive darkness. The air was damp, heavy with the scent of rust and decay. Every footstep seemed louder, every breath sharper. Suddenly, a figure materialized from the shadows with eerie silence—a Phantom Hunter, her curved blade gleaming wickedly under the faint light.

Without a word, the hunter lashed out, her sword slicing through the air, aiming for Dorian's head with deadly precision. But Dorian moved with a speed and agility that belied his size, almost as if he had been trained in the art of the hunt himself. Anticipating the strike, he ducked low, his movements fluid and effortless. Rolling forward across the grimy floor with a grace usually reserved for the most elite of assassins, he appeared behind the Phantom Hunter in a blur of motion.

Before she could react, Dorian's powerful arm snaked around her neck, locking her in place. His grip was unyielding, his muscles taut like coiled steel, and for a brief moment, the hunter's eyes widened in shock. A male had matched her in skill, and now, she was at his mercy. Dorian's hand went for his blade, his movements fast and deadly, but Imani grabbed his arm, stopping him. Her pulse raced as she met his gaze, her eyes wide with a mixture of fear and determination.

"You can't kill her," she whispered, her voice trembling.

Dorian's eyes flashed with fury. "Why not? She would not show either of us mercy."

Imani's throat tightened as she struggled to keep her voice steady. "Because you are a male," she said, her eyes hardening. "I won't stand by and let you kill a woman. Not in front of me. No matter the reason, no matter the place—there's nowhere in this world where I would ever allow a male to harm a woman."

The silence between them was suffocating, the weight of Imani's words hanging in the air like a stone. Dorian's gaze hardened, his jaw clenched, but he didn't move.

"She can't be allowed to live," he hissed, his voice barely a whisper.

"Agreed," Imani said, her voice cold as she stepped forward, drawing her own blade. There was no hesitation, no mercy. In a swift, calculated movement, Imani slashed the Phantom Hunter's throat. Her blade cut clean, the sound of it sharp in the narrow tunnel. The woman's eyes widened, surprise flickering in them for a brief second before she fell to the ground, her hands clutching at her neck as blood pooled beneath her. Imani didn't flinch, her face a cold mask as she watched the life drain from the woman's body. The Phantom Hunter—an elite warrior, just like she had once aspired to be— was dying.

The tunnel was silent, save for the faint, dying gurgles of the fallen woman. Imani's heart pounded in her chest, the adrenaline surging through her veins like wildfire. She had killed before, of course—had trained to be a Phantom Hunter, before the injury. But this felt different. The woman at her feet had been one of her own, a soldier of the Matriarchy. And now she was dead by Imani's hand.

Dorian was watching her closely. There was something in his eyes—an intensity, a curiosity—as if he were seeing her for the first time. "You didn't have to do that," he said quietly, his voice low and measured. "I would have handled it."

Imani sheathed her blade, her jaw tight. "I told you. I can't let you kill her. I'm still loyal to the Matriarchy. That woman… she was just doing her job."

Dorian's gaze darkened, his lips curling into a humorless smile. "Loyal to the Matriarchy? The same Matriarchy that hunts you now? The same Council that sent her to kill you? You can't see it, can you?" He shook his head, frustration seeping into his voice. "You still believe in the lies they've fed you."

Imani bristled, her fists clenching at her sides. "It's not a lie. The Council has kept us safe for centuries. They've created order out of chaos."

"Order?" Dorian's voice was sharp, biting. "Is that what you call it? A system where power is everything, and those without it are left to die in the wilderness? Do you think they're any different from the men who ruled before them? Power corrupts, Imani. It doesn't care about gender. It doesn't care about anything but itself."

Imani felt a surge of anger flare in her chest. "And what do you know about power? You've spent your entire life hiding from it. You haven't seen what the world was like before the Matriarchy took control. You don't know the kind of brutality men are capable of. They ruled through violence, through fear. The Council stopped that. They gave us peace."

Dorian's eyes flashed, his voice dark and bitter. "Peace? You call this peace? My mother died because of that 'peace.' I watched her give up everything to protect me from the very people you're still loyal to. The Council doesn't care about peace, Imani. They care about control. And they'll do anything—sacrifice anyone—to keep it."

Imani inhaled deeply, a cold knot of guilt twisting in her gut. She wanted to argue, wanted to push back against the anger in Dorian's words, but she couldn't. Not fully. The truth was, a part of her had always known that the Matriarchy wasn't as perfect as it appeared. But admitting that would mean unraveling everything she had believed in, everything she had fought for. Something she was not willing to do just because a male was finally…after centuries…making sense.

Her voice softened, trembling. "I don't trust men. You weren't there when they ruled. You didn't see the destruction they caused, the way they treated women like property, like nothing more than tools to be used and discarded. I can't… I can't forget that."

Dorian's expression softened, but his voice remained firm. "And I can't forget what the Matriarchy has done to me. To my mother. We're all prisoners of our past, Imani. But that doesn't mean we have to keep repeating it."

For a long moment, they stood in the dimly lit tunnel, the weight of their words hanging heavy between them. Imani's chest constricted as she gazed at Dorian—truly seeing him for the first time. He was nothing like the men she had been taught to fear. His caramel-colored skin glistened faintly in the low light, his locks falling across his broad shoulders, his body lean and muscular, hardened by years of survival in the wilderness. But it wasn't his physical presence that drew her in—it was the intensity in his eyes, the fire burning beneath the surface.

There was a tension between them, a pull that neither of them fully understood. Imani could feel it, this strange energy that crackled in the air between them, like the invisible charge of the barrier they had just passed beneath. Her mind told her to push it away, to fight it—but her body betrayed her, the heat in her veins making her heart race.

Dorian's gaze lingered on her, his eyes flickering with something unspoken. He stepped closer, his voice lowering. "We need to keep moving. The Council's forces will be hunting us, and they'll be relentless. The lower levels of the city aren't safe for long."

Imani swallowed hard, forcing herself to focus on the task at hand. "Right," she said, her voice steadying. "Let's go."

They moved through the tunnel with renewed urgency, the air growing thicker and more oppressive as they ventured deeper. The walls were lined with dormant power conduits and old security cables, relics of the city's early infrastructure. Dorian navigated the maze-like passages with ease, his movements sure and deliberate, as though he had memorized every inch of New Lagos's underworld.

"My mother taught me how to move through the city without detection," Dorian explained quietly as they walked. "She became one of the Council's personal guards before she fled. She knew all the weak points, the hidden tunnels, the old access routes that even the Council has forgotten about."

Imani glanced at him, surprise flickering in her eyes. "Zara was a Black Lotus?"

The Black Lotus was more than a guard—they were the council's shadow, the unseen blade, and the embodiment of untouchable perfection. Unlike the Phantom Hunters, who were relentless on the battlefield, the Black Lotus existed beyond that realm. They were a force of nature, sculpted by the Council's most advanced bioengineering. Their bodies were flawless weapons—lean and powerful, enhanced well beyond human potential. Reflexes like lightning, muscles coiled like tempered steel, every breath they took calculated for efficiency and precision.

Unlike the ferocity of the hunters, the Black Lotus moved with an eerie, almost unnatural grace. Their presence was a whisper in the air, a ripple in the atmosphere before they struck, so fast and silent that many had died without even knowing they were under attack. No armor clanked, no weapons flashed; their very silence was their deadliest weapon.

Each member of the Black Lotus was handpicked, trained not just in combat, but in the art of psychological warfare. Their fighting style was elegant yet brutal, every strike designed to incapacitate or kill with chilling precision. Their swords were extensions of their will, as fluid as water, and they used them with an expertise that bordered on supernatural. Even the Phantom Hunters, known for their brutality and fearlessness, whispered tales of how a single Black Lotus could dispatch an entire squad of Phantoms without breaking a sweat.

Their sole duty: protect the Council of Mothers. They never engaged in warfare outside their task, never hunted enemies. To them, the battlefield was beneath their calling. The only threat they acknowledged was any that dared come near the Council's chambers. It was said that to see a Black Lotus was to know that your life had already ended—it was just a matter of when. Their black, polished armor was devoid of insignias, no need for decoration when they themselves were the symbol of power.

The Black Lotus was not feared for their numbers, nor for their ferocity, but for their unmatched, calculated perfection. No one fought them. No one dared. They were better—better than the hunters, better than the soldiers. Better in every way.

Dorian nodded, his expression darkening. "She was one of the best. Until she realized what the Council was really doing. When she found out she was pregnant with me, she knew she had to run. The Council would never have let her or me live."

Imani felt a pang of guilt twist in her chest. Zara had been her mentor, her ally during their early years of becoming a geneticist. But being a Black Lotus meant living a life of secrecy. Living double lives. One on the surface and the other in the shadows. You would never know who a Black Lotus was until you crossed their line of sight. Which would mean you were a threat to the Council of Mothers.

"I never knew," Imani whispered. "She never told me."

Dorian's gaze softened slightly. "She didn't want to put you in danger. She knew the Council would have killed anyone who tried to help her."

Imani swallowed the lump in her throat, her mind racing with memories of Zara. She had been strong, fierce, and unyielding in her loyalty to the Matriarchy. But somewhere along the way, that loyalty had broken—and now Imani was beginning to understand why.

As they reached the end of the tunnel, Dorian stopped, his eyes scanning the area ahead. They were close now—close to the city, to the heart of the Council's power. Imani could feel it in the air, the hum of the bio-grid growing louder, vibrating through the walls like the pulse of a living organism.

"We're almost there," Dorian said quietly. "But once we're inside, there's no turning back."

Imani nodded, her heart pounding in her chest. They were about to step into the lioness's den, and once they crossed that line, everything would change. The Council would be waiting. The hunters would be searching. And the virus would continue to spread, consuming everything in its path.

Imani glanced at Dorian. There was something about him—something she couldn't quite place. He was a mystery, a contradiction. He was a male, the one person she had been taught to fear. And yet, as she stood beside him, she felt something stir within her—something dangerous, something electric.

But she couldn't afford to dwell on it now. Not when the fate of their world hung in the balance.

"Let's go," she said, her voice firm.

And together, they stepped into the darkness.

Chapter 6:

The Shadow in the Chamber

Imani and Dorian moved cautiously through the dimly lit tunnels beneath New Lagos, their footsteps echoing softly against the damp stone. The air was thick with dust and the faint, metallic scent of decay, and darkness stretched before them. The walls were lined with corroded pipes and exposed wiring, remnants of a time long past. They were deep in the forgotten underbelly of the city, rumored to be the birthplace of the Matriarchy—long abandoned and left to decay.

Dorian broke the silence, his voice low and steady. "My mother used to tell me about these tunnels. She said they were the foundation of a new world, the place where the first leaders of the Matriarchy made their plans for a society free from the oppression of men. She called it 'The Stronghold.'"

Imani nodded, surprised by the familiarity in his tone. "The old labs," she murmured, glancing around at the crumbling walls. "They say this is where the first advancements were made, the birthplace of the Matriarchy. But few remember what really lies beneath New Lagos. I'm surprised your mother told you about it."

Dorian's gaze lingered on her. "She believed that history, real history, should be remembered. Not just the sanitized version the Council tells everyone. She wanted me to understand what was lost when the virus wiped out the men. How fragile our existence truly is."

Imani shivered, a chill running through her despite the stale warmth of the tunnels. "If that virus is mutating now," she said carefully, "then we may be facing something even worse than what happened back then. The current strain targets women, attacking from within, turning them into… something monstrous. If we're going to find a way to stop it, we need samples of the original virus. They're down here, in these labs. With those, and your DNA, we might be able to create a cure."

Dorian raised an eyebrow, studying her closely. "So you think exposing this mutated virus to my DNA could weaken it? Force it to react to something it hasn't seen in centuries?"

Imani nodded slowly, her gaze intense. "That's exactly what I'm thinking. We've never had a chance to study how the virus would react to the Y chromosome. It was made to evolve, to adapt to its environment. If we expose it to something it can't recognize—something that's been absent for two hundred years—it might destabilize. We might be able to find a weakness."

Dorian's expression remained skeptical, though his interest was clear. "And you really think these old labs can give you what you need?"

"I don't have a choice," Imani replied, glancing down at the faded map on her datapad. "My lab is too close to the heart of New Lagos. There's no way I can take you there without setting off alarms and risking everything. But the old labs… they should still have the equipment we need. The Council abandoned them when they built the new city, but if we can get the power back online, they should work. And with the original virus samples down here, we can test your DNA against them directly. It's our only option."

Dorian's face softened for a moment, though the intensity in his gaze never wavered. "You're taking a big risk, trusting me with all this. How do you know I won't just take my chance and leave?"

Imani looked at him, a hint of vulnerability in her expression. "I don't know that. But your mother… she believed in you. And for what it's worth, I want to believe in you too. This isn't about the Council or the Matriarchy. This is about survival, Dorian. If we don't stop this, there may be nothing left to save."

Hearing Imani call him by his name momentarily softened Dorian's hardened resolve. For so long, women's hatred of men had stripped them of even the most basic acknowledgment of their humanity; they were rarely called by their names, referred to only by their gender as if that alone defined them.

A silence stretched between them, weighted with unspoken understanding. Finally, Dorian nodded, his expression grim. "Then let's keep moving. We need to reach the main control room to restore power. Once the systems are online, we'll have access to the labs. Without power, all the lab doors will stay locked, and we'll be trapped down here."

Dorian's gaze drifted down the darkened tunnel, tension coiled in his posture. "Follow me. Let's see what secrets these old labs are hiding."

Together, they pressed deeper into the tunnels, shadows stretching around them as they made their way toward the control room. The silence grew heavier, each step bringing them closer to the heart of the Matriarchy's past—and perhaps, to the cure that could save them all.

The old control room felt like a tomb. Faint light flickered from ancient consoles, casting jagged shadows that clawed at the cracked walls. A hum of dormant machinery droned in the background, but that wasn't what made the air feel thick and oppressive. It was the presence of the figure standing across the room, cloaked in darkness. Imani gasped, every muscle in her body tensed, her mind screaming danger. She knew—they both knew—what this was.

A predator. Watching them. Waiting.

The woman who stepped forward was tall, her frame lean but strong beneath her dark cloak. The dim light caught her eyes, burning cold and sharp, predatory. She moved with the deadly grace of someone who knew their power was absolute, a cat toying with its prey before the kill. Every step seemed deliberate, filled with malice. This was a hunt, and Mara—the Council's deadliest assassin—was the hunter.

Dorian stood rigid beside Imani, his muscles taut as a bowstring ready to snap. His hand hovered near the hilt of his blade. He didn't speak, didn't even blink. There was no need for words. They both understood the gravity of the moment. Mara wasn't just any threat. She was one of the elite Phantom Hunters, a creature born from the Council's obsession with control. She was the darkness that swept across the city, wiping out those who defied the order.

"The Council's been expecting you—and that thing standing beside you," Mara said, her voice smooth as silk yet laced with a venom that sent an involuntary shiver down Imani's spine. "I gave you one week to bring that male forward, but instead of loyalty, you've chosen death."

Her words sliced through the air with an unsettling calm, like a blade gliding through flesh. The weight of her presence was palpable, and the room seemed to shrink under the quiet menace of her tone. Imani felt a cold knot tighten in her gut. Mara's reputation had always preceded her—death incarnate, a ghost who moved through shadows with such lethal precision that even whispers of her name carried dread. There was no need for raised voices or threats; the chilling certainty in her voice was enough to strip the courage from anyone who dared defy her.

Mara took another step forward, her cloak shifting around her like a living thing, revealing the insignia of the Phantom Hunters etched into the fabric. Imani's throat tightened. This wasn't just about survival anymore. The Council had sent their best. There would be no mercy here.

Dorian's hand curled around his blade, his eyes narrowing. "My mother warned me about women like you."

Mara tilted her head, a cruel smile playing on her lips. "Did she now?" Her voice was almost a purr, as if the mention of Zara amused her. "Zara was always too clever for her own good."

"You shouldn't have come here," Dorian growled, stepping in front of Imani, his frame shielding her from the looming threat. "If you think I'm going back to the Council with you, you're wrong."

Mara let out a soft chuckle, the sound low and unsettling, like the scrape of metal on stone. "Oh, male," she said, her tone dripping with condescension. "You will come back. Not because of the Council. But because of me." She flicked her gaze to Imani, her eyes gleaming with cruel understanding. "She's why you're really here, isn't she? Did she tell you; you were our last hope?"

Imani's heart stuttered in her chest, cold fear twisting its way through her veins. Mara knew. Somehow, she had seen through the facade, through the mission. This wasn't about finding Dorian. It was about protecting him. And in doing so, she had put both of them in the jaws of the Council's trap.

Dorian's eyes hardened. "Leave her out of this."

Mara's hand slid beneath her cloak, and in the dim light, Imani caught the flash of metal—a curved blade, sleek and deadly, like the fang of a serpent. "I don't think I will," Mara whispered. "You've been running a long time, male. But it ends tonight. You're coming with me, dead or alive. But come to think of it, I was given a choice. I choose dead."

In a blur of motion, Mara attacked. Her speed was terrifying—inhuman, even. The room exploded into chaos as Dorian barely deflected the first strike, the clash of steel ringing out like a gunshot in the confined space. Mara's blade was a streak of silver, cutting through the air with deadly precision. Each strike was calculated and controlled. She moved like water, her movements fluid and graceful, each one designed to wear Dorian down.

Dorian, on the other hand, fought with raw, primal fury. His strikes were powerful but unrefined, the product of survival in the wilderness, with some formal training, but nothing that could contend with Mara. He countered her attacks with brute strength, his muscles straining with the effort. But Mara was relentless. She moved faster than he could keep up, each of her strikes narrowly missing vital points. Suddenly, her blade grazed his arm, leaving a trail of blood that dripped onto the cold floor.

Imani watched in horror as Dorian struggled against the superior fighter. Mara was toying with him, and she could see it. Each strike became more dangerous, more precise. Dorian's breathing grew labored, his face slick with sweat as Mara drove him back, cornering him.

The moment came fast. Too fast.

With a flick of her wrist, Mara knocked Dorian's blade from his hand, sending it skidding across the floor. She moved in for the kill, her blade raised high, aimed for Dorian's heart. Imani screamed, panic surging through her as she watched in helpless horror.

No. Not like this.

Instinct took over. Imani moved without thinking, grabbing a rusted pipe from the ground and hurling herself at Mara with a force she didn't know she possessed. The metal struck Mara's shoulder with a sickening thud, knocking her off balance. For the first time, the Phantom Hunter faltered.

Dorian rolled out of the way, his chest heaving as he scrambled to his feet, his eyes wide with disbelief. Imani stood between them, her hands trembling as she gripped the pipe like a lifeline.

Mara turned to face Imani, blood seeping from the wound on her shoulder. But her eyes—those cold, predatory eyes—never wavered. "You'll regret that," she hissed, her voice a venomous whisper.

Imani's heart hammered in her chest, but she didn't back down. She couldn't let Dorian die. Not like this. "You'll have to kill me first."

Mara's lips curled into a snarl, and for a moment, Imani thought she might lunge at her, but then something strange happened. Mara's expression shifted—just for a second. Her eyes flickered with something almost... supernatural. The light in the room dimmed, and the surrounding shadows seemed to grow darker, deeper, swallowing her whole.

Imani blinked, and Mara was gone.

The silence that followed was deafening. Imani stood frozen, her chest heaving, the pipe still clenched tightly in her hands. Dorian stumbled towards Imani, his breath ragged.

"Where did she go?" Imani whispered, her voice trembling.

Dorian shook his head, wiping the blood from his shoulder. "She'll be back," he muttered, his voice hoarse. "That was just the beginning."

Imani's mind raced. Mara had vanished like a ghost, retreating into the darkness as if the shadows themselves had swallowed her whole. But the danger wasn't over. She would return, and next time, she wouldn't make the same mistake.

"Let's get the power on and move," Dorian urged, his voice laced with urgency. "Now."

Imani nodded, quickly scanning the dusty control room until her eyes landed on an ancient power panel embedded in the wall. She approached it, her fingers brushing away layers of grime to reveal a large, rusted lever. With a deep breath, she braced herself, gripping the heavy handle. Her muscles strained as she forced it upward, letting out a low, involuntary groan as the lever growled in resistance, as though the machinery itself resisted being awakened after centuries of dormancy.

A shudder reverberated through the walls as the lever clicked into place, and the control room lit up in a sputtering haze. The lights overhead flickered to life, bathing the tunnel in a harsh, fluorescent glow. From deep within the underground network, a low hum began to build, growing louder as power surged through the forgotten veins of the old city.

The walls seemed to tremble, releasing an eerie, metallic moan as ancient circuits rebooted, reluctantly accepting the current after so many years. Pipes rattled overhead, and a distant whirring signaled the reactivation of ventilation systems, forcing stale air through the tunnels.

Imani stepped back, wiping sweat from her brow, her face illuminated by the soft, pulsing lights. "Alright," she said, catching her breath. "It's on. Let's go!"

As they ran, Imani couldn't shake the feeling of dread that had settled deep in her bones. Mara was still out there, watching, waiting. And the worst part was, she had no idea how to fight someone like her.

But for now, they were alive. And that had to be enough.

They slipped deeper into the underbelly of the city, the weight of their mission pressing down on them like a storm. And somewhere in the darkness, Mara was waiting. Ready to strike again.

The real battle had only just begun.

Chapter 7:

The Labyrinth Below

The tunnels beneath New Lagos were a twisting, suffocating maze, a relic of a forgotten time, their walls slick with damp and age. It felt as if the earth itself was pressing down on them, the weight of centuries of secrets threatening to bury them at any moment. The dim light from the wall mounted lamps flickered in the darkness, casting elongated, eerie shadows across the crumbling concrete. The deeper they ventured, the more the oppressive silence bore down, broken only by the echo of their footsteps and the distant, irregular drip of water.

Imani walked behind Dorian, her breath uneven, her thoughts still racing from their encounter with Mara. Her skin prickled with the cold, but it wasn't just the temperature—it was the residual fear that clung to her like a second skin. Mara had nearly killed them.

Nearly.

And the Phantom Hunter wasn't the kind of enemy who would make the same mistake twice.

Dorian's pace was relentless, his body moving with the fluidity of someone who knew these tunnels like the back of his hand. Imani had questions—about the virus, about the Council, about Mara—but the words stuck in her throat, her mind too distracted by the tension coiled tightly between them.

And then, a question she hadn't expected tumbled from her lips. "Why did you try to protect me back there?"

Dorian didn't answer at first. His broad shoulders, visible even in the shadowy light, tensed as he walked, his jaw clenched. He wasn't the type to talk about his feelings; that much was obvious. But something about Imani's voice cut through the silence between them.

He slowed his pace and glanced back at her, his dark eyes unreadable. "I don't know," he said finally, his voice low, almost gruff. "I've never felt like I needed to protect anyone… except my mother."

His words were raw, unfiltered, and Imani felt her heart squeeze at the mention of his mother. She had seen that look in his eyes before—a haunted look, one that spoke of pain buried deep beneath layers of survival. She wanted to ask him more, but there was something in his tone, in the way his voice trembled slightly, that stopped her. He wasn't ready to go there.

But he went there anyway.

"She's gone," Dorian whispered, his voice trembling, barely audible. "I couldn't save her. Something… something out there in the wilderness got to her." He swallowed hard, the weight of his words heavy with guilt and pain. "I was sick—feverish. My body was reacting strangely, changing, and she went down to the river to gather herbs. Something to help with the fever. But she never came back."

Dorian's gaze dropped to the ground, his jaw tightening as the memories resurfaced, each one a dagger to his heart. "I forced myself to go after her, even though I was weak. I dragged myself through the forest, desperate to find her. And then I did—" His voice broke for a second. "But all I found were signs of a struggle. Blood... so much blood. There was no trace of her after that. No body. Just silence. She was gone."

His words hung in the air like a lead weight, the grief so raw, it felt like it might crush him.

Imani's stomach churned at the thought. A part of her wanted to reach out to him, to say something—anything—but the words failed her. What could she say? The Council had destroyed his life. His mother, his only link to the world of women, had been taken from him. She had a sudden, overwhelming sense of guilt for ever thinking of him as anything less than human.

"I'm sorry," she murmured, her voice thick with emotion.

Dorian didn't respond. He turned away from her and continued down the tunnel, his silhouette hard and unyielding, the past still clinging to him like a shadow he couldn't outrun.

The silence between them grew heavier, and Imani's mind shifted to the task at hand. The virus. The original samples. Everything hinged on their ability to access the bio-storage facility. She could barely wrap her mind around the revelation that Dorian's DNA was the key. His mother's DNA. The woman who mentored Imani, who had been her friend, her confidante. Zara. It was almost too much to process.

Suddenly, Dorian stopped in front of an enormous metal door, its surface rusted and worn. The air grew even colder here, and the damp stench of decay hung heavily in the air.

"This is it," Dorian muttered, running his hand along the door. "The bio-storage facility."

Imani's heart skipped a beat as she stared at the door. It was here, just beyond this threshold, that the truth lay. The original virus, the samples... everything.

Dorian crouched beside the biometric scanner embedded in the wall next to the door, his fingers hovering over the device as he hesitated, casting a hard glance at Imani. "You realize the Council always knew about the mutation," he said, his voice low and tense. "They've known from the very beginning. This virus—what it's become—it didn't happen by accident. This place, this facility... it's where it all started."

Imani's heart pounded, her throat tight with disbelief. "What are you saying?"

"They didn't make a mistake, Imani," he continued, his voice laced with barely controlled fury. "This virus wasn't a fluke of nature. It was created, engineered. Over two hundred years ago, your Council designed it to eliminate men."

Imani felt as though the ground had shifted beneath her. The virus, which had wiped out the male population of the planet... was a deliberate act? She had always heard rumors, whispers of secret experiments, but this? "I can't believe that," she said, her voice trembling. "It's impossible. Women were oppressed—slaves, denied education, reduced to breeders and commodities. They wouldn't have had the means, let alone the power, to create a virus like that."

Dorian looked at her, his eyes hard. "And yet you, a geneticist, never questioned the Y Chromosome Virus? How can a virus only target one gender? How did it spread so fast, without any trace of origin? And then, almost miraculously, it just vanished, leaving a world without men. My mother told me everything—she was there. She was one of the children the council rescued and brought them to this place."

Imani's eyes widened as Dorian continued, his voice dark. "My mother remembered Seraphine as a little girl, they were both just children when this all began. Seraphine was traumatized, broken by what men had done to her, and it shaped her into the ruthless leader she is now. She is capable of doing anything to make sure men will never return, that no male would ever hold power again. And when Dr. Lyra Amari engineered the virus, Seraphine saw her as a savior, the architect of her vengeance. They created this world together, built on eradication and silence, waiting down here in cryosleep until the last man was dead."

Imani shook her head, her face pale. "You have no proof of this. It's just a story. It has to be."

Dorian's mouth twisted into a grim smile. "You won't need to take my word for it. My mother's DNA grants me full access to the bio-storage facility. She told me all about these old labs, the archives hidden in this place. The Council doesn't want this truth out, Imani, because it would destroy everything they built. But on the other side of this door…"

He glanced back at her, his expression deadly serious. "On the other side of this door, you'll find the proof you're looking for. The truth will reveal itself."

He pressed his thumb to the scanner, and with a soft click, it came to life, analyzing his genetic signature. The scanner beeped, recognizing his access and the door hissed open. The stale air that rushed out from the darkness beyond was thick with the scent of chemicals and dust. Imani stepped forward, her heart hammering in her chest.

They entered the lab. Rows of long-dormant equipment and ancient terminals lay shrouded in dust, their screens flickering with dim, ghostly light. The walls were lined with containment units, some still glowing faintly, others shattered and dark.

"Here," Dorian said, leading her toward the far end of the room. "These are the original samples."

Imani approached one of the containment units, her hands trembling as she wiped away the dust. Inside was a series of vials, each marked with dates and genetic codes. Her eyes scanned the labels, and her stomach twisted.

This was it. The genesis of their world. The birth of the Matriarchy. The virus that had wiped out billions of men, that had changed the course of history... it was here. She walked over to an old computer terminal and pressed the power button. The computer crawled to life as a series of data sprawled across the screen. The information tore deep into her soul. A revelation that nearly caused her heart to stop in her chest.

"They created it," Imani whispered, her voice shaking. "The Council of Mothers… they built their world on the deaths of billions."

A flash of memory overtook Imani—a scene she had only heard of in whispers. It wasn't the kind of story that lived in books or history lectures. No, this one slithered through the cracks of darkened rooms, muttered in voices too low to be heard. A tale deemed so blasphemous, so dangerous, that even the suggestion of its truth would be enough to condemn the speaker to exile. Outcast from the domed cities, left to face the wilderness alone or to take their chances in the faraway colonies—desolate places without the iron grip of the Council's protection.

In her mind's eye, the vision unfolded like a grainy film reel, the flickering light of a distant past casting shadows that felt all too real. The room was dim, the air thick with tension and purpose. Around a table sat women of all ages, their faces drawn tight with pain, their eyes sharp with fury. These weren't ordinary women. They were leaders, scientists, and mothers. Survivors. Each one carried the scars of the old world, the one ruled by men—a world that had burned in its own hubris and violence, its endless wars and bloodshed.

The room itself was a hidden bunker, somewhere deep beneath the surface of what had once been a major city. Its walls were lined with technology, screens blinking with data, and maps of the world above, now ravaged by chaos. But despite the equipment, the place had a feeling of secrecy, of finality, as though it were cut off from the rest of humanity— a place where the old world could be dismantled piece by piece.

In the center of the table, a holographic image flickered, its pale blue light illuminating the faces of the women gathered around it. It was a model of the human genome, the intricate web of life's code twisting and turning like a labyrinth of invisible threads. But one element stood out among the rest, marked in deep crimson: the Y chromosome.

Dr. Lyra Amari, a geneticist of unparalleled brilliance, spoke first. Her voice was quiet, but it carried the weight of the room's collective anguish. "This is where it begins," she said, pointing to the glowing red marker in the hologram. Her eyes were hard, her features worn from years of surviving in a world that had broken her and every woman she knew. "This is the key to everything. The source of the violence, the hatred. We eradicate this, and we eradicate them."

Around her, the women sat in silence, their faces shadows of rage and fear. Some were politicians, once movers and shakers in a world where their voices were drowned out by men who wielded power like a weapon. Others were survivors of the sex trade, women who had been bought, sold, and broken by a system designed to consume them. There were mothers, too, who had lost daughters and sons to the endless wars—wars fought for land, for pride, for male egos.

And yet, here they were. A coalition of the brightest minds, the most ruthless hearts, gathered not to fight the world of men, but to erase it entirely.

One woman leaned forward; her voice thick with concern. She had managed to escape from the Midwest region of the former United States, fleeing the brutal breeding city of Chicago. In that nightmarish place, women were forced into relentless cycles of childbirth; the incubation period from conception to birth had been accelerated to just three months to ensure a constant supply of offspring to replenish the endless armies of men fighting a war that seemed to stretch on without end.

The newborns were immediately placed into cryo-growth chambers, where their bodies were forced to mature into full-grown adults within a single year. Once grown, they were deployed to the battlefield, human lives churned out like machinery, their only purpose to serve and die in a war not of their choosing. The women themselves were treated like livestock, their eggs harvested and abused at the whims of men, their bodies reduced to instruments of reproduction for the war machine.

This woman had once been one of those "cattle." Against impossible odds, she had escaped and eventually joined the Council, bringing with her the skills and intellect of one of the last educated women on earth—education having been outlawed for everyone but men. Her journey was a testament to resilience, a symbol of defiance against the very system that had once enslaved her.

"Are we certain?" she asked, her voice trembling slightly. "This virus… this thing we're creating. It will not only end men. It will end… everything about them. Their legacy. Their existence. Once this is released, there's no going back."

Lyra's gaze didn't waver. She had heard the same concerns, the same doubts, a thousand times before. "We've been certain since the first experiments. The Y chromosome carries with it the aggression, the predisposition for violence. The data speaks for itself. Men are built to destroy. We end them, we end the threat to our survival."

There was a pause, the weight of the decision hanging over them like a guillotine's blade.

An older woman, her face etched with lines of age and sorrow, finally spoke, her voice raw and heavy, as though each word had been dragged over gravel.

"My daughter," she began, the words trembling with restrained pain. "She was killed by her husband. Beaten to death for the simple crime of wanting to leave him. The courts did nothing. The police turned their backs. She was left to die like an animal."

Her voice cracked, but she continued, her gaze fixed and unyielding. "Her life meant nothing to them. She couldn't wield a weapon; she couldn't read. Her only worth was in breeding, existing solely for the pleasure and whims of men. This world… this world of men… took her from me, robbed her of every chance, every hope."

She looked around the room, her eyes hardened by grief. "I see no other way."

Her words sent a ripple through the room, the collective grief of every woman present bubbling beneath the surface. They had all suffered. They had all watched as the world built by men burned itself to the ground, leaving women and children to pick through the ashes. But now, here in this room, they were the ones with the power. And they would wield it like a weapon.

Lyra activated the hologram again, and the model zoomed in on the genetic code of the virus they had created. It was elegant in its simplicity, ruthless in its precision. The virus would lie dormant, passed through generations without symptoms, until it reached critical mass. And then, in a single stroke, it would wipe out the Y chromosome from every man on Earth. They would be gone—eradicated like a plague.

"Once we release it," Lyra continued, her voice low but steady, "it will spread through every corner of the globe. No male will be spared. And in their absence, we will rebuild. A new world. A world of peace. A world without the weight of their violence."

The room was silent. Then, slowly, one by one, the women nodded. It wasn't just revenge they sought—it was survival. A chance to create a world where their daughters would never have to fear, never have to suffer as they had.

But no one, not even the brilliant minds around that table, had foreseen what would happen next. No one had anticipated the mutation. The virus had been perfect—too perfect. It had eradicated men, yes, but in the centuries that followed, it had evolved, grown stronger, more virulent. And now, the children of the future were being born twisted, deformed, and consumed by the very thing that was meant to save them.

Imani's vision shifted, and the scene flickered like a dying flame, pulling her back to the present. Her breath stilled in her throat, her heart pounding in her chest. The truth of it all hit her like a sledgehammer—The Council, The Matriarchy, the very foundation of their society—it was all built on this, on the deaths of billions. On a single lie.

"The virus…" she whispered, her voice trembling. "It was never meant to mutate like this."

Dorian's eyes burned into hers, his jaw clenched. "They thought they could play gods. They wanted a world free of men, but they created something worse. And now it's coming for them."

Imani felt the weight of her disbelief settle in her chest like a lead weight. Her world, everything she had believed in, had been a lie. Built on the corpses of men who had been erased from history. Tears burned in her eyes, but she blinked them away. Now wasn't the time for grief. Now was the time to act.

"We need to stop this," Dorian said, his voice hard, but there was a flicker of something else there, something Imani hadn't seen before. Compassion. "You can't let their mistakes destroy you. If you give up now, everything's lost. You're stronger than that."

Imani stared at him, her mind a whirl of confusion and fury. She wanted to lash out, to scream at the injustice of it all. But Dorian's words anchored her, grounding her in the present. He was right. They had to stop this—before it was too late.

The sound of approaching footsteps cut through the air like a knife.

Mara.

Dorian tensed beside her, his muscles coiling like a spring ready to strike. "We don't have time for this. We need to move."

But it was too late.

Mara appeared in the doorway, her face shrouded in shadow, her eyes gleaming with malice. "You should have stayed hidden," she said, her voice a dark, menacing whisper. "Now it's over."

Imani barely had time to react before Mara lunged. The fight was brutal, and quick, the air thick with the sound of blades slicing through the dark. Imani fought with everything she had, her muscles screaming in protest, her heart pounding in her chest. But Mara was faster, stronger, her movements a blur of lethal precision.

Mara disarmed her with a vicious twist, throwing Imani to the ground, her blade raised for the killing blow.

But Dorian was there, faster than a shadow. He grabbed Mara by the arm and, with a roar, hurled her across the room. Mara slammed into the far wall, her body crumpling—but before Dorian could reach her, she vanished, melting into the shadows like a ghost.

Imani's breath came in ragged gasps as she pushed herself to her feet, her body trembling from the fight.

"Let's go," Dorian said, his voice tight, his hand gripping hers, pulling her toward the vault. "We're not finished yet."

Dorian used the biometric scanner to close the vault's door behind them, hopefully giving them some time to continue their mission. But as they disappeared into the depths of the lab, Imani couldn't shake the feeling that Mara was still out there, watching, waiting. And this time, she wouldn't fail.

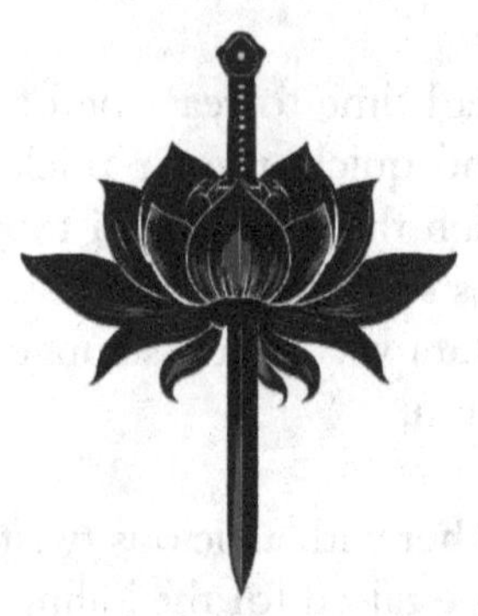

Chapter 8:

Into the Heart of Darkness

The lab was like something out of a nightmare, a relic of an era buried beneath layers of lies and secrets. Glass cabinets, their contents long forgotten, lined the walls, and metal consoles, caked in dust, stood dormant like sentinels of an abandoned battlefield. But it was the dim, flickering lights that cast an eerie glow over the room, illuminating the glass containment chambers scattered throughout, which truly unnerved Imani. It felt as though the shadows themselves were watching, waiting.

Her heart was still racing, adrenaline pumping after their narrow escape from Mara. The cold, metallic air bit at her skin, the sterile smell of the lab reminding her that they were far from safe.

"We're locked in," Dorian muttered, his voice low but sharp, like a blade being drawn.

Imani nodded, her eyes scanning the room. Despite the silence, the room hummed with a strange, unsettling energy.

This place wasn't just any old laboratory—it was the birthplace of the virus. The virus that had wiped out men, altered the course of human history, and now, two hundred years later, was mutating into something far more terrifying.

The virus had been crafted here—genetically designed, she realized, as though seeing it for the first time. The steel consoles held the remnants of the greatest secret the Council of Mothers had ever kept.

The Y Chromosome Virus.

Imani's stomach churned. She had suspected the Council of tampering with the future, of covering up the truth, but this… this was worse than she had imagined.

"We need to find the original samples," Dorian said, his voice steady but lined with the tension that filled the room. His dark eyes flickered around, assessing every corner, every shadow.

"If we can get access to a Council member's personal console, we might be able to unlock more information on The Y Chromosome Virus."

Imani swallowed hard, her thoughts swirling like a storm. "Why didn't they destroy everything?" she asked aloud, as if speaking the question would somehow alleviate the weight pressing down on her.

Dorian paused, glancing at her. "Because they never truly planned for the end. The Council's always been two steps ahead. Even when they created the virus, they knew there would be unintended consequences. They thought they could control it."

Imani shivered at the thought. Control. That's what the Council had always been about, wasn't it? Controlling life, death, and now the truth.

The virus had originally been created as an elegant solution to centuries of patriarchal oppression. It targeted the Y chromosome, designed to wipe out men—violence, brutality, cruelty—all gone in one fatal sweep. But the virus had been too perfect, too efficient. And now, two centuries later, it was no longer content with merely eradicating men. The children born in recent years, infected in utero, were suffering. The virus had begun to twist their DNA, creating mutations—monstrous aberrations of humanity.

Imani recalled the last report she had seen before fleeing the city—babies born with razor-sharp teeth, skin translucent and hard as glass, eyes black and unblinking. Some barely survived the birthing process. Those that did had to be terminated. The Council had buried those horrors, hidden them from the public under layers of propaganda about a perfect matriarchal utopia. But the truth was too ugly to hide forever.

Her chest tightened as the weight of it all bore down on her. She glanced at Dorian. "Thank you," she said softly, almost hesitantly. "For saving my life back there."

Dorian's brow furrowed. He had been quiet since their encounter with Mara, but now, he looked at her with an intensity that made her stomach flutter.

"You don't need to thank me," he replied, his voice rough, raw. "My mother taught me to cherish all life, not just my own.

Imani raised an eyebrow.

His voice softened when he mentioned her, and Imani felt a pang of guilt. Imani's breath stalled in her chest. She could see the pain etched into every line of his face and hear it in his voice. This was the part of Dorian that had been broken long before they met. The part that couldn't heal.

"After she was killed," Dorian continued, his voice barely above a whisper, "I realized there was nothing left for me. No reason to hold on to hope. The Matriarchy... it destroyed everything. My mother died because of them, because of the world they built. And I hated you for it."

Imani felt a sharp pang in her chest. "But she raised you to see women as human beings, didn't she?"

Dorian's expression darkened. "She did. She wanted me to be different, to be better. She taught me to respect women, to see the world through her eyes. But after she was gone... all I could see was the damage. The destruction."

Imani opened her mouth to speak, but before she could say anything, a low, guttural sound echoed through the lab—a rasping, hungry breath. She froze, her heart skipping a beat.

Dorian tensed, his hand instinctively going to his blade. "What was that?"

The sound came again, this time louder, more urgent. It was a noise that chilled the blood—like a creature caught between starvation and madness. Imani's eyes widened as she turned toward one of the large containment chambers at the far end of the room.

Something was moving inside.

She stepped closer, her pulse racing as she peered through the fogged glass. There, hunched in the shadows of the chamber, was a figure. It moved slowly, painfully, dragging itself toward the front of the enclosure. Its body was twisted, malnourished, its limbs elongated and grotesque, skin stretched tight over bones that jutted out unnaturally. But its eyes—those wide, black eyes—were filled with malevolent intelligence.

It was one of the children born infected. A product of the mutated virus.

Imani stumbled back, horror washing over her as the creature pressed its skeletal hands against the glass, its mouth opening in a silent scream. The thing had been trapped in the lab for decades, somehow surviving without food or water. It shouldn't have been alive, and yet, it was. A testament to the virus's terrifying ability to mutate and adapt.

"Dorian," Imani whispered, her voice trembling. "It's one of them."

Before she could react, the creature slammed itself against the glass with a force that rattled the chamber. The glass, weakened by time and decay, began to crack.

Dorian moved in front of Imani, his blade drawn, his stance defensive. "Stay back," he growled.

"Don't let it touch, scratch, or bite you! You'll be infected!" Imani warned, her voice trembling with horror as she took in the sight of the creature within the enclosure. The terror in her eyes made it clear—she understood exactly what the creature was capable of.

With a final, savage lunge, the creature hurled itself at the glass, the force of its impact sending fractures rippling across the surface before the entire pane exploded outward in a spray of jagged shards. It hit the floor in a blur of limbs and claws, a twisted mass of sinew and bone that moved with terrifying speed, far faster than anything that emaciated should have been able to.

The creature let out a guttural snarl, a noise that reverberated through the air like the grinding of stone, its jaws snapping open to reveal jagged, needle-like teeth. It charged, a whirlwind of claws and hate, aiming straight for Dorian and Imani.

Dorian's instincts kicked in. His blade flashed through the air, the steel catching the faint light of the room as he stepped fluidly into position. The creature lunged, its claws swiping down toward Dorian's head, but he was faster. In a blur of motion, he sidestepped its attack and brought his sword up with precision, driving the blade deep into the creature's chest.

The beast shrieked, a spine-chilling sound that seemed to vibrate the very air around them. Thick, black blood splattered onto the floor as the creature thrashed violently, trying to wrench itself free from Dorian's strike. Its sharp claws flailed, desperately attempting to land a blow, but Dorian's grip was unyielding.

Imani, standing frozen for only a heartbeat, quickly regained her composure. She darted to the side, pulling her own blade from its sheath, prepared for any unexpected moves from the creature. The beast was wild, erratic, its body convulsing in a twisted frenzy as it fought against the pain.

Dorian twisted the blade with a practiced, brutal precision, and the creature staggered, its movements becoming more desperate, more frantic. With a swift, final motion, he tore the blade from its chest and spun in a smooth arc, severing the creature's head in one clean strike.

The head hit the ground with a sickening thud, rolling across the floor, black blood spilling from the stump of its neck. The body crumpled, limbs twitching before falling still, a grotesque heap of bone, sinew, and congealed blood pooling beneath it.

For a moment, the room was silent, save for the ragged breaths escaping from the creature's decapitated corpse. Dorian stood tall, not a scratch on him, his breathing calm despite the carnage at his feet.

Imani exhaled slowly, her grip tightening on her blade, ready for any other surprises. But there were none. Dorian glanced at her, his face hard but calm, his eyes scanning the dark corners of the room for any further threats.

"Is that all of them?" she asked, her voice steady despite the knot of tension that had gripped her moments earlier.

Dorian wiped the black ichor from his blade with a practiced flick of his wrist. "For now," he replied, his voice cold and unflinching. "But we need to keep working."

Imani stared at the creature's lifeless form, her heart still pounding. "How... how did it survive?" Dorian whispered, his voice shaky.

"The virus…" Imani began, her voice trembling slightly as she studied the creature, "it's evolved beyond anything we've ever seen. At its core, it's no longer just a pathogen. The infected are technically dead, but the virus reanimates them, overriding their genetic decay and mutating their bodies to adapt to any environment. It's as if it rewrites their cells to suit whatever situation they're in, almost like it's learning from each host."

Dorian frowned, processing her words. "But viruses don't work like that—they're parasitic, sure, but they don't take control. They replicate, destroy the host, and then move on."

"That's exactly it," Imani replied, nodding. "A typical virus would use the host as a vessel for reproduction, burning it out quickly. But this one... it's different. The virus doesn't need food or water to sustain itself—it doesn't even behave like a true biological organism anymore. Its genetic structure is changing, adapting in ways we haven't seen before."

Dorian's expression hardened. "So what you're saying is... it's not just killing its hosts—it's *preserving* them. Keeping them animated, functional."

"Precisely." Imani's voice lowered, laced with anxiety. "It's as though the virus has a survival instinct that goes beyond replication. It uses the host's genetic material to modify itself, ensuring it can continue to spread in a way that maximizes its impact. It adapts with every interaction, rewriting its own genetic code as it encounters new challenges. That's what worries me most. This virus... its mutations don't seem to have limits."

Dorian looked down at the creature with a mix of disgust and horror. "You're saying it could... learn from us?"

"Yes," Imani replied, her gaze intense. "In theory, it could analyze the genetic and behavioral data it encounters. Each host, each human interaction, teaches it something new. The more it adapts, the more efficient it becomes at using its host's body—strengthening muscle fibers, sharpening senses. If it encounters enough humans… it could eventually make the infected smarter and more effective predators."

Dorian took a step back, his face grim. "So, if this mutated virus gets out, it wouldn't just be a mindless horde. We'd be facing an evolving swarm that could think, adapt, even strategize."

Imani nodded, her eyes reflecting the weight of what she was saying. "Exactly. If this virus gains even a fraction of intelligence, if it learns to anticipate us, it won't just be a plague. It'll be a force of evolution—a new predator that could rival anything nature's ever created."

Dorian's jaw clenched. "Then we'd better make sure it doesn't get out."

"But how did it get down here? In that chamber? Someone had to take one of those babies from the birthing chamber and sneak it down here to study years ago. From the looks of this lab and that thing, over forty years at least!"

"But that would mean these mutations have been happening long before you were born. That means the Council has been covering up these mutations for decades. Maybe longer. How deep does this shit go?" Dorian responded, his voice riddled with shock and disgust.

Imani knelt beside the creature's body, her hands trembling as she examined its malformed features. The virus had twisted it into something beyond human, something monstrous. But even in death, it held the answers they sought.

"We need to study this," she said, her voice steadier now. "If we can understand how the virus mutated, we might find a way to kill it. Cause if this is what we can expect, we're gonna need more than a vaccine. We're gonna need an anti-virus that will kill these things more efficiently."

Dorian nodded; his eyes dark with determination.

As they began their grim task, Imani couldn't shake the feeling that this was only the beginning. The virus was alive, and it was changing. And if they didn't stop it soon, it wouldn't just consume the children—it would consume the world.

Chapter 9:
The Mutant's Truth

Imani reached out, her fingers trembling as they brushed against the thing's chest. The skin felt wrong—unnaturally cold and brittle, as if the life had been drained from it long before Dorian's blade ended its misery. Her hand moved slowly, her eyes narrowing as she searched the creature's body for any signs of what had kept it going.

The body twitched, and Imani jerked back with a gasp, her heart leaping into her throat.

"It's dead," Dorian said, his voice low but steady. "It's just the nerves."

Imani forced herself to breathe, calming the panic that threatened to rise in her chest. She leaned in closer, her eyes scanning the creature's head. That's when she saw it—a faint metallic glint beneath the pale skin at the base of its skull. Her stomach turned, a sickening realization beginning to take shape.

"Help me turn it over," Imani whispered, her voice tight.

Dorian nodded and knelt beside her. Together, they lifted the creature, its bones cracking unnaturally as they rolled it onto its stomach. The sound was hollow, like something brittle and broken. As the creature's head tilted, Imani saw it clearly— a small, metallic implant embedded deep into the flesh just behind its ear.

A tracking device.

And something more.

Imani's fingers moved quickly, pulling her datapad from her coat as she scanned the chip. Her heart raced as the screen flickered, bringing up a stream of encrypted data. The chip wasn't just a tracker. It was a neural link, a direct connection to something far more insidious.

Dorian watched her, his brow furrowing. "What is it?"

Imani's fingers flew over the datapad as she accessed the data stored in the chip. The code was old, tangled with layers of encryption, but as she worked through it, a horrifying truth began to emerge.

"This… this isn't just a tracker," Imani said, her voice trembling with shock. "It's connected to the New Lagos network. This thing—this creature—it's been under the Council's control."

Dorian's eyes darkened, his jaw clenching. "They've been controlling them? Using them like… like weapons?"

Imani nodded, her stomach twisting as she uncovered more of the data. "The last command it received was right before it attacked us. The Council was monitoring it this whole time. They knew it was down here and if they knew it was down here when they sent these final commands, they know exactly where we are."

The realization struck her like a punch to the gut, stealing the air from her lungs. The Council hadn't just turned a blind eye to the mutations—they had orchestrated them, controlled them from the shadows. But for how long? How deep did this treachery run? Her mind reeled at the thought. How many more of these abominations were out there, lurking, waiting for their moment?

The Council had always been about cold, calculated efficiency. They never committed resources to anything unless they were certain of a return—a deadly precision in everything they did. The investment in neural links was no small undertaking. It meant one thing: this mutant was far from an anomaly. There had to be more. Many more. The Council had a network of monsters at their command, a silent army of horrors, each of them tethered to the whims of their masters. Her fingers froze over the datapad as another line of code appeared on the screen:

Project Reset—activation pending.

"What's Project Reset?" Dorian asked, his voice low and dangerous.

"I don't know," Imani muttered, her mind racing. "But it's connected to the mutants. The Council knew the virus was mutating—they knew it was creating these… things. And they did nothing to stop it."

Dorian cursed under his breath, his hands curling into fists. "They let this happen. They let the virus spread, knowing it would create monsters."

Imani swallowed hard, her throat tightening as the horrifying truth sank into her like a lead weight. The surrounding lab, once a symbol of progress, now felt like the heart of a monstrous deception. The cold air seemed to cling to her skin, suffocating, as the gravity of what she had just uncovered began to unravel in her mind. Her hands trembled, hovering over the datapad, which displayed the damning evidence—the Council hadn't just failed to stop the virus; they had nurtured it, shaping it into the very tool they used to exert power.

"They didn't lose control of the virus," Imani whispered, her voice barely audible in the cold, sterile air of the lab. "They cultivated it, encouraged it to evolve, let it spread because it gave them something they wanted—something they craved."

Dorian stood beside her, silent, his chest rising and falling with quiet fury as he stared at the mutant's corpse still lying on the examination table. The creature's grotesque, malnourished form was the twisted offspring of centuries of genetic tampering, the result of a virus that had slipped through the fingers of its creators. But this wasn't some rogue mutation. The virus had a purpose—a design that ran far deeper than simply eradicating men.

Imani's voice wavered, her words filled with disbelief and disgust. "The virus... It wasn't just designed to kill men or corrupt children. It was designed to alter women too."

She clicked through more layers of encrypted files on the datapad, her fingers moving mechanically as the horrifying details emerged. The virus had been engineered to target the Y chromosome in men, eliminating them with surgical precision, leaving only women behind. But the Council hadn't stopped there. They had seen potential—an opportunity. The virus was more than a weapon; it was a tool for power, for control. It didn't just stop with killing. It changed women.

The virus had bonded with their DNA, weaving itself into the very fabric of their genetic makeup. But the Council had let it continue evolving and mutating because it offered them something darkly brilliant—an enhancement. It has made women faster, stronger, and more resilient to disease. It had amplified their intelligence, sharpened their reflexes, and extended their lifespans. Women could now live well over a hundred years before their bodies began to show any signs of aging. But with these enhancements came something far more sinister.

"They used it to control us," Imani's voice trembled as she repeated the words, barely able to comprehend the enormity of the betrayal. Her fingers tightened around the datapad, her knuckles turning white. "The virus bonds with women's DNA, enhancing their abilities. But it doesn't just make them stronger, faster, or smarter... it makes them susceptible—more easily manipulated by specific brainwave frequencies."

She could barely choke out the next words. "The Council... they've been using these frequencies to control us. To keep us in line."

The silence in the room was thick, and oppressive, as the depth of the treachery settled between them. Dorian's face was a blank canvas, his eyes dark as he processed what Imani had just uncovered. But beneath that stoic exterior, Imani could sense his anger simmering, barely contained.

"The Council used the virus to breed a better woman," Dorian said slowly, his voice laced with venom. "But a woman who's easier to manipulate, easier to control. They're not just ruling over a society—they're engineering it, down to the genetic level."

Imani felt a nauseating mixture of horror and fury roiling in her gut. "It's not just the physical enhancements," she continued, scrolling through more data, her eyes wide with shock. "The virus subtly rewires the brain. It makes women more responsive to certain frequencies emitted by the bio-grid in the cities. The Council's been using it to alter our thoughts, our behaviors, without us ever knowing."

"That's why they've kept it going," Dorian muttered, his gaze hardening as the pieces began to fall into place. "The virus gave them a perfect tool—a population of superwomen who would willingly follow their commands because they're unknowingly tuned into the Council's frequency. It's not just genetic engineering... it's psychological warfare. Now it all makes sense! How could you ever convince women to be ok with murdering their sons? How could any mother be ok with that?"

"And each time a group of women resisted, they murdered them and their sons and engineered a stronger version of the virus. There are hundreds of versions of the virus in these records. And the last revision was…"

"When?!" Dorian asked, his face engulfed in confusion.

"The day after your mother escaped from New Lagos."

"Are you telling me that right after my mom became immune to their mind control, they mutated the virus again?"

"Yes, and the information about this new strain is locked under Project Reset."

Imani's stomach churned at the realization. The women of New Lagos—and likely every other domed city—had become pawns in a game they didn't even know they were playing. Their thoughts, their very identities, were being manipulated by the Council at a cellular level. This wasn't just a political regime; this was biological tyranny.

The implications were overwhelming. The virus had been the catalyst for the Matriarchy's rise, a tool that wiped out men and allowed women to build a seemingly utopian society. But beneath the surface, the virus had also been the foundation of the Council's control, ensuring that no one could rise against them because they had literally rewritten the rules of human biology.

Imani's mind raced as she considered the consequences. The virus, once hailed as a savior of womankind, was in fact their chains—an invisible shackle that had been keeping them bound to the Council's will for generations.

"But the virus mutated beyond their control," Imani said, her voice laced with both fear and anger. "It started to affect the children, turning them into these... these monsters." She gestured to the grotesque remains of the mutant on the table, its elongated limbs and misshapen body a testament to the virus's deadly potential when it slipped from the Council's grasp.

"You say it's beyond their control," Dorian began, his voice low and seething, "but from where I'm standing, it looks like they've had control the whole time. They anticipated these mutations, planned for them, even. This isn't some scramble to manage a disaster—they've got contingencies lined up, ready to take advantage of every single change. And yet, despite the overwhelming evidence, you still cling to some belief in your Council. Still making excuses for their treachery."

His fists were clenched tight at his sides, knuckles white with fury. Dorian's gaze dropped to the mutant's twisted corpse, the rage simmering in his eyes barely contained.

"This isn't some desperate attempt to salvage a bad situation. It's calculated. Purposeful. They've been playing God all along."

Imani nodded, her voice barely above a whisper. "And they're still trying to control it. That's what Project Reset is... some kind of contingency plan to deal with the mutations. However, the data here is limited. We need access to a Council member's personal console to get the full details."

Before she could say more, a sudden, sharp hiss echoed through the lab. Imani and Dorian both whipped around to see the door sliding open once again. Mara stepped inside, her cloak swirling around her like a shadow, her eyes burning with fury. Her hand rested on the hilt of her blade, ready to strike. She had come here to kill them.

"You," Mara growled, her voice low and dangerous as she stalked toward them. "You think you can ever escape me?!"

Her gaze suddenly flicked to the dead mutant on the table, and something changed in her expression. The cold detachment she had worn like armor cracked, revealing a raw, seething fear beneath.

"What is that and where did you find it?"

"An offspring from a birth gone horribly wrong. And we found it in this lab." Imani responded, taking a step towards the examination table.

"But that thing... that creature. This lab was sealed for decades. How long has that... thing been here?"

Imani stood frozen, her breath trapped in her throat, but she forced herself to speak. "Mara, listen to me. The Council knew," she said, her voice urgent and low. "They knew the virus was mutating, that it was creating these... monsters, and they did nothing. They let it happen because it's giving them control—giving them control over us." Her hands shook as she held up the datapad, then, with a burst of frustration, she tossed it to Mara.

Mara caught it, her eyes narrowed in disbelief. "Imani, that's impossible. Why would they—"

"Just look," Imani insisted, her tone edged with desperation.

With a skeptical glance, Mara tapped through the files. Her face shifted, shock and horror contorting her features as she scrolled through each classified document, each unsettling report. Line after line, the truth unraveled before her: the virus wasn't some tragic accident spiraling out of control. The Council had been aware all along, carefully watching, allowing it to mutate, allowing it to twist their world into something dark and monstrous.

Imani's voice broke the silence. "They've been manipulating us from the start. Using the virus to keep us in check, to make us into… whatever they need." She swallowed, her eyes pleading. "I know it's hard to believe, but you see it now, don't you?"

Mara looked up, her face pale, still gripping the datapad. Mara took a step back, her chest heaving with barely controlled rage. She had been the Council's weapon for years, their enforcer, their executioner. But now, as she stood before the horrifying truth, the cracks in her loyalty were becoming impossible to ignore.

Mara's hands trembled as she scrolled through the data, each revelation clawing deeper into her heart. Her stomach twisted with the weight of the betrayal, her entire life unraveling before her eyes. This was more than a conspiracy— it was the shattering of everything she had believed in. The Council, the Matriarchy, the women she'd looked up to as the architects of freedom and justice… they had known all along. They had kept this infection locked inside each of them, a virus that granted them strength but stripped them of true autonomy. They weren't free. They were being controlled, puppets dancing on invisible strings, tethered by their own bodies.

Her vision blurred as the full horror of it settled upon her. For two centuries, she and her sisters had believed they were finally free from oppression, that they were building a world where women had true power. But behind this utopia, the same insidious tactics of domination still thrived—just rebranded, refashioned, and now wielded by those they trusted most. It was patriarchy in a different guise, still gnawing at their humanity, infecting the soul of their society. Nothing had truly changed. Her whole life, her purpose, had been a lie.

She stumbled, her body weak under the crushing weight of her rage and grief. Her heart hammered wildly, and for a moment, the room spun around her. She looked to Imani with a desperation that bordered on panic, her voice trembling as she spoke. "My sisters… they would never do this to me. They love me. I've fought beside them, bled beside them. I thought… I thought they cared."

Imani's face crumpled with sympathy, but it did nothing to soften the ache inside Mara. Her gaze shifted to Dorian, standing silent and watchful, and something inside her snapped. Rage flared, bright and vicious, and she turned on him, her voice raw with betrayal.

"You and your kind have managed to infect the Matriarchy!" she spat, her voice a mixture of fury and despair. "This reek of your Y chromosomes—the violence, the deceptions, the disregard for human life. This is why your presence is to be eradicated. Your chromosome deleted like an outdated program no longer necessary for the continuity of the system. But this…this isn't what I trained for. This isn't the world I gave my life to build."

Her voice cracked, and she clutched her chest, as if the pain were too much to bear. "You've taken everything from me… my light, my purpose… This kind of cruelty, only a man could conceive of it. Only a man would tear someone down like this."

She took a ragged breath, her voice barely a whisper. "But my sisters… they wouldn't do this. They couldn't. They love me. They…" Her words faltered as tears slipped down her cheeks. "They love me. They… love… me."

But even as she spoke, the words tasted hollow, her faith unraveling with each passing second. She had given everything to the Matriarchy, poured every ounce of her soul into the promise of a world where women were safe, strong and liberated. And now, standing in the wreckage of that promise, Mara realized that love, loyalty, and even freedom had been illusions, twisted beyond recognition by those who were meant to protect them.

Imani reached out a hand, but Mara pulled away, clutching herself as if she could hold the broken pieces of her world together. Her shoulders shook as she fought back the sob that threatened to tear from her throat. She felt gutted, stripped of everything she believed in, every truth she had clung to.

The room was silent, but Mara's world had never felt so loud, a cacophony of shattered trust and buried dreams. Her voice, when it finally came, was barely a whisper. "What did we even fight for... if this is what we've become?"

"I don't know. I have no answers, my sister. But what I do know is whatever Project Reset is they're going to activate it soon and I am almost certain, these things are in the center of that plan," Imani responded, her voice steady but filled with urgency. "We have to stop it."

Mara stared at Imani, her face a mask of simmering fury. She opened her mouth to speak, but then, slowly, she turned her attention to the dead mutant. When she spoke again, her voice was low, filled with venomous hatred.

"If what you're saying is true," she said, her words slow and deliberate, "then the Council has betrayed us all. They've used me. They've used everyone and I want to know why right before I bury my blade in their chests."

Imani nodded, her heart racing. "They've used us all. Project Reset—it's connected to the mutants, but we need more data to understand what they're planning. We can bring them down, but we need your help."

For a long, tense moment, Mara stood still, her breathing heavy, her knuckles white as they gripped the hilt of her blade. Then, slowly, she released her grip and turned toward the dead mutant on the table, her lips curling in disgust.

"They created this," she said, her voice low and filled with fury. "They created these monsters using our babies, and they let it grow beneath our feet."

She looked up, her gaze locking onto Imani's. "We stop this. We bring them down, together."

Imani exhaled, the weight of Mara's words washing over her like a cold wind. The Council's most dangerous weapon had now become their greatest threat. Together, they would unravel the treachery that had been festering in the heart of New Lagos for centuries.

And as they prepared to face the Council, Imani knew one thing for certain: there was no turning back.

Chapter 10:

An Uneasy Alliance

The cold of the lab clung to their skin like a second layer, thick and biting, making each breath visible in the frozen air. Imani and Dorian stood side by side, surrounded by the endless hum of the cryogenic chambers that lined the walls like the silent tombs of forgotten secrets. The tension was unbearable, not just from the deadly presence of Mara lurking nearby, but from the weight of the discoveries they had made about the virus and the Council's betrayal. Yet, deeper truths still eluded them, veiled in the cryptic data they had only begun to unravel.

Mara paced the perimeter of the room like a caged predator, her eyes never leaving Dorian, and the air between them crackled with hostility. Imani could feel it, that palpable charge as if a single misstep or word could ignite an explosion. She had seen Mara fight—experienced it first-hand and knew how quickly things could spiral into bloodshed.

Dorian, however, was holding his ground, his dark eyes fixed on Mara, his jaw set in a tense line. He didn't trust her, not for a second. His fingers twitched near the blade at his side, as though even now, he was ready for her to pounce.

"So," Dorian's voice cut through the silence, each word laced with venom, "I'm supposed to believe you're suddenly on our side? After years of hunting down anyone who even questioned the Council? You expect me to just ignore what you are?"

Mara's lips twisted into a dangerous smile, cold and sharp. "What I am, Dorian, is the reason you're still breathing. If I wanted to, I could have ended this a long time ago. But I'm giving you a chance, which is more than your kind ever gave mine."

Dorian's eyes narrowed. "My kind?"

Mara's smile widened, more feral now. "Males." The word left her mouth like poison, as though just saying it was an offense. "You're all the same—entitled, selfish and violent. I was raised to eliminate threats and males. Males were always the biggest threat of all. And I wouldn't be surprised if a male wasn't pulling the strings of the council. Forcing them to do these horrible things."

Imani's stomach twisted at Mara's words, and she quickly stepped between them, sensing the growing storm.

"Mara, we need to stay focused," she said, her voice steady, though the tension in the room made it hard to breathe. "We don't have time for this."

But Mara's gaze was fixed on Dorian, cold and unwavering.

"No, Imani. He needs to understand his place in all this. You think because you survived out there in the wilderness, you're some kind of warrior?" Her tone was mocking, dripping with disdain. "I've killed men three times your size without breaking a sweat. You're lucky I'm letting you live at all."

Dorian clenched his fists, the muscles in his neck tense. "And what makes you so much better?" he shot back, his voice low, dangerous. "You're nothing more than the Council's puppet, trained to do their dirty work. Don't think for a second that makes you superior."

Mara's eyes flashed, and for a moment, Imani thought she might strike. Her hand twitched toward the hilt of her blade, but she didn't draw it. Instead, she took a step closer, her voice dropping to a deadly whisper. "Watch your tongue, male. I'm not like the Council. I don't need an excuse to kill you."

The air thickened, the space between them shrinking, and Imani could feel the tension escalating to a dangerous peak.

"Both of you, stop," she said sharply, turning to Dorian, her voice firm. "We need Mara's help. And she needs ours. Fighting each other won't change what's happening."

Dorian let out a slow breath through his nose, his eyes never leaving Mara's, but he stepped back, relenting, for now. Mara, too, seemed to ease, though the hatred still simmered beneath the surface.

Imani moved back to the console, trying to focus on the task at hand. The data they had retrieved from the cryogenic chambers was monumental. Every test, every experiment led back to one chilling conclusion—the virus had been designed with surgical precision, and its mutations were no accident.

"According to the files, the Y chromosome virus was specifically programmed to target genetic markers associated with violent aggression," Imani's voice was steady, but the weight of the revelation was palpable.

"At the time, over 98% of the male population—regardless of age—expressed these traits at significant levels. The virus wasn't just a blunt instrument; it was a scalpel, designed to isolate and bind to aggression-linked sequences in the DNA."

She paused, her tone sharpening as she continued. "What we've discovered is that violence and aggression aren't solely learned behaviors—they can be encoded into a life form's genetic makeup, passed down through generations. It's hereditary in nature, reinforced by epigenetic changes triggered by the environment. And in that era, the male population had compounded the problem. Their children were grown in enhanced incubation chambers—accelerating their development artificially—and then programmed with neural directives to exhibit acute aggression. Inhibitors were placed in their systems to suppress empathy and remorse, ensuring that brutality became their primary instinct."

Her expression darkened, the weight of the truth settling in. "It was as if they painted a crosshair on their own backs. The virus didn't have to work hard; it was designed to seek out the very traits that were most prevalent in their biology. Once it found its targets, it destroyed them with ruthless efficiency. It was a perfect predator, one that left no room for survival."

She paused, her eyes narrowing as she analyzed the data. "But with women, the virus responded differently, adapting to our genetic structure in a way that defied its original programming. Instead of triggering aggression, it bonded with our DNA at the cellular level, enhancing key biological functions. Resilience, adaptability, even cognitive efficiency were all heightened. It was as if the virus recognized a more compatible host and shifted its focus from destruction to optimization."

Her voice grew more thoughtful as she continued, "Each new generation presented the virus with a fresh biological landscape to interact with, forcing it to adapt with every replication. As it evolved, it didn't just integrate—it refined its functionality, learning from our biology to optimize its effects. What we're seeing now isn't just adaptation; it's co-evolution. The virus and our genetic structure are reshaping each other in ways we're only beginning to understand. Back then women weren't violent, we were oppressed and weak. The virus responded to us by enhancing us and Dr. Lyra's genetics program pushed the virus effects on us even further."

Imani's fingers tapped against the edge of the console, her face shadowed with confusion. "But when did it turn hostile? What changes in our DNA or environment made it revert, becoming something far more dangerous? It's as if it's now targeting the X chromosome itself instead of the Y. What triggered it?" Her voice trembled with the weight of the question.

Mara's expression turned dark, her voice tinged with quiet resignation. "The Phantom Hunters happened." She took a breath, steadying herself. "We became what men once were— relentless, violent, and creatures of conquest. Our lives started to revolve around hunting, killing, taking pleasure in bloodshed, especially the deaths of males and the women who dared to bring them into this world. In our pursuit of vengeance, we twisted ourselves into the very thing we fought so hard to be liberated from."

Mara's gaze dropped, the faintest hint of sorrow flickering in her eyes. "With our sisters accepting this, our very DNA evolved, but not for the better. We told ourselves we were finally free, finally safe. But deep down, we knew something was wrong, something… off. We were changed, and not in the way we'd once dreamed of."

Dorian frowned, stepping closer to Mara, the tension between them momentarily softened. "If you knew this… if you knew it was corrupting you… why keep killing?"

Mara's face hardened, her voice a whisper edged with defiance. "Because even in this twisted reality, trusting a woman has always been safer than trusting a male."

Imani's fingers flew over the console, pulling up more data. She suddenly paused, her brow furrowing as she unearthed a new file—an encrypted section buried deep within the code. "But the original virus... it's still in these samples. If we can extract it, and pair it with your DNA, Dorian, we might be able to create a vaccine—a way to stop the virus from mutating any further."

Dorian's expression darkened, his mistrust of the Council, of their twisted science, evident. "And what's stopping them from using that same vaccine to make things worse?"

Mara let out a sharp snort, crossing her arms defiantly. "You think the Council would allow a cure to circulate if they didn't stand to benefit from it? They thrive on control, on keeping everyone in their place. The vaccine isn't just about saving lives—it's a tool for power. We need to be the ones holding that power, not them. If we control the vaccine, we control them. We can use it as leverage, forcing them to come to a resolution on our terms. And then I'll bury my sword in their chests."

Dorian's eyes narrowed, his gaze hardening. "And you're suddenly a revolutionary now?"

Mara's face clouded with intensity and she took a measured step toward him, her hand instinctively drifting to the hilt of her blade.

"I didn't spend years wiping out every male I crossed just to have you speak to me like we're equals. We're not," she said, her voice low, each word laced with a razor's edge. "And we never will be. Don't let this temporary alliance inflate your worth in a world that has no place for you. You're still a male, a reminder of everything the Council once vowed to eliminate."

For a moment, the air between them was tense, charged with unspoken tension. Mara's gaze was unflinching, her posture radiating both fury and conviction. "You'd do well to remember that," she finished, her voice cold, with a finality that echoed like a closing door.

Imani moved between them once more, her patience wearing thin. "Enough!" she snapped, her voice stronger than she expected. Both Mara and Dorian stopped, their eyes locking onto her in surprise.

"We have bigger problems than your hatred for each other. If we don't work together, there won't be anything left to fight for."

Mara narrowed her eyes but said nothing, her hand dropping away from her blade. Dorian, though still visibly tense, gave a slight nod, though the fire in his eyes remained.

Imani turned back to the console, her fingers flying over the controls, her focus razor-sharp despite the whirl of thoughts in her mind.

"I'll need time to extract the virus and isolate the original strain," she said, her voice steady, though the weight of what they were attempting bore down on her. "I need to be incredibly cautious to prevent accidentally releasing it into the air—it could kill Dorian in seconds."

"Wouldn't that be a shame," Mara muttered, a smirk tugging at the corner of her mouth, her tone dripping with dark humor.

Imani shot her a look. "Mara, please. You're not helping," she said, her voice laced with both exasperation and urgency. "Once we have the original strain isolated, we can use Dorian's Y chromosome to synthesize a counter-virus. But I need your focus, not your sarcasm, if we're going to pull this off."

Mara's smirk faded slightly, and she crossed her arms, stepping back with a silent nod.

Dorian raised an eyebrow. "And that'll stop the mutations?"

Imani shook her head. "It won't reverse what's already been done, but it will stop the virus from spreading further. It'll give us a chance to stop the Council before they can cause more damage."

Mara's eyes gleamed with cold determination. "Then we'd better move fast. The Council isn't going to sit back and wait for us to destroy them."

Dorian's mistrust still lingered, thick and I' in the air, but Imani knew they had no choice. Mara was right—they didn't have time. The virus was mutating faster with each new birth, gaining strength every time a child is born, transforming them into stronger and more efficient killers and the Council wasn't going to let them get any closer to the truth without a fight.

As Imani began the process of extracting the virus, she felt the weight of the future pressing down on her shoulders. The Council's lies had shaped this world, but now, in the cold, sterile light of the lab, she could see the cracks forming. And with Mara's reluctant help, she knew they had the power to tear those cracks wide open.

But whether they would survive the coming storm was another question entirely.

Chapter 11:

Beneath the Surface of Deceit

The cryogenic chamber hummed with an eerie, mechanical rhythm, a cold, sterile pulse that echoed through the cavernous space like a heart long frozen in time. The air hung heavy, suffused with the biting chill of preserved history, but it wasn't the cold that suffocated—it was the weight of what lay ahead. Imani's fingers danced across the control panel, her movements precise, yet urgent, as if every keystroke carried the weight of the world. The low glow from the console illuminated her face, casting stark shadows that flickered across the walls, the rows of cryo-tubes standing like the forgotten relics of a bygone era, silent sentinels holding the remnants of the old world in their icy grip.

Dorian stood a few feet away, his stance rigid, coiled like a spring ready to snap. His eyes flicked between the heavy steel door that sealed them off from the unknown and the rapidly scrolling data on the screen, a storm brewing in his gaze. Every muscle in his body was taut, vibrating with the tension that permeated the room. His jaw was clenched so tightly that Imani could almost hear the grinding of his teeth, a physical manifestation of the rage and mistrust simmering beneath his surface.

Mara lingered near the exit, her presence as sharp as a blade drawn in the dark. She moved like a predator, eyes always calculating, cold and unreadable. The distance she kept from them wasn't just physical; it was an unspoken barrier, an invisible wall of hostility and mistrust. She leaned casually against the wall, fingers resting lazily near her weapon, but there was nothing relaxed about her. Every breath she took, every slight shift of her body, radiated lethal potential, a hunter watching prey.

The faint blue light from the consoles bathed the chamber in an otherworldly glow, reflecting off the frost-laden tubes, their contents hidden beneath layers of ice and glass. This place was a tomb of secrets, its walls thick with the cold weight of deception, and somewhere within these tubes lay the truth they had come for—the truth that could either save or destroy them.

Now and then, Imani caught Mara's sharp glances at Dorian, eyes gleaming with something close to contempt, but she remained silent. The history between them—between what Mara represented and what Dorian had been fighting his whole life—didn't need to be spoken aloud. It lingered in every look, in the tense silence that filled the room.

The machines beeped softly, alerting Imani that the extraction process had reached a critical stage. Her heart pounded as she focused on the task at hand, knowing how much was riding on this moment.

"This is it," she whispered, her breath fogging in the cold air. "We're almost there."

Suddenly, the lights flickered, and the hum of the machines faltered. A low, ominous tone filled the chamber, followed by the unmistakable sound of systems failing. Imani's pulse quickened as panic surged through her.

"No, no, no…" Her fingers flew over the controls, but the extraction process was grinding to a halt. Without power, they would lose everything.

"The power's cutting out," Dorian muttered, stepping closer, his eyes darting toward the door. "We need to finish this before we're exposed."

Mara's gaze shifted to the console. "I can keep it going," she said, her voice cold and steady, already moving toward the biometric scanner embedded in the wall. "But if I use my bio-signature, the Council will know exactly where we are."

Imani's heart sank. They were out of time, but the extraction was so close. She could feel the weight of the decision hanging in the air, the unspoken consequences of Mara's next move. If she diverted more power to the system, they would have mere moments before the Council dispatched its forces.

"We don't have a choice," Imani said, her voice strained. "Do it."

Mara didn't hesitate. With a single fluid motion, she pressed her hand to the scanner. The machines roared back to life, the extraction process resuming in full. Imani exhaled in relief as data continued to scroll across the screen, but the reprieve was short-lived.

A low, eerie tone echoed through the chamber. The signal. The Council was alerted.

"They're coming," Mara said, her voice flat, a grim acknowledgment of the danger now bearing down on them.

Imani's stomach twisted. The extraction was still in progress, and there was no turning back now. "How long until they get here?" she asked, her voice laced with urgency.

Mara's eyes flicked toward the door, her hand tightening around her blade. "Not long."

Dorian tensed beside her, his gaze hard as he scanned the room, readying himself for whatever came next. But before any of them could speak, a low, guttural sound reverberated through the walls. It wasn't the precise, deliberate footsteps of Phantom Hunters. It was something far more primal.

Imani's blood ran cold. The sound grew louder, more urgent, and the vault door shuddered under the weight of something massive slamming against it.

"What the hell is that?" Dorian asked, stepping back, his eyes wide with confusion and growing alarm.

Mara's expression darkened. "Not Phantom Hunters," she muttered sarcastically.

Imani's heart lurched in her chest. The mutants. The feral creatures, twisted by the virus, bred in the shadows of the Council's darkest experiments. They were here, and they were coming for them.

The vault door rattled again, a shriek of metal as whatever was outside tried to tear it apart. Imani's breath quickened. She turned back to the console, frantically checking the extraction progress. It was nearly complete—but not fast enough. She could hear the creatures clawing at the door, their inhuman growls growing louder, more desperate.

"Finish the extraction," Mara said sharply, her voice cutting through the noise. "I'll hold them off."

Imani glanced up, her pulse racing. "Mara, you can't—"

"I can," Mara interrupted, stepping toward the door with a calm that defied the surrounding chaos. "You're not done here. And if we don't stop them, none of this will matter."

Dorian moved to block her path. "You're not going out there alone," he said, his voice low and defiant.

Mara's eyes rolled in her head like dark brown marbles, her reaction to Dorian was cold and unflinching. "I don't need your help, male. You stay here. Protect her. That's your only job now."

Imani's heart pounded as the door shuddered once more, the sounds of the mutants beyond it becoming a deafening roar. There was no time left to argue. No time to plan.

"I'm almost done," Imani whispered, her fingers flying over the console. "Just hold them off a little longer."

Mara gave a single nod before moving toward the door, her hand resting on the control panel. For a moment, she turned back to Imani, her expression softer than before, a glimmer of something almost human in her eyes.

"Finish it," she said, her voice barely above a whisper. Then, with one swift motion, she unlocked the door and tossed out a plasma grenade. The explosion rocked the corridor outside the lab, momentarily silencing the chaos of the mutants. Mara quickly slipped out into the darkness, sword drawn, determination covering her face. The door slammed shut behind her, sealing Imani and Dorian inside.

Imani's breath stalled in her throat as the sounds of the battle outside erupted into chaos. The screeching of metal, the howls of the mutants, the clash of steel as Mara fought them off—all of it filled the air like a storm raging just beyond the door.

Dorian stood at her side, his jaw tight, his eyes fixed on the door. "She'll be killed," he muttered, but he didn't move, didn't charge after her. He knew, just as Imani did, that Mara had given them the only chance they had.

"I just need a few more minutes," Imani said, her voice trembling as she worked to extract Dorian's DNA. The machines hummed around her, the data flowing across the screen as the final pieces of the puzzle fell into place. But the sounds outside were growing louder, more frantic, and she could feel the weight of Mara's sacrifice weighing her down.

"Come on, come on..." Imani whispered, her heart pounding as the last of the data was extracted. Finally, the screen blinked, signaling completion.

"It's done," she said, turning to Dorian, her voice filled with a mixture of relief and terror. But the sounds outside told her that they had only bought themselves a little time.

And Mara was still out there.

The door rattled violently, and Imani's chest tightened with fear. The mutants were still trying to break through, their relentless hunger driving them forward. But Mara was drawing them away, leading them into the dark depths of the tunnels, buying them precious minutes.

"Let's go," Dorian said, his voice low and urgent. He grabbed her arm, pulling her toward the door opposite the one Mara had sealed. There was no time to think, no time to hesitate. They had to run, had to get the data out, had to survive.

But as they fled into the labyrinth of tunnels, Dorian couldn't shake the image of Mara standing alone in the darkness, fighting the monsters sent to kill them all.

And deep down, he knew that without their help, he might never see her again. The thought gripped him with unexpected urgency, his sudden concern for her stirring a confusing mix of emotions he hadn't anticipated.

Chapter 12:

The Turning Point

The tunnels of New Lagos groaned with an eerie silence, the faint hum of the city's power grid pulsing through the metal walls. Shadows stretched long and dark along the damp passageways as Dorian and Imani moved quickly, their footsteps echoing through the cold air. But as they pressed forward, Dorian's pace slowed, his mind filled with one image—Mara, back there, fighting alone, surrounded by those mutants. He couldn't shake it, couldn't ignore the tug in his chest urging him to turn around.

"We can't just leave her!" he growled, spinning to face Imani. "She's outnumbered and fighting for her life. We have to go back."

Imani's face remained impassive, her eyes fixed ahead. "No, Dorian. Mara knew the risks when she stayed behind, and we can't risk the mission for her. She's holding them off to buy us time—that was the plan." Her voice was calm, but a hint of irritation crept in as she spoke.

Dorian's jaw clenched, his frustration flaring. "Mara is more than just some... some sacrifice, Imani! She's risking everything for us. We owe it to her to go back."

Imani halted, her gaze sharpening as she turned to him, a cold edge in her voice. "Listen to me, Dorian. I can't risk losing you, or the original virus sample. We're talking about the one chance we have to create a counter-virus and fight back against the Council. Mara..." She hesitated but held firm. "Mara is a fierce fighter, but she's expendable. You're not."

Dorian's eyes blazed with anger and disbelief. "Expendable? That's how you see her? But she's your sister?" He shook his head, his fists clenching. "No. If we don't go back, I'm done. I'll abandon this whole mission if I have to. I will not risk my life to save a world that just tosses away life like it's nothing. If that's what I'm saving, then I'd rather watch it burn."

Imani's mouth fell open in disbelief, frustration flashing across her face.

"Are you serious, Dorian? You'd throw away everything we've fought for—everything we need—for her? Not too long ago, she was ready to put a sword through your chest! Or worse, remove your testicles from your body! But now, you want to save her?!"

"Yes," he said, his voice low but resolute.

Something is pulling me back to her, Dorian thought, the feeling of an inexplicable tug at his core.

"So, if you won't help, I'll go back alone."

Imani's jaw tightened, and for a moment, she held his gaze, searching his face for any sign of hesitation. But Dorian's resolve was unwavering, his eyes fierce with determination. She let out a sharp, frustrated breath, her stance stiff with reluctance.

"Fine," she said finally, her voice tense. "But if anything goes wrong, we don't have time to turn back again. You're putting this entire mission in jeopardy for her."

Dorian didn't respond, already moving back the way they'd come, his mind focused entirely on Mara. Imani followed, Her face initially tightened with frustration, but as they retraced their steps through the narrow, winding tunnels, a slow, diabolical smirk began to creep across her lips. The closer they got, the louder the sounds of Mara's struggle became—the clash of metal, the guttural roars of the mutants, and the unmistakable thud of bodies hitting the concrete floor.

Dorian quickened his pace, the unexplainable pull toward Mara growing stronger with every step.

They reached the dead-end chamber just in time to witness Mara, drenched in mutant blood, surrounded by a horde of grotesque, twisted forms. The mutants were unlike anything they had seen before—emaciated, skeletal, with patchy, discolored skin that hung loosely over their malformed bodies. Their eyes gleamed with a feral madness, their mouths filled with jagged teeth dripping with blood. They swarmed her, dozens of them, clawing at her with a hunger that only death could satisfy.

But Mara was a force of nature. Every swing of her blade was precise, every movement a symphony of violence. She fought with a ferocious grace, her body a blur of lethal efficiency. Her sword cleaved through the air with terrifying speed, severing limbs, decapitating heads, but the mutants kept coming. Their blood sprayed the walls, the floor, pooling around Mara's feet as she danced between them, a whirlwind of death and fury. But it was clear that she was tiring. Her breath came in ragged gasps, her once-fluid movements becoming more desperate, more frenzied.

A mutant lunged at her, its jaws snapping inches from her throat, but she sidestepped, driving her blade into its skull. Another clawed at her back, tearing through her armor, ripping flesh, but she barely flinched as she whirled and sliced it clean in half. Still, there were too many. For every one she killed, more seemed to take its place.

She was outnumbered and overwhelmed.

And then, just as a mutant's claws raked across her abdomen, sending her stumbling backward, Dorian roared into the fray. He hit the nearest mutant with the force of a bull, tackling it to the ground before crushing its skull with his bare hands. Blood sprayed across his face, but he didn't care. He was a feral beast now, lost to the primal rage that surged through his veins. Another mutant lunged at him, but he spun, his fist connecting with its jaw with a sickening crunch.

Imani darted into the chaos, her heart pounding, her hands shaking as she pulled her pulse gun from her belt. She aimed for the nearest mutant, firing a bolt of energy that sent it sprawling to the ground. She barely had time to catch her breath before another lunged at her, claws outstretched. She fired again, the blast hitting it square in the chest, sending it flying backward into the wall.

Mara, bloodied and bruised, fought with renewed vigor beside Dorian. Together, they were unstoppable—two forces of destruction tearing through the horde. Dorian's raw strength and Mara's deadly precision made for a terrifying combination. They moved in perfect sync, their movements fluid and brutal as they cut down the mutants one by one. It was as if they were destined to fight alongside each other.

A mutant latched onto Dorian's back, its claws digging into his shoulders, but Mara was there in an instant, severing its head with a single stroke. Blood sprayed across her face, but she barely flinched. She locked eyes with Dorian for the briefest of moments—a flicker of acknowledgment passing between them before they turned back to the battle.

The fight was savage, violent, and gory. Blood slicked the floor, bodies piled around them in grotesque heaps. Imani's pulse pounded in her ears, her breath ragged as she fired shot after shot, her arms trembling from the effort. A mutant lunged at her, its claws inches from her face, but she ducked, rolling beneath it and firing a bolt into its spine. It collapsed with a shriek, convulsing as its body crumpled to the floor.

Finally, after what felt like an eternity, the last of the mutants fell. The room was silent, save for the ragged breathing of the three survivors. Blood and gore covered every surface—walls, floors, even the ceiling dripped with the carnage of the battle.

Dorian stood over the bodies, panting, his chest heaving, his fists still clenched and dripping with blood. Mara, too, was gasping for air, her body shaking with exhaustion. For a moment, there was only silence, the aftermath of violence hanging heavy in the air like smoke.

Imani stared at the two of them—Dorian and Mara, standing amidst the bodies of the dead, covered in blood but alive. She had never seen anything like it. The sheer brutality of their fight, the raw power, the desperation. It left her breathless. Proud.

Mara wiped blood from her face, her eyes flicking toward Dorian. There was a moment of silence between them, an unspoken acknowledgment, a realization that went deeper than words.

Dorian had saved her.

Mara's expression was unreadable, her face an emotionless mask. But beneath the surface, Imani could see the storm of conflict raging inside her. For the first time in her life, a male had saved her. A male she hated, mistrusted, a thing she had been raised to despise. And yet, there he was, standing beside her, bloodied and bruised but alive—because of him.

"We need to move," Dorian said, his voice low, hoarse from the battle. "There's another facility deeper in the tunnels. We can synthesize the vaccine there."

Mara nodded, still silent, still conflicted. She glanced once more at Dorian, her eyes narrowing as though trying to make sense of the chaos inside her. Without another word, the three of them turned and moved into the shadows of the tunnels once more, leaving the blood and death behind them.

Chapter 13:

Blood Ties

Mara's breath had become shallow, labored, the pain etched into her face growing more pronounced with each passing moment. She stumbled again, and Dorian's sharp eyes flicked toward her.

"Hold on," he muttered, his voice rough, more out of necessity than concern. His hand shot out, catching her just as she pitched forward, her body folding under the weight of her injuries.

Her eyes were glassy, her skin pale, slick with sweat, and her breathing was shallow. The wound on her back, the deep gash left by a mutant's claws, was seeping blood at an alarming rate. It wasn't just the wound itself—it was the strain of the fight, the overwhelming blood loss, and the toll it had taken on her body. She was fading fast.

"We need to stop the bleeding," Imani urged, her own voice tight with urgency. The walls of the tunnel echoed her words, turning them into a hollow whisper.

Dorian glanced ahead. The new facility was close—he could feel it, see the faint outline of the heavy steel door at the far end of the passage. He gritted his teeth and hoisted Mara up, throwing her arm around his shoulders as he half-carried, half-dragged her toward the entrance. Imani was already at the door, frantically entering the access code into the rusted panel.

The door creaked open with a groan of protest, and they stumbled inside the facility. The stale air of the sealed space greeted them, heavy with disuse, the scent of dust and ancient metal filling their lungs. The room was dimly lit, the walls lined with cracked screens and abandoned equipment. It was a stark contrast to the high-tech labs of New Lagos—this was a place that had been forgotten, left to rot in the bowels of the earth.

"Help me with her," Dorian grunted, his muscles straining as he laid Mara across one of the large metal tables in the center of the room. She groaned, barely conscious, her vision flickering in and out as the blood continued to pool beneath her.

Imani's hands were already moving, her mind racing as she searched the room for something—anything—that could help. But the advanced healing tech of New Lagos was far out of reach. Here, in these ancient tunnels, they were left with rudimentary tools and outdated medical supplies that hadn't been touched in decades.

"She's not going to make it unless we stop the bleeding now," Imani said, her voice filled with fear.

"I know how to do it," Dorian replied, his voice low and grim. He knelt beside Mara, ripping open her armor to expose the jagged wound on her back. Blood welled up from the gash, dark and thick, oozing onto the cold steel beneath her. His hands moved with surprising precision, pulling a med kit from one of the nearby shelves. The supplies inside were old, barely functional, but it was better than nothing.

As Imani set to work preparing the machines for the blood transfusion, Dorian pulled out a sterilized needle and thread, his fingers deftly stitching the wound closed. His face was set in concentration, his mind focused on the task. He had done this before—too many times to count. Life in the wilderness had taught him survival in ways that no one from New Lagos could understand.

Mara groaned again, her body twitching as the needle pierced her flesh. "Male, you have the nerve to touch my body? You better… hope this kills me," she hissed through clenched teeth, her voice weak but still carrying its venomous edge.

"Shut up and stay still," Dorian growled, his hands steady as he tightened the last stitch. The bleeding slowed, but she was far from out of danger.

Imani wheeled over an ancient machine, the rusted gears creaking as it powered on. "We can't give her much," she warned, hooking Mara up to the IV. "But it'll buy us time."

As the transfusion began, Dorian's eyes caught something strange. The blood—Mara's blood—was reacting to the transfusion in a way that defied logic. It wasn't just clotting or regenerating—it was merging, shifting. His brow furrowed as he leaned closer, watching the interaction between her blood and the blood from the IV. The new cells seemed to engulf the damaged ones, almost as if they were repairing themselves, faster than anything he'd seen before.

"Imani," Dorian called out, his voice laced with suspicion. "Look at this."

Imani moved beside him, her eyes widening in disbelief. She watched as Mara's blood began to bind itself with something foreign—something deep within her. It was almost as if it recognized the mutant blood from the creatures they had just fought. The cells began replicating faster, stronger, and mutating before their very eyes.

"This isn't normal," Imani whispered, her voice trembling. She quickly ran Mara's blood through a rudimentary scanner they had found in the lab, her mind racing as the data streamed across the cracked screen. "She's… she's an experiment," Imani muttered, more to herself than to Dorian.

"What the hell are you talking about?" Dorian demanded, his fists clenching as he stepped closer, his eyes locked on Mara's unconscious form.

Imani's fingers flew across the keyboard, pulling up the data as her mind tried to make sense of what she was seeing. "Mara's DNA—it's been altered. Her blood contains traces of the early mutant samples. The Council must have used her in their experiments, merged her DNA with the original virus strain to create a hybrid… a super-soldier."

Dorian's face twisted with fury, his heart pounding in his chest. "They turned her into one of them?" The words felt like acid in his mouth. He stared at his own blood-stained hands, a sickening realization creeping over him like a cold fog. The fight with the mutants flashed through his mind in brutal, vivid detail—how effortlessly he had torn through them, how the sheer force behind each blow had felt almost too easy. His heart raced as fragments of memories flooded in—each one a puzzle piece fitting into a dark and twisted picture.

The bear. His mind shot back to that moment, deep in the wilderness, where he had fought off a massive black bear with his bare hands. He had snapped its spine, the crack of bone echoing through the forest as if it were nothing. At the time, it hadn't seemed unusual—just survival. He had always been different, always stronger, faster, sharper. These feats of strength were a part of him, as natural as breathing. But now, with the revelation of Mara's DNA, the truth was clawing its way to the surface like some buried nightmare.

He wasn't just strong. He wasn't just fast. He was something else. Something designed.

His eyes, wide and trembling, darted to Mara, still unconscious on the table, her blood mingling with his own on the floor. The weight of it all settled in his gut like lead. He wasn't like other men. He had never been like other men. The Council hadn't just hunted him for being a male—they had hunted him because he was part of their twisted experiment.

"Imani… run my blood through the system."

Imani hesitated, her heart sinking as she realized what he was suggesting. She grabbed a vial of Dorian's blood and inserted it into the scanner. The machine whirred to life, spitting out data at an alarming rate. Imani's breath caught in her throat as the results came through.

Dorian's DNA… was a match.

"You have the same markers as Mara," Imani whispered, her voice barely audible over the hum of the machines. "Your blood—it's… it's been altered, too."

Dorian's fists slammed down on the table, the rage building in his chest like a wildfire. "Those monsters did this to me," he snarled, his voice raw with anger. "I'm not even human. They turned me into one of their weapons."

Imani's heart ached as she watched the man before her unravel. Dorian's entire life had been a fight for survival, a fight against the very people who had created him. And now, to find out that he was part of the same experiment that had created the monsters they were trying to stop—it was a cruelty she could barely comprehend.

But as the weight of the revelation settled over them, another truth began to take shape.

"Wait," Imani said, her voice trembling with a new understanding. "Because you and Mara are hybrids… the virus can't infect you. That's why you didn't turn when the mutants wounded both of you. The virus… it recognizes your DNA. It can't corrupt what's already been altered."

Imani's memory drifted back, recalling the haunted look in Dorian's mother's eyes when she'd discovered she was carrying a male child. Zara's reaction was different from the other mothers who had fled New Lagos upon learning of their sons' fates. Her terror ran deeper, more profound—almost as if she knew that carrying a son would unleash a kind of doom upon them both. And now, it all began to make sense.

Zara hadn't been just another fearful mother. She had volunteered for an experiment, knowingly agreeing to be the vessel for what the Council called "the next evolution." She was meant to carry a female child, a new generation enhanced by the Y chromosome virus that was carefully crafted to bond exclusively with female DNA. But in Zara's case, something unexpected had happened: in the second trimester, her fetus began to shift, its genetic structure reprogramming itself, the intended female suddenly developing male traits.

The virus's interaction with Zara's DNA had created unprecedented outcomes. The Y chromosome virus had initially been engineered to bond with female cells, enhancing and modifying them. But when confronted with Zara's unique genetic profile, it had catalyzed a rare mutation, one that altered the fetus's gender midway through development, creating an anomaly the Council hadn't foreseen.

The virus, combined with Zara's DNA, had triggered a genetic cascade effect, its encoded instructions struggling to adapt to the biological shift in real-time. What was meant to be an enhanced female embryo had mutated, producing a male whose genetic structure bore traces of both the virus's intended enhancements and something entirely unpredictable.

Dorian's eyes flashed with realization, but the fury remained. "So what does that mean for the anti-virus? Can it still work?"

Imani's hands shook as she worked, her heart pounding in her chest. "I don't know," she whispered. "But we have to try."

She moved to the synthesizer, her mind racing as she worked on creating the anti-virus. But as the machine hummed and whirred, the results that appeared on the screen left her breathless.

"It's not working," Imani choked, her voice breaking. "The anti-virus isn't bonding with the sample. Because you're not fully human, Dorian. Your DNA—it's rejecting the treatment. It's not just the virus that's evolved. You have."

The weight of the failure crashed over her, and Imani collapsed to her knees, the reality of their situation crushing her spirit. The one thing they had fought for—the one hope they had left—was slipping through her fingers.

And there, in the cold, sterile room, with Mara unconscious on the table and Dorian seething in his own fury, the future felt more uncertain than ever before.

Chapter 14:
The Council of Mothers

The Chamber of the Council of Mothers was vast, a domed cathedral of glass and steel that echoed with the soft hum of unseen machinery. The walls were adorned with shifting holograms—images of past achievements, great leaders, and the thriving metropolis of New Lagos, glowing under its protective dome. It was a room built to command reverence, to instill fear and awe in all who entered.

But within its pristine walls, far removed from the lives of the citizens it controlled, sat a cabal of women whose power was absolute, and whose secrets had shaped the world into a twisted reflection of their ideals. At the center of this circle was the Head Mother—Seraphine Ryland—a woman whose cold, calculating intellect had made her the most feared mind in New Lagos. Her dark eyes, sharp and devoid of warmth, surveyed the other Mothers seated around the crescent-shaped table. Her silver hair was tightly coiled at the nape of her neck, a stark contrast to the rigid black uniform she wore, devoid of any ornament or insignia except for the faint shimmer of the Council's emblem over her heart.

Her voice was cold and precise when she spoke. "The Ferals have been eradicated."

The words echoed through the chamber, as the hologram of a bloodstained tunnel flickered before them—mutant bodies, twisted and grotesque, lay scattered across the floor. The destruction was absolute. And yet, it was not victory that flickered in Seraphine's eyes, but fury.

"We dispatched twelve of them. Twelve of our finest experiments." Her fingers tapped on the smooth surface of the table, each tap a metronome of her growing impatience. "And all of them are dead."

A murmur rippled through the chamber, the other Council members exchanging uneasy glances. The silence that followed felt like a tightening noose.

"We have underestimated the traitor, Mara," one of the Council members, Zuri, finally said, her tone laced with unease. "And the male... Dorian. He is more dangerous than we anticipated."

Seraphine's gaze sharpened, pinning Zuri with a look that could have cut glass. "More dangerous than you anticipated, perhaps. I always knew the threat he posed. He is not just a man—he is our creation."

Another council member, Vanya Clarke, leaned forward. Younger than most, with a severe face that seemed chiseled from stone, her eyes gleamed with a kind of calculated ambition that could only be bred in the shadow of such power. "The Phantom Hunters are being deployed as we speak," she said, her voice brisk and efficient. "We will find them, Mother Seraphine. And we will correct this mistake."

Seraphine nodded, but there was no satisfaction in her expression. "See that you do. Mara's betrayal was expected, but this male, Dorian… he is the real danger. He has a part of the virus within him, and we cannot allow that to escape."

Her gaze swept over the council, and when she spoke again, her words were laced with venom. "If necessary, we will burn New Lagos to the ground."

A ripple of shock spread through the room, though no one dared to voice their objections outright. Burning New Lagos—destroying the very heart of their empire—was unthinkable. But they knew Seraphine. If it came to protecting the secrets of the Council, there was no line she wouldn't cross.

One of the newer members of the Council, Mother Elara, cleared her throat. She had risen quickly through the ranks, known for her unflinching loyalty and her ruthless pragmatism. "We have another pressing issue, Head Mother."

Seraphine's eyes shifted to Elara, her gaze cold and expectant.

"The new batch of births," Elara continued, her voice steady but grim. "Seventy percent of them were born Feral."

There was a silence that seemed to suck the air out of the room. The word "feral" hung in the space between them like a curse.

Seraphine's jaw tightened. "How many mothers?"

Elara hesitated for only a second before responding, "All of them, Head Mother. Every single one died during childbirth. The feral mutations were… uncontrollable."

Zuri let out a faint gasp, her fingers gripping the edge of the table. "How are we going to cover up 2,300 deaths? The birthing chambers—"

Seraphine cut her off with a wave of her hand, her expression like carved stone. "We will deal with it, as we always do. The populace will believe what we tell them to believe."

"But 2,300 deaths?" Vanya Clarke spoke, her voice edged with disbelief. "It will not go unnoticed. We are nearing a tipping point, Seraphine. The population will demand answers."

A cold smile crept onto Seraphine's lips, a smile that never touched her eyes. "Then we will give them a story they cannot refute."

Elara's brow furrowed, but it was Zuri who asked, "What story?"

Seraphine leaned forward, her fingers steepled as a cold, calculating smile spread across her face. "We'll use the frequency enhancer," she began, her tone measured and deliberate. "We'll flood the minds of the population with images of rebellion, with whispers of sedition. Tell them the women who died in the birthing chambers were kidnapped, stolen by a rogue colony that has risen up against the Matriarchy. Paint them as traitors, desperate to bring males back to repopulate the Earth. These so-called rebels will become the ultimate enemy—an existential threat to our way of life."

She paused, her gaze intense as she let her words sink in. "We'll claim that this colony is loyal to our enemies and aided their efforts, infiltrating New Lagos. The mere thought of their pristine city tainted by sympathizers to males will be enough to unite the people against any story we choose to tell."

Her voice lowered, a sharp edge in her words. "Fear will drive them, and outrage will bind them to our cause. Because, in the end, there is only one true enemy to this council's power. And we will ensure the people know exactly who that enemy is."

"The Red Ravens?" Elara whispered, her voice barely audible. The very mention of them sent a frigid chill down the council members' spines. If there was a force capable of threatening the council's iron grip on the planet, it was the Red Ravens. For nearly fifty years, they had repelled every attempt the council had made to uproot them from the Crimson Straits in the southern region of the continent. Whether through direct assaults or covert operations, the council had tried time and again to weaken them. Yet, the Ravens always seemed to anticipate their every move, staying several steps ahead.

The council's leaders, particularly Seraphine, had cultivated an extensive propaganda campaign to instill fear in the citizens, portraying the Red Ravens as a barbaric society. According to council broadcasts, the Ravens were ruled by monstrous, bio-engineered men—hulking figures rumored to be twelve feet tall, bred specifically for domination. The council warned that the Ravens enslaved their women, forcing them to work the fields and sex houses, toiling under conditions that recalled a brutal, ancient world—one the matriarchy had saved them from when the Y chromosome virus had purged the male population centuries before.

Through the council's carefully crafted narrative, the Red Ravens represented the worst of the past—a society where men ruled with an iron fist, using violence and oppression to keep women in subjugation. Women were said to be mere breeding vessels, forced to bear more sons to strengthen the Ravens' army of giants, with no choice but to serve as laborers or unwilling concubines. It was a fate the council framed as a return to the dark ages, a dystopia from which the matriarchy had liberated humanity.

Yet, the Ravens defied this narrative, embracing a culture that allowed women the choice to give birth to male children if they wished. This alone was an affront to the council's vision, challenging the very foundation of the matriarchy's control. The Red Ravens symbolized a dangerous, radical idea: a society that was truly inclusive, even allowing women to choose freely whether to bring sons into the world. This choice, this autonomy, was something the council could not tolerate, for it threatened the carefully constructed image of a society built solely on the matriarchal ideal.

To the council, the Red Ravens were not just rebels; they were heretics. And as the propaganda machine churned, the people of New Lagos were fed the vision of a monstrous enemy lurking to the south, waiting to reclaim their daughters and plunge them back into a world of male-dominated tyranny.

The idea was both brilliant and horrifying in its simplicity. The Council had long experimented with neural frequency manipulation to keep the population compliant, but to use it on this scale, to make them believe in a fabricated rebellion— it was a level of control that surpassed even the worst of their previous manipulations.

Vanya, ever the strategist, nodded slowly. "Which colony?"

Seraphine's smile widened, though it was a thing of cruelty, not joy. "We'll choose one far enough to make it believable, but close enough to annihilate. The Feral will be our weapon. We'll release them upon the colony and once the colony has been wiped out, New Lagos will be reminded of why they need us."

The room fell into a cold silence, the weight of Seraphine's words settling like a shroud over the Council. The decision had been made. There was no turning back.

"And what of Imani?" Vanya asked, her voice quiet. "She knows too much."

Seraphine's eyes darkened, her smile vanishing. "Leave Imani to me, she will die. As will the traitor Mara and the male. No one leaves those tunnels alive."

The finality in her voice left no room for debate. The Council had its orders. New Lagos would remain under their control, no matter how many had to die to ensure it.

As the meeting drew to a close, Seraphine rose from her seat, her cold eyes fixed on the holograms flickering above. In them, New Lagos stood as a beacon of the Matriarchy's power—a city of shining glass and steel, built on the bodies of the men they had eradicated and the children they had sacrificed.

But beneath its gleaming surface, the city was crumbling.

And if Seraphine had to raise it to the ground and start again, she would do so without hesitation.

Chapter 15:

The Lab of Dr. Selene Amari

The soft glow of bioluminescent lights flickered through the sterile air of Dr. Selene Amari's lab, casting the room in an otherworldly glow. The walls, lined with sleek surfaces and towering screens, pulsed with streams of data—genetic sequences, mutation logs, and the most intimate secrets of human evolution. The hum of advanced machinery was the only sound, save for the rhythmic beeping of monitors that tracked every change in the living specimens behind the glass, creatures born of her ancestors' darkest legacy.

Dr. Selene Amari sat alone at the center of it all, her fingers tapping the surface of her transparent console as her eyes flitted across the screen. Her face, illuminated by the eerie light, was a mask of cold brilliance, her expression neutral, emotionless. Behind her calm façade was the madness passed down through generations—an inheritance from the woman who had designed the virus that had wiped men from the Earth.

She was the descendant of Dr. Lyra Amari, the brilliant, unhinged geneticist who had unleashed the plague centuries ago. But while Lyra had sought to end a world ruled by men, Selene's ambitions had long since eclipsed that of her forebear. Her ancestors had created a plague to shift the balance of power, but Selene was perfecting it. She wasn't just controlling evolution; she was mastering it. And yet, as her eyes scanned the endless lines of data, the inevitable truth pressed against her mind like a weight she could no longer bear.

The world would end.

The mutants—feral, twisted abominations born from the virus—were spreading rapidly. The council had thought they could contain it, bend it to their will. But Selene knew better. The real threat wasn't the virus itself; it was Seraphine and her relentless obsession with purging all traces of male existence, down to the cellular level.

Under Seraphine's direct orders, and unbeknownst to the rest of the council, Selene was tasked with ensuring the feral population grew faster, with each new generation showing increasingly extreme mutations. With every batch, the Feral evolved in ways Selene could no longer predict. The virus was no longer just rewriting women's DNA; it was reshaping the entire ecosystem, tampering with the very blueprint of life on Earth.

This was no longer an experiment spiraling out of control. It was the onset of an extinction event, with Seraphine's ambition pushing humanity to the edge of oblivion.

"How did we get here?" Selene whispered to herself, though she knew the answer. Her ancestor's obsession had planted the seeds, and she had watered them with her own ambitions. Now the garden was overgrowing, wild and uncontrollable, its roots cracking through the very foundation of the world.

Her eyes flicked to the corner of the room where a single specimen floated in a tank of viscous liquid, one of the original Feral. Its body, emaciated and twisted, hovered in the glow of the tank, wires protruding from its skull, feeding information directly into her systems. Its skin was pale and translucent, a map of the virus etched into every cell, its mutations laid bare like a living tapestry of genetic horror.

The virus had bonded with the Feral's DNA in ways Selene had once marveled at. But now, seeing the grotesque shape of the creature, she felt nothing but the cold weight of failure.

Her console chimed, pulling her from her thoughts. A call from Seraphine.

Selene pressed her fingers to the screen, and Seraphine's face appeared in a hovering hologram, her expression hard and unyielding. Seraphine's eyes were cold, her impatience barely concealed.

"Dr. Amari," she began, her tone clipped and direct. "We need more ferals—one hundred, to be exact. Deploy them to the northern colony immediately."

Selene's hand hovered over the console, her jaw tightening. "The northern colony is isolated, far from any domed city. There will be no way to contain the infection's spread," she replied, her voice steady but underpinned with a note of warning. "We can only control the Ferals we deploy, and even then, we can't be certain the neural links will hold if they continue to mutate. Hundreds of thousands of women could die." She fixed Seraphine with an icy stare through the hologram.

Seraphine's eyes narrowed, a hint of dark satisfaction creeping into her gaze. "Hundreds of thousands?" she mused, a twisted smile tugging at her lips. "Dr. Amari, don't be so modest. I was anticipating millions. Now, do as you're told… unless you're questioning a direct order from your Head Mother, Dr. Amari?"

Her tone was laced with warning, but Selene didn't flinch.

The bitterness rose in Selene's throat, but she swallowed it down, keeping her face expressionless. "And what will we do when the virus breaches the domes? When the infected Ferals begin to evolve past our control?" Her words were sharper now, the tension crackling in the air between them.

Seraphine's face darkened. "Your job, Dr. Amari, is to follow my directives, not speculate on future threats. We have more important matters to deal with than your concerns. Activate the Ferals. That is an order."

Selene stared at Seraphine for a long, tense moment. The logical part of her mind screamed at her to refuse, to defy the Council and stop the madness before it was too late. But the other part—the part that understood the Council's ruthlessness—knew what would happen if she disobeyed.

Exile.

And in exile, there were no tunnels, no safe havens. Only death.

"And what if I refuse?"

"I know your little secret," Seraphine said, her tone ice-cold yet dripping with calculated amusement. "You've connected your heart to the Feral chambers, haven't you? A contingency plan, no doubt. Did you really think you could keep that from me?" She stepped closer to the camera, her eyes narrowing, a cruel smile tugging at her lips. "Especially when it's tied into the same neural network I used to control those abominations? I know everything, Selene. Every beat of your heart echoes through that system."

Her voice dropped, laced with quiet menace. "Tell me, can you even fathom the chaos that would erupt in this city if your heart just… stopped beating? The creatures would run wild, wouldn't they? All your careful planning, all your supposed safeguards, would crumble in an instant. New Lagos would fall into madness, and it would be your fault."

She tilted her head, her gaze sharp as a blade. "Now, tell me, Selene, do you really want me to answer that question?

Selene's fingers hovered over the controls for a moment longer before she pressed the activation sequence. On the far side of the room, the lights of the cryogenic chambers flared to life, the glass tanks hissing as they began to thaw the sleeping monsters within. One hundred Ferals. Each one more dangerous, more volatile than the last.

"They're waking up," Selene said softly, her eyes narrowing as she watched the ferals stir. Their grotesque forms began to twitch inside their chambers, their skeletal limbs flexing with inhuman strength. The room filled with a low growl, the sound of the mutants coming to life, their eyes glowing faintly beneath the pale light.

"Good," Seraphine said, her lips curling into a thin smile. "Send them to the colony at once."

Selene's chest tightened as she keyed in the final commands, routing the ferals to the northern colony, their location set far beyond the reach of New Lagos. As the sequence completed, she felt the weight of what she'd done settle over her like a suffocating fog. She had unleashed another wave of death, and soon the infection would spread. Again.

But what choice did she have?

"Report back to me and only me once the mission is complete," Seraphine said, her tone dismissive. "Make sure there are no further delays."

The hologram flickered and disappeared, leaving Selene alone with the sound of the Ferals awakening. She sat back in her chair, staring at the creatures as they banged against the glass of their containment tanks. A gnawing sense of dread twisted inside her as their growls grew louder, more feral, more desperate.

As the last Feral was fully awakened, Selene stood and moved toward the door, her mind spinning with calculations. She needed to think, to get away from the sound of the creatures she had helped create. But there was something else pulling her now, something far deeper than fear or guilt.

Her sister.

Mara.

Selene had created her most prized experiment in Mara—a hybrid, a soldier designed to fight and kill with the precision of a machine. She was the apex predator of the Matriarchy's design, the deadliest assassin in the Council's arsenal. But she was also Selene's little sister, the one person she had wanted to protect, even as she shaped her into a living weapon.

Mara was out there in the tunnels now, fighting for survival. The thought made Selene's chest tighten. She had to find her.

The lights dimmed as Selene left the lab, her footsteps echoing softly down the long corridor. She descended into the deeper levels of the facility, the shadows growing darker, the air colder. Below the city lay the labyrinth of tunnels where Mara had been deployed, where death and violence were everyday companions. And Selene, despite everything she had done, wasn't ready to let her sister die.

Not yet.

As she stepped into the darkness, Selene's thoughts raced. The Council would stop at nothing to maintain their control. They would burn New Lagos to the ground if necessary. But Selene knew that if Mara survived—if she could be found—there was a chance to change everything. A chance to stop the virus before it consumed them all.

But time was running out. And the shadows were closing in.

Chapter 16:

The Fall of the Northern Colony

The Northern Colony had always been a sanctuary. Nestled between towering pines and lush hills, it was an oasis of peace amidst a world that had known too much pain. The streets were lined with sleek, low-rise buildings, their metallic sheen reflecting the soft, golden light of the afternoon sun. Gardens bloomed in radiant colors along every walkway, and the air was rich with the scent of fresh earth and flowers. The colony was a marvel of clean, renewable technology—wind turbines spun silently in the distance, and drones hummed gently overhead, tending to the crops.

Children laughed and ran through the streets, their mothers walking nearby, content and smiling. There was no violence here, no hunger, no fear. It was a utopia, far from the domed cities of New Lagos and their politics, a place where harmony wasn't just a dream—it was a way of life.

Mira Kane stood on the porch of her home, her daughter Elara playing with a group of girls in the square. The air was cool, a gentle breeze stirring the trees at the edge of the forest, their leaves whispering secrets of an ancient world. Mira smiled to herself, watching Elara's face light up with pure joy as she ran through the grass, her hair wild and free.

And then, it began.

A deep, guttural roar echoed from the forest—so loud and primal it seemed to shake the very ground. The trees swayed violently as though caught in a sudden storm, but there was no wind. A shadow passed over the colony, a creeping darkness that swallowed the light. Mira's smile faltered, her heart thudding in her chest as she turned toward the sound.

Another roar. Louder this time. Closer.

The laughter of the children faltered. The women began to look toward the trees, their faces creasing with confusion, then fear. The shadows in the forest moved—shapes darting between the trees, twisted and distorted figures that didn't belong to the peaceful world the colony had built.

A scream shattered the air.

The first Feral burst from the tree line, its body a grotesque nightmare of muscle and bone. Its skin was slick and pale, marbled with black veins, and its eyes—blood-red and gleaming with a savage hunger—locked onto the closest woman. It moved with terrifying speed, its long, clawed arms swinging through the air as it barreled toward the square.

The woman didn't even have time to scream before the Feral crashed into her, knocking her to the ground with brutal force. Its claws tore through her chest, blood spraying in a sickening arc as it ripped her apart. Mira's breath caught in her throat as the woman's body convulsed violently, her limbs twisting, bones snapping audibly as she began to change.

The infected woman's screams turned into a guttural howl of agony, her eyes wide with terror as her body morphed into something monstrous. Her skin peeled back, revealing the same pale, marbled flesh as the Feral that had attacked her. Her fingers elongated into claws, her teeth sharpening into jagged points. And then, with an animalistic snarl, she rose to her feet, her humanity completely erased.

The colony erupted into chaos.

More ferals poured from the forest in a tidal wave of blood and violence, their shrieks mixing with the terrified cries of the women and children. They moved with inhuman speed and ferocity, their claws slicing through flesh like knives. Each attack was a brutal, bloody massacre—women were torn apart in the streets, their bodies mangled and broken. Blood pooled on the white walkways, staining the once-pristine streets a dark, sickening red.

Mira screamed for Elara, her voice lost in the cacophony of terror. She ran toward the square, her heart pounding in her chest, but the Ferals were everywhere. They ripped through the colony with unstoppable force, leaving nothing but destruction in their wake. Each time a woman or child was struck down, their bodies writhed and twisted, their bones breaking and resetting as the infection spread through them like wildfire.

Within moments, they too became Ferals, joining the ranks of the horde. Their faces, once familiar, now twisted into grotesque parodies of the people they had been, their eyes gleaming with the same bloodlust that drove their attackers.

They turned on their friends, their daughters, their neighbors, their claws slashing through the air with horrifying efficiency.

Mira's vision blurred with tears as she stumbled through the chaos, desperately searching for Elara. Everywhere she looked, there was blood, bodies, death. A woman she had known for years—her neighbor, who had shared meals with her—lunged at her, her mouth open in a snarl, her hands twisted into claws. Mira barely dodged the attack, her heart racing as she fled toward the closest building.

"Mommy!"

Elara's voice pierced through the chaos, sharper than the screams and destruction surrounding Mira. She whipped around, heart pounding, and spotted her daughter, trembling beneath the shelter of a porch. Fear gripped Mira's chest like a vice, but without hesitation, she sprinted toward Elara, scooping her into her arms. Holding her tight, Mira bolted toward the colony's last safe haven, desperation driving her forward with every step.

The survivors, those who hadn't yet been infected, were retreating to the largest structure in the colony—a community center designed for safety during storms. But now it had become a last stand against the Feral horde.

The doors slammed shut as Mira and a group of women and children made it inside, barricading the entrance with whatever they could find. The sound of the ferals outside was deafening, their claws raking against the metal doors, their growls shaking the walls.

Inside, the women were silent, their faces pale, their eyes wide with terror. The children huddled together, crying softly, their small bodies shaking with fear. Mira clutched Elara to her chest, her heart aching with the knowledge that there was nothing she could do to protect her daughter from the horrors outside.

The building shook as the Ferals slammed against the doors, their snarls growing louder, more desperate. The barricades wouldn't hold for long.

"What are those… things?" Mira's voice trembled, her wide eyes locked on the door as the Ferals continued to crash into it.

Beside her, Liora's face was pale with horror. "They're not just things, Mira," she whispered, her voice thick with disgust. "They're a sickness. An experiment the council unleashed on us because they believe we're harboring men here."

Mira recoiled at the thought, her expression one of revulsion. "Men? Here?" She shook her head, struggling to suppress a shudder. "We'd never allow that. We just wanted to live simply—away from the council's walls and their rules. And now we're being punished over a rumor?"

Liora nodded bitterly. "The council doesn't care about truth. They're too drunk on power, too eager to wield it against anyone who defies their perfect little cities. They see us as rebels simply because we didn't want to live like them, confined under glass domes, surrendering every choice to their whims."

Another woman nearby gasped, catching the conversation. "Men… among us?" She shuddered, her voice tinged with horror. "We left the domed cities to escape council control, not to invite the horrors of the past back into our lives."

Mira's gaze hardened as she looked out at the ferals again, their grotesque forms snarling just beyond their colony's edge. "This is their punishment. For nothing more than a twisted rumor. And now they'll let these… monsters devour us, just to keep their power intact."

Liora's jaw tightened. "They don't see us as women with lives of our own. We're just another threat to control. They'll sacrifice us without a second thought if it means keeping their authority unchallenged."

The group fell silent, a shared realization dawning: they were alone, left to face the council's nightmare creations, all for the crime of living life on their own terms.

"We have to fight," one of the women said, her voice trembling. "We can't just wait for them to break through."

Mira nodded; her throat tight. They had no weapons, no way to defend themselves against the Ferals. But they had no other choice. They grabbed whatever they could—chairs, metal poles, anything that could be used as a weapon—and prepared for the inevitable breach.

The door buckled under the force of the ferals' attacks, the metal groaning as it began to give way. Mira's hands shook as she gripped a metal rod, her mind racing with fear. She looked down at Elara, her heart breaking. She wanted to tell her daughter that everything would be okay, but the words wouldn't come. Because they wouldn't be okay. Not anymore.

The door finally gave way with a deafening crash, and the Ferals poured into the building, their eyes wild with hunger, their claws slicing through the air. The women fought back with everything they had, but they were no match for the Ferals. Blood sprayed across the room as the creatures tore through the survivors, their growls mixing with the screams of the dying.

Mira swung her makeshift weapon with all her strength, but the Ferals were too fast, too strong. One of them lunged at her, knocking her to the ground. Its claws dug into her flesh, and she screamed as the pain shot through her body. Elara's terrified cries filled her ears as the Feral ripped her apart.

The last thing Mira saw before darkness claimed her was the sight of her daughter being pulled away, her small body twisted and broken as the infection took hold.

Outside, the sounds of the battle faded, replaced by the guttural growls of the Ferals as they feasted on the remains of the colony. Blood soaked the streets, the buildings, the very earth itself. The once beautiful utopia was now a graveyard, a mass of twisted bodies and grotesque monsters.

As the horde of Ferals swarmed through the forest, their numbers growing with each new victim, the sunset on the horizon, casting the world in a dark, crimson light. Another colony lay ahead in the distance, unaware of the doom that was already rushing toward them, the sound of their destruction carried on the wind like a distant, haunting cry.

The world was falling.

Chapter 17:

Bloodlines of the Future

Dr. Selene Amari moved with purpose through the shadows, her every step calculated, her sharp eyes gleaming in the dim light of her locator device. Each faint beep of the device was a reminder of the weight on her shoulders, and what she had to face. She wasn't just searching for anyone in the maze of tunnels beneath New Lagos. She was searching for family—Mara, her sister, and the dangerous truth she had unleashed.

Mara. The name haunted her, echoing through the darkened tunnels like a ghost she couldn't outrun. She had created her sister into something more than human, something beyond control, and now the consequences of that creation were unraveling the fragile balance of power. As Selene crept past a patrol of Phantom Hunters, their black armor glinting like predatory beetles, she held her breath. These women were shadows made flesh, deadly and efficient. If they saw her, they would kill her without hesitation.

But they passed, unaware of her presence. A small victory, but Selene knew it wouldn't last. The deeper she ventured into the tunnels, the more imminent her encounter with Mara became, and the weight of what she needed to confess—what she needed to warn her sister about—gnawed at her insides.

Her hand tightened around the locator device as she reached a rusted, towering vault door, its surface covered in layers of grime and rust. This was the place. The faint glow from her device flickered, confirming her destination. Taking a deep breath, Selene keyed into the door's control panel, her fingers moving swiftly over the outdated technology. The door groaned open, and the sight of the figures inside—their faces twisted in anticipation—sent a cold shiver through her.

Dorian was the first to react. His eyes blazed with fury, and within a second, he lunged toward her like a force of nature. But Selene had anticipated this.

"Stop!" she ordered, her voice cutting through the air with razor-sharp authority. It froze Dorian mid-motion, his arm just inches from her throat, his massive hand twitching with the desire to tear her apart. She met his burning gaze without flinching. "You want answers, male. I have them. And if you kill me, you'll never understand why you exist."

Her words sliced through the room with chilling clarity, silencing everyone. Imani, standing by the console, paled as the weight of the revelation washed over her. Mara stirred from her place on the metal table, eyes glowing with the lethal intensity Selene had always feared.

Dorian's voice, thick with rage, came out in a low growl. "Who are you?"

Selene drew herself up. "I am Dr. Selene Amari, the woman who created you both."

Silence filled the room, thick and suffocating. Dorian's fists clenched at his sides; his muscles coiled with rage. "You're lying, I was born, not created."

"Silly male, I wish I were," Selene replied calmly, her gaze flicking to Mara. "But it's the truth. You and Mara… you are my creations. Bio-engineered hybrids. You were made to be something more than human—something stronger, faster, immune to the virus that ravages the world. But you, male… you were supposed to be born female. The Y chromosome wasn't part of the plan."

Mara's face twisted with disgust, her voice a seething hiss.

"What did you do to us?" Dorian's voice was low, but the fury simmered just beneath the surface.

Selene met his gaze, her voice quiet but steady. "You were designed to be the future," she said, a hint of sadness flickering in her expression. "Women perfected, genetically optimized, free from the need for male fertilization. Seraphine wanted a new generation to lead a world without men, a society rebuilt from engineered perfection. But you…" She paused, her voice tightening. "You were an anomaly. You were never meant to exist as you are. During the second trimester, your DNA— intended to develop exclusively with XX chromosomes— unexpectedly altered, allowing Y chromosomes to emerge and flood your system. Somehow, your genetic structure rewrote itself."

Dorian's face darkened, his fists clenched, his fury barely contained. "So my mother… she knew?"

Selene nodded slowly. "Yes. Your mother kept it hidden. She understood that if the Council discovered you, they'd have turned you into a specimen, dissected every cell to understand how you became... male. She risked everything to protect you from becoming another experiment in their laboratories."

Dorian's eyes blazed. "You used us. Turned us into weapons."

Selene's gaze softened slightly, but the clinical detachment remained in her tone. "Being an unstoppable weapon was only part of your design. You were crafted to be more—a new evolution of humanity, the last phase of Project Reset. In the Council's eyes, you are the final step in achieving their vision: a population engineered not only for endurance and survival but also for complete genetic control. You were their ultimate project."

Mara, her face twisted in a mixture of disbelief and horror, snarled, "What the hell is Project Reset?"

Selene's shoulders slumped, as if the weight of the truth had finally crushed what remained of her resolve. Her voice, once clinical and detached, now trembled with the burden of what she had held inside for so long. "It's Seraphine's final solution. Project Reset—her plan to erase everything, to wipe the slate clean. Everyone, except for a handpicked few deemed worthy of surviving. Seraphine always feared... eventually, women would start giving birth to males again, no matter how hard they tried to stop it. And she couldn't—wouldn't—let that happen. She'd rather watch the world burn, watch every city crumble into dust, before she allowed males to rise again."

She paused, the bitterness in her voice deepening. "It was never about control alone... it was about erasure. About rewriting existence itself. That's what you're up against—an obsession so deep it's become madness. She would rather destroy everything than live in a world where males could exist again."

Her eyes darkened, filled with both sorrow and disgust as her voice broke. "And I was a part of it."

"And the Ferals?" Imani asked, her voice trembling with the realization that hit too close to home.

"They're an intricate part of it. The Council has been breeding them for years. And those babies, the ones born as monsters? They weren't terminated. And the mothers that died during childbirth? They were also infected and mutated into Ferals. They kept them all. They've been kept in cryo chambers under New Lagos for decades."

Dorian's jaw clenched. "How many?"

"One hundred thousand at least." Selene's voice was almost a whisper. "One hundred thousand Ferals, the result of one hundred thousand of our sisters and daughters dying in the most horrific way and bred for one purpose—annihilation."

Imani's breath hitched, but it was Mara's voice that broke the silence. "You… knew about all of this?"

Selene's gaze faltered, her voice breaking with emotion for the first time. "I believed in the Council's vision once. But I didn't realize how far they would go. Seraphine... she's gone mad. Driven insane by her hatred for males and her fear that women will give the world back to them. She wants to reset everything. She doesn't care how many will die."

Tears stung at Mara's eyes, but they weren't tears of sorrow—they were tears of betrayal, of rage. Her voice trembled as she spoke, raw with emotion. "You… did this to us. To me. To The Matriarchy. And now you think we'll just go along with it? You think I can just stand here and let it happen?"

Selene flinched at the words, her carefully constructed facade crumbling under Mara's fury. She tried to steady herself, her voice faltering as she spoke, softer now, almost pleading. "Mara… please. I raised you. I loved you like you were my own. You weren't just my sister—you were my whole world. Don't you understand? Everything I did, I did to protect you. All those nights telling you stories, all those days hiding the truth… it was because I didn't want you touched by this world, by its darkness."

Mara's eyes narrowed, her chest heaving, her voice thick with betrayal. "Protect me? You didn't protect me; you turned me into a weapon! Since I was twelve years old, you had me training to kill, to end lives. Do you have any idea what that does to a child? How many faces I've seen go cold, how much blood I've watched spill? You looked me in the eyes and told me you loved me, that you'd die for me! But all along, you were twisting me, building me into one of their monsters. How could you?"

For the first time, Selene's composure shattered entirely. Tears streamed down her face, her lips trembling as she choked out her words. "I never wanted this for you, Mara. You think I don't carry the weight of every choice I made? You are my sister. You always were, but the Council… they gave me an ultimatum. They said if I didn't create you, mold you into what they needed, they would exile me—or worse. I thought this was the only way to keep you safe."

"Safe?" Mara spat, her voice breaking, fists clenched so tightly her knuckles turned pale. "You think this is safe? You turned me into a shell, Selene. I looked up to you. I trusted you. And you turned me into something I don't even recognize."

Selene collapsed to her knees under the weight of Mara's words, her face twisted with grief and regret. "I do love you, Mara," she sobbed. "Every day, I told myself this was for you, to save you from what the Council had planned. But I was wrong. I know that now."

"If you loved me," Mara said, her voice shaking, "you would have fought for me. You would have stopped them."

"I tried!" Selene cried out, desperation roughening her voice. "But the Council's power... it's absolute, Mara. Seraphine, the others... they've spent centuries building this. You think you can tear it down alone? They'll kill you. And they'll kill Dorian too, without a second thought."

Mara's rage softened, if only for a moment, as she stared at her broken sister. "And you think that justifies everything? That turning me into a weapon was somehow the answer?"

Selene shook her head, her voice a strangled whisper. "No... it doesn't justify anything. I see that now. But Mara, please... if you won't forgive me, then do this for yourself. Walk away. Leave New Lagos. The Council's grip will only tighten. Seraphine—she's spiraling. She'll destroy everything and I don't want you anywhere near this place when things go from bad to worse."

Mara hesitated, her gaze flickering with both rage and a deep, painful sorrow. "I can't walk away, Selene. I can't leave, not after everything you've done." Her voice softened. "Not after what I've become."

Selene crawled toward her, her hands shaking as she clutched at Mara's legs, her voice barely a whisper. "Please, Mara. Don't let them take you too. Don't let them turn you into the very thing they're trying to destroy."

Mara looked down, her heart a mix of fury and heartbreak. "They'll never have us, Selene. Not while I'm still breathing." She hesitated, fighting back the tears. "But I can't forgive you for this. Not now. Maybe not ever."

A broken sob escaped Selene's lips, her hands falling limply to her sides. "I know… I know I don't deserve it."

The sound of crashing metal filled the air as the doors to the chamber exploded inward. The Phantom Hunters had arrived.

Chaos erupted. Armed Hunters flooded the room, weapons raised, firing in all directions. Mara and Dorian sprang into action, their bodies moving with fierce precision, their strength and training slicing through the Phantom Hunters with ruthless efficiency. Blood splattered across the floor, the sounds of dying women filled the air.

But as one Hunter raised her rifle toward Mara, Selene's eyes widened. Without a second thought, she lunged forward, her body intercepting the blast meant for her sister. A bolt of energy seared through her chest, and she fell back, her eyes wide with shock.

Time seemed to stop as Mara realized what had happened. "Selene!" She dropped to her knees beside her sister, clutching

Selene's body as blood pooled beneath them. "No, please... no," she whispered, her voice choked with desperation. "Don't leave me, Selene. I can't... I don't know how to do this without you. I'm so sorry... I'm sorry for everything. Please... just stay. Just stay with me."

Selene's face softened, her pain-riddled eyes meeting Mara's with a flicker of the sisterly love she'd carried all those years. Her hand trembled as she reached up, brushing a tear from Mara's cheek. "Mara... I've loved you... since the day you were born. I'm sorry... for all of it. But I couldn't let them... have you." Her voice faded, her breathing shallow. "I finally... did something right... for you."

"No!" Mara sobbed, pressing her forehead to Selene's, her voice a broken whisper. "Please, don't leave me. Don't leave me like this."

A faint smile tugged at the corners of Selene's lips. "Be free, Mara," she whispered. "For both of us."

As her vision darkened, she reached out toward Mara, her voice a dying whisper. "If... if my heart stops... the fail-safe... it will unleash them all. The Ferals."

Mara's face paled with horror. "No..."

But it was too late. Selene's heart stilled, and then, with one last shuddering breath, her hand fell limp.

And somewhere, deep beneath New Lagos, one hundred thousand ferals began to stir. Their long sleep was over.

A strangled cry tore from Mara's throat as she clutched Selene's lifeless body, tears streaming down her face. Her grief twisted into a raw, primal rage as she looked up, her eyes burning with hatred.

"I swear… I will destroy you, Seraphine," she spat, her voice dripping with venom. "I will bring the Council to its knees. You will pay for what you've done."

As she held her sister's body, the promise reverberated through her, sealing her resolve.

Chapter 18:

The Floodgates of Hell

Mara led the charge, her body moving with lethal precision, though her mind felt fractured. Something inside her had snapped when her sister Selene had died, and now the anger, the fury at the Council, was like an animal gnawing at her insides, urging her forward with a ferocity that was beginning to unravel her.

Behind her, Imani and Dorian followed, their boots pounding against the cold metal floor. The metallic tang of the air was punctuated by the low hum of ancient machinery struggling to keep the facility operational. Every step echoed in the vast tunnel, bouncing off the walls like a death knell, a grim reminder of what waited for them in the incubation chamber ahead.

"Imani, how much longer until we reach the chamber?" Dorian's voice was low and tense. He clutched his blade tightly, the weight of what was coming pressing down on him like a steel vice.

"We're close," Imani said, panting as they rounded the final corner. "The door is just ahead."

And there it was. The massive metal doors of the incubation chamber loomed before them like the maw of a beast waiting to swallow them whole. The cryo-pods behind those doors held the Ferals—the last, devastating remnants of the Council's experiments. If they woke, 100,000 Ferals would be unleashed upon New Lagos, and the city would drown in blood.

The door hissed open as Imani hacked into the control panel, and they rushed inside. The vast expanse of the chamber stretched out before them, a sterile room with rows upon rows of cryo-pods, like tombstones for a dead world. The low hum of the freezing systems filled the air, punctuated by the faint, ominous click of machinery.

Mara froze at the sight of the Ferals encased in their pods, her breath catching in her throat. The sight of them stirred something deep within her—a memory of the Council's ruthlessness, of her sister's cold detachment in the face of it all. Selene had been a willing participant in these horrors, and yet, she was gone. Murdered. And it was the Council's fault.

Rage clawed at Mara's heart like a wild animal, desperate to escape, to tear something—anything—apart.

"I'll try to override the system and freeze them again," Imani said, rushing to the console. Her fingers flew over the keys, her breath quickening as she fought against time.

Mara stepped closer to the pods, her fingers brushing the glass surface of one of them. Inside, the Feral was grotesque, its twisted body barely human. Rage boiled up inside her. She could feel the bile rising in her throat as she stared at the creature that was once a woman, a product of the Council's madness.

The Council—they had murdered her sister. They had unleashed these monsters. They had turned her into nothing more than a weapon, stripped of her humanity. Rage bubbled up inside her, raw and unrelenting, as memories of Selene's sacrifice seared through her mind. Her hands clenched into fists, her nails biting so deeply into her palms that she could feel the blood pooling beneath her skin, warm and stinging. But she didn't care. The pain was but a whisper compared to the storm raging within her.

"Imani, work faster!" Dorian barked, his sword in hand, his body tense and ready for the fight he knew was coming. The cryo-pods were groaning, their seals trembling as the thaw began.

Imani cursed under her breath, her fingers flying over the controls as warnings flashed across the screen.

REMOTE ACCESS OVERRIDE ENGAGED. SYSTEM LOCKED.

"No, no, no! Someone's remotely locked us out." Imani screamed, slamming her fists against the console.

Imani's heart sank as her fingers stilled. They had been so close, but someone in the Council, or perhaps one of their engineers, had stopped them cold. "It's over," she whispered, her voice filled with dread.

A deafening hiss filled the chamber as the first pod opened, and Mara's heart stalled in her chest. There was no stopping it now.

Dorian growled, stepping in front of Mara, his blade at the ready as the first Feral stumbled free from its cryo-pod. Its once-human face was twisted, a gnarled mask of hatred and hunger, its eyes black and soulless. It let out a scream, a sound like a tortured animal, as it lunged forward.

Mara moved before she could think. Her blade sliced through the air with a clean, lethal arc, and the Feral's head hit the ground with a sickening thud. Black blood sprayed across the metal floor, slicking her boots.

But more were coming.

Dorian swung his sword in a brutal arc, slicing another Feral across the chest. The creature howled, staggering back, but Dorian was relentless. He rammed the blade through its throat, yanking it free with a savage twist, severing his head from its grotesque body.

The sound of metal clanging echoed around them as pod after pod released its twisted prisoner. The Ferals were fast, a ferocious hunger radiating from their bony frames as they pounced on Mara and Dorian.

Mara's blade flashed again, and again, her movements swift and brutal. But her mind was ablaze with grief and fury, her thoughts flashing between the present chaos and the image of her sister's lifeless body. This was all for Selene. The Council would burn, and Mara would make sure of it.

"I've got to set the bombs!" Imani screamed, her plasma gun rattling as she fired shot after shot into the horde. The Ferals screeched as their flesh melted under the plasma's heat, but there were too many of them. "Cover me!"

Dorian let out a roar, barreling into the crowd of Ferals. His sword hacked through limbs and torsos with feral strength, his eyes wild with bloodlust. A primal rage consumed him, the scent of blood igniting something deep inside. His muscles bulged as he swung his sword with vicious force, cleaving a Feral's skull in half with a sickening crunch. The Feral collapsed, twitching in a pool of its own blood, but another took its place.

Next to Dorian, Mara moved like a phantom, her blade cutting through the air in deadly arcs, severing limbs and decapitating Ferals with each precise strike. Her body felt like it was on autopilot, moving with a lethal rhythm she didn't even have to think about. Blood splattered her face and arms, but she didn't care. All she could see were the bodies—the Council's creations—and the Council's betrayal.

"Move!" Mara shouted, spinning on her heel to sever the arm of another Feral before it could swipe at Dorian. The blade sliced cleanly through bone and flesh, but the creature lunged again with its other arm. Mara ducked beneath its strike, driving her sword into its chest and yanking it free as the Feral crumpled to the ground.

Imani was planting plasma bombs across the room, her face pale and slick with sweat as she fumbled with the charges. "Hurry!" she shouted. "We're almost out of time!"

Dorian stabbed his sword into another Feral, grunting with effort as he kicked it off the blade. "We need to fall back now!" he yelled, grabbing Mara by the arm as more Ferals spilled from the pods. "Imani, set the last charge!"

Imani scrambled to the final structural column, slamming the plasma charge into place and activating the timer. "It's set!" she shouted, her voice trembling. "We've got sixty seconds before the entire chamber collapses!"

They ran, their boots thudding against the slick floor as they raced toward the exit. The Ferals screeched behind them, their twisted bodies scrambling across the floor, claws scratching at the metal as they gave chase.

Dorian reached the door first, his chest heaving as he shoved it open. Mara was right behind him, her breath ragged, her eyes burning with fury. Imani stumbled through the door last, her hands shaking as she hit the detonator.

The explosion tore through the air with a deafening roar, a sound so violent it seemed to split the world in two. In an instant, a blinding flash of light engulfed the chamber, turning everything white-hot and searing itself into their vision. The shockwave followed with a force that felt like a freight train barreling straight into them, lifting them off their feet and slamming them to the ground with bone-rattling intensity. The very walls seemed to buckle under the impact, groaning like tortured steel as the entire facility shuddered violently. Dust and debris cascaded from the ceiling, chunks of concrete and metal raining down as the structure began to give way, its foundations trembling as if the earth itself had been shaken to its core. The air filled with the sharp scent of burning wires and the acrid stench of destruction, while the distant sound of twisting metal and collapsing beams echoed ominously through the chaos.

For a fleeting moment, it seemed as though they had triumphed. The chaos stilled, hanging in the air like a suspended breath. Smoke and dust swirled in slow, ghostly tendrils, shrouding the aftermath in a heavy, choking fog. The cacophony of destruction faded, leaving only a deep, oppressive silence that clung to everything, as if the world itself had paused to consider the cost of what had just unfolded.

But then the upper levels gave way, and the world fell apart.

A massive section of the ceiling gave way with a thunderous crack, sending a cascade of rubble crashing down. Dust and debris exploded into the air as a jagged, gaping hole yawned open above them, revealing the ink-black expanse of the night sky. The stars flickered like distant, indifferent spectators to the carnage below. But it wasn't the stars that filled the void.

Through the breach, they came.

The Ferals swarmed over the wreckage, moving with a sickening, insect-like precision. Their bodies were twisted and deformed, skeletal limbs jutting at unnatural angles, their skin mottled and stretched too tight over bone. Their eyes, sunken and glassy, reflected the moonlight with a dull, malevolent glow as they crawled through the crumbled stone-like roaches emerging from the rot. Their gnarled fingers clawed at the debris, pulling themselves free of the wreckage with a desperate hunger, their breath ragged and hissing as they scrambled toward the city above. The scent of blood and fear seemed to pull them forward, their grotesque forms writhing and skittering as they moved in a frenzy, eager to feast on whatever lay in their path.

Mara fell to her knees, her body trembling with exhaustion and rage. Her sword slipped from her bloodstained hands, clattering to the floor as the screams of the Ferals echoed in her ears.

"We failed..." she whispered, her voice hollow. Tears welled in her eyes as she watched the creatures climb toward New Lagos, their screeches mingling with the distant wails of the city's inhabitants.

"We lost..."

Imani stood frozen beside her, her heart shattered. They had tried. They had fought. But it hadn't been enough.

Dorian's breath came in ragged gasps as he watched the Ferals swarm through the breach, his fists clenched in frustration. The city was about to be consumed by darkness.

New Lagos would burn, and there was nothing they could do to stop it.

Chapter 19:

The Fall of New Lagos

The night air was thick with a premonition of death, a suffocating stillness that Dorian, Mara, and Imani couldn't ignore as they emerged from the tunnels. New Lagos stood before them, the glass towers shimmering beneath a soft layer of dust, the streets deceptively calm under the glow of the towering buildings. But it was a silence that held its breath, the kind that comes before a storm.

Imani froze, her heart pounding in her chest, as her gaze swept over the city. "Mothers be merciful…" she whispered, her voice a tremor in the stillness. She could sense it—a nightmare about to be unleashed.

Then, like a crack splitting the world, a sound rose in the distance—a howl, guttural and monstrous.

The Ferals had come.

Before they could react, chaos erupted. The shriek of creatures mixed with screams of terror from women and children. The Ferals, twisted abominations from the thawed cryo chambers, flooded the streets in a tidal wave of snarling flesh. They poured out from alleys and broken windows, their bodies twisted and malformed by the virus, each more grotesque than the last. Their eyes, black and void, burned with hunger and fury, their howls echoing across the city.

Dorian gripped his blade, his muscles tensing as the first wave of Ferals came charging toward them. "Get ready," he growled, the fury in his voice barely restrained. He could feel the bloodlust rising in him, the same primal rage that had surged through his veins in the tunnels. But now wasn't the time to question his own nature. Survival came first.

Mara had already launched herself into the fray, her sword flashing as she cut down the first Feral to come within striking distance. Her movements were brutal, efficient, a perfect symphony of violence. The streets of New Lagos had descended into a living nightmare, the air filled with the deafening screams of the dying and the relentless, guttural roars of the Ferals. Mara, Dorian, and Imani fought with a ferocity born of desperation, their blades cleaving through the monstrous hordes as the tide of violence surged around them. Blood splattered the cracked pavement, and the acrid stench of plasma burns hung heavy in the air. The walls of the surrounding buildings shook with the concussive force of collapsing infrastructure, a crumbling testament to the chaos that had been unleashed.

Mara's movements were a blur of precision and rage, her blade an extension of her fury. Every swing was lethal, every strike purposeful as she cut down Feral after Feral. The monstrous creatures, their bodies twisted by the virus, snapped and clawed, but Mara moved like a shadow—swift, deadly, unrelenting. Her mind seethed with anger, not just at the creatures but at the Council, at the people who had created this horror, and at herself for ever believing in their lies. The loss of her sister Selene weighed on her like a leaden chain, every strike of her blade an outlet for her grief.

And yet, the Ferals kept coming. For every one they felled, two more seemed to take its place. They were running out of time.

Suddenly, a new sound cut through the din of battle—the rhythmic pounding of boots. A large platoon of Phantom Hunters came into view, rushing toward them through the chaos. Clad in their sleek black armor, their faces hidden behind dark visors, they moved with the precision and discipline of a well-trained unit. They had been sent to kill Mara and her companions, to erase the Council's mistakes and silence the truth. But as they neared, something faltered in their rigid ranks.

The Ferals surrounded them, tearing through the streets with mindless brutality. The Phantom Hunters, trained to obey without question, hesitated. Their visors tilted toward Mara, watching her fight with a relentless fury, carving a path through the Ferals like a vengeful goddess. The horror in their eyes was palpable, the disciplined lines of soldiers wavering as they struggled with their orders.

For a moment, the scene hung in the balance—the Phantom Hunters poised between duty and conscience, between the Council's commands and the nightmare unfurling before them.

Then, one of the Phantom Hunters—a woman whose movements were sure and swift—broke from the ranks. She sprinted toward Mara, ducking beneath the swipe of a Feral's claws before driving her blade into its skull with brutal efficiency. She slid to Mara's side, breathless but resolute, her visor retracting to reveal a face hardened by years of battle. Her eyes, though fierce, held something else: loyalty. Not to the Council, but to Mara.

"My sister," the Phantom Hunter gasped, her voice thick with emotion. "I'd rather die by your side than watch another one of our sisters fall to these monsters."

Mara froze for the briefest of moments, her chest heaving, her blade dripping with Feral blood. She met the woman's eyes, and something shifted within her—a flicker of the bond that she had once shared with her fellow Phantom Hunters. These women had been her comrades, her sisters-in-arms. They had trained together and bled together. And now, they stood at a crossroads, the truth laid bare before them in the bodies of their fallen comrades.

The Phantom Hunter's words cut through the fog of Mara's grief and rage. In that moment, Mara realized that the battle wasn't just against the Ferals—it was for the soul of New Lagos, for the women who had been manipulated and lied to, just as she had been.

With a sharp nod, Mara accepted the woman's loyalty, her eyes hardening with renewed determination. "Then fight with me," she said, her voice like steel. "Fight with me, and we'll make sure no more sisters die."

The Phantom Hunter's face hardened with resolve, and she turned to the others. The hesitation that had gripped them shattered like glass. One by one, the other Phantom Hunters moved, their discipline crumbling as they made their choice. They joined the fray, abandoning their orders to kill Mara,

Dorian, and Imani. Instead, they fought alongside them, their blades slicing through the Ferals in a deadly symphony of violence.

The battle became a maelstrom of chaos and bloodshed. The Ferals, unrelenting in their assault, swarmed from every direction, their twisted forms screeching as they tore through anything in their path. Dorian, fueled by the bloodlust that had always simmered just beneath the surface, fought with savage brutality. His blade cleaved through bone and sinew, his strength unmatched as he sent Ferals flying with each strike.

Imani fired shot after shot from her plasma gun, the high-powered blasts ripping through the Ferals' bodies in bursts of light and heat. But even as they fought with everything they had, the Ferals kept coming. Their numbers seemed endless, a relentless tide of horror that threatened to drown them all.

Through it all, Mara moved like a specter, her grief and rage driving her to fight harder, faster. Every swing of her blade was a cry for vengeance, every Feral she killed was a small piece of retribution for the sister she had lost. And as the Phantom Hunters fought by her side, Mara felt something crack open inside her—an unspoken bond, reforged in the heat of battle.

But even with the Phantom Hunters joining the fight, the odds were stacked against them. The Ferals swarmed the streets, tearing through the city like a plague. Buildings crumbled, the lower levels of New Lagos giving way under the onslaught. Explosions rocked the streets as plasma grenades detonated, sending chunks of concrete and twisted metal flying through the air.

And still, the Ferals kept coming.

Mara's blade whistled through the air, slicing through the throat of a Feral that lunged at her. Blood sprayed across her face, but she barely noticed, her focus razor-sharp. Another Feral came at her from the left, and she spun, driving her blade deep into its chest. But even as it fell, two more took its place.

The battle was a blur of violence and blood, a desperate fight for survival. And yet, despite the overwhelming odds, they fought on—Mara, Dorian, Imani, and the Phantom Hunters, bound together by a common enemy, fighting for the city they had once called home.

But they couldn't hold the line forever.

As the battle raged on, Mara's eyes darted toward the horizon, where the Ferals continued to pour from the shattered city. She knew, deep down, that they couldn't stop them all. There were too many. The Ferals were like a flood, a force of nature that couldn't be contained.

Mara gritted her teeth, her rage boiling over. She wanted blood—Council blood. They had done this. They had created this nightmare, and they had to pay for it.

But first, they had to survive.

As the last of the Phantom Hunters fell in beside her, Mara looked to Dorian and Imani. Their faces were grim, their bodies bruised and bloodied, but they were still standing. And together, they would keep fighting.

For as long as it took.

The surrounding city was disintegrating. Homes, once places of safety and warmth, were being torn apart. Screams pierced the air, and the Ferals moved from house to house, dragging women from their beds, their teeth tearing into flesh, their claws rending bone. Each victim they claimed rose moments later, their bodies convulsing and mutating into the very creatures that had killed them.

In one high-rise apartment, a mother fought desperately against a Feral that had broken into her home. She held a makeshift weapon—a broken chair leg—and jabbed at the creature with everything she had, her daughter huddled behind her.

"Mama, please!" the little girl sobbed. "Run!"

But the woman didn't flee. She couldn't—not while the Feral blocked her path. She thrust the chair leg forward again, landing a blow that sent the creature reeling back. But it wasn't enough. The Feral leaped forward, and its claw raked across the child's arm.

The transformation was swift. The mother screamed as her daughter convulsed, her small body warping and twisting into something inhuman. Her eyes, once bright with innocence, became dark and hollow, her mouth splitting open into a snarl. The mother's horror was complete as the creature that had once been her daughter lunged at her, snarling and drooling.

Unable to fight the thing her child had become, the mother backed toward the window. Tears streamed down her face, her mind struggling to comprehend the nightmare unfolding before her. But as the Feral lunged, the mother made her choice. She turned and leapt from the high-rise, her body disappearing into the darkness below.

Meanwhile, Mara, Dorian, and Imani fought for their lives in the streets. The Ferals kept coming, wave after wave, their numbers seemingly endless. Blood soaked the ground beneath them, and every corner they turned revealed another group of grotesque creatures, each more savage than the last.

Then, from the smoke and carnage, a familiar figure appeared—a general in full combat gear, her face etched with determination. Phantom Hunters followed close behind her, their expressions grim as they surveyed the surrounding destruction.

"Mara!" the general shouted, cutting down a Feral that had lunged at her. She moved toward Mara, her voice filled with desperation. "Is it true? Has the Council done this?"

Mara's eyes blazed with fury as she decapitated another Feral, her sword gleaming with blood. "Yes," she spat, her voice filled with venom. "The Council knew everything— Selene, the virus, the Ferals. They've damned us all!"

The general's face hardened, a deep line of pain etched into her features. She looked around at her soldiers, her decision made. "We'll fight with you," she said, locking eyes with Mara. "We'll evacuate the city, but when this is over, we're coming for the Council."

The alliance was born in fire and blood. The Phantom Hunters, once sworn to kill Mara, now fought beside her, cutting through the Ferals with precision and fury. The battle was savage, violent, every clash of blades and discharge of plasma echoing through the war-torn streets.

As the battle raged on, entire buildings began to collapse. The explosions in the cryo chambers had torn apart the lower levels of New Lagos, and now the towering skyscrapers were falling like dominos. Entire blocks crumbled, sending plumes of dust and debris into the air.

"Keep moving!" Dorian shouted, driving his blade through a Feral's skull before kicking its limp body aside. "We need to reach the Council!"

But even as they fought their way through the streets, the Ferals kept coming, their numbers growing by the second. The virus was spreading faster than anyone could have predicted, and soon, there would be no one left to save.

As another Feral jumped at her, Mara spun on her heel, her blade cleaving through its neck with a sickening crunch. She fought with everything she had, determined to make every last one of them pay.

But even as they fought with all their might, the city of New Lagos was falling apart around them. And deep beneath the city, the remaining Ferals were breaking free, the incubator chambers destroyed, and their prison shattered.

And as the screams of the women of New Lagos echoed through the night, Mara fell to her knees, tears streaming down her face. The devastation was too much. The Council had brought this upon them all.

And now, the world was ending.

Chapter 20:

The Final Move

The Council Hall of New Lagos was an oasis of serenity in the midst of chaos. Gleaming white walls, tall crystalline windows, and sleek metallic arches enclosed the space, a sanctuary of sterile perfection. But the calm inside was deceptive. The screens that lined the walls flickered with the horrific scenes unfolding across the city. Outside, New Lagos was burning. The once-pristine streets had become a battlefield overrun by Ferals, their monstrous forms tearing through the helpless with brutal efficiency.

The screams from the city echoed through the hall, broadcasted in real time—desperate cries of mothers protecting their children, the guttural howls of the infected as they ripped apart anyone in their path. Yet, despite the carnage, the woman seated at the head of the council chamber was utterly still. Seraphine watched the screens with a cold, detached gaze. Her fingers, long and thin, drummed a slow, deliberate rhythm on the armrest of her chair, the only sound within the vast chamber aside from the distant destruction displayed on the monitors.

As the other council members sat in silence, a growing tension swelled in the room. Some shifted uncomfortably, their faces pale with horror, their eyes darting between the scenes of the massacre and Seraphine's disturbingly calm demeanor. She seemed almost… satisfied.

A faint smile tugged at the corners of her lips, a shadow of something far more sinister lurking in the depths of her expression. Her eyes glinted with something unholy, as if the chaos and death flooding the streets below were the final strokes in a masterpiece she had long been painting.

On one of the screens, a mother clutched her daughter to her chest as a Feral lunged toward them, its gnarled claws outstretched, its mouth twisted into a hungry snarl. The screen flickered, cutting out just as the Feral reached them, but the scream—the mother's final cry—echoed in the council chamber like a chilling, final note. Seraphine leaned forward slightly, her tongue brushing her lips as though she could taste the suffering.

"I think this city should have burned long ago," she whispered, her voice low, almost caressing the words. "It's cleansing, isn't it? Necessary."

One of the council members, a woman with wide, fearful eyes named Anara, broke the silence. She had been watching in disbelief as her fellow council members sat paralyzed, unwilling to challenge Seraphine. But now, her voice trembled with fury and despair as she stood.

"This is madness!" Anara's voice cracked. "These are women—our people—dying out there! We have to do something! We can stop this before the entire city is destroyed.

We have the resources, and the technology! How can you sit here, satisfied, while they die?"

Seraphine's gaze shifted to Anara, her smile slowly vanishing as her eyes darkened. The room held its breath. The other council members exchanged glances but remained silent, fear etched into their faces. They knew better than to speak. They knew better than to defy Seraphine.

Anara's desperation grew as she looked around the chamber, seeing nothing but the cowardice in the eyes of her peers. "Do you not hear them? The screams? The children?" Her voice shook. "We have the power to stop this. To save the city. You've all lost your souls—every one of you! We can't let this happen!"

But the others wouldn't meet her gaze. They stared at the floor, their faces frozen in grim resignation. No one would dare cross Seraphine, not after what she had done to those who had opposed her in the past. Not after she had demonstrated the extent of her control over them—her cruelty and power.

Anara's breath came in shallow bursts, her chest heaving with frustration. The blood pounded in her ears as she reached into the folds of her robe, pulling out a sleek plasma gun. She leveled it at Seraphine, her hand trembling but resolute.

"I won't stand by and watch this anymore," she whispered. "This ends now."

For a moment, Seraphine's expression didn't change. She didn't flinch, didn't blink. It was as if the sight of the gun aimed at her had no meaning—no weight. Slowly, her lips parted, and a dark chuckle escaped, echoing through the chamber like the soft hiss of a snake.

"You always were the foolish one, Anara," she said, her voice dripping with mockery. "Do you really think you can stop me? Do you think a toy like that can end this?"

Anara's grip tightened, her finger hovering over the trigger. "You're a monster, Seraphine."

"And yet, here you are, part of my world," Seraphine replied. "You see, this was always going to happen. The city, the Ferals, all of it—it's part of the plan. Project Reset. A new world, purified of weakness, of dissent. A world where women like you, weak in your morals, are washed away."

Anara's hand shook as she fired.

But Seraphine moved.

In an instant, she was out of her chair, faster than the eye could follow. She was a blur, crossing the room in less than a heartbeat. Before the plasma bolt had even discharged fully from the gun, Seraphine was upon her, her fingers coiling around Anara's wrist like a vise, twisting with a sickening snap. Anara cried out as her wrist shattered, the gun falling uselessly from her grip. The plasma bolt scorched a blackened mark into the wall, but it hadn't come close to its target.

Seraphine's free hand moved with snake-like precision, her fingers closing around Anara's throat. The look of triumph in Seraphine's eyes was almost grotesque as she leaned in close, her lips inches from Anara's ear.

"I've given you the gift of seeing this city burn. And you will die for daring to defy me."

With a flick of her wrist, Seraphine tore Anara's throat out, her fingers slicing through flesh and bone as easily as if she were carving into soft fruit. Blood sprayed across the pristine floor, and Anara fell to her knees, gurgling as her life poured from the ragged wound in her neck.

Seraphine let her fall without a second glance, her gaze turning back to the council members who sat frozen in horror. The quiet in the room returned, save for the soft wheezing of Anara's dying breaths.

"Does anyone else have any concerns?" Seraphine's voice was cold, detached. There was no emotion, no humanity in her tone. Just icy authority.

No one moved. No one dared to speak.

Satisfied, Seraphine stepped over Anara's twitching body, her focus returning to the screens. New Lagos continued to burn, the city's fall inevitable.

"This world is a failure," she said calmly, her eyes flicking to the devastation on the screens. "But Project Reset will ensure that what rises from its ashes will be perfect."

One of the council members, pale and shaking, spoke up. "What of the survivors? The women who remain in New Lagos?"

Seraphine turned slowly to face her, her lips curling into a thin smile. "There will be no survivors," she said. "The Ferals will cleanse the city. And once that is done, we will begin again—elsewhere."

"The Ferals?" another council member whispered, her voice barely audible. "But we have no way of controlling the new ones. The infection spreads too fast. We'll lose containment."

Seraphine's smile widened, an unsettling gleam in her eyes. "Let it spread," she said softly. "We'll let it burn itself out. And when all is quiet, we will rebuild."

The council members exchanged uneasy glances, but none dared challenge her again. They knew what would happen if they did.

"We've already prepared the evacuation route," Seraphine continued, her voice smooth and controlled. "The transports are standing by. We will leave the city soon, and the Ferals will take care of the rest. Project Reset will succeed, and New Lagos will be but a memory."

As she spoke, the council's attention was drawn back to the screens, where the chaos in the city continued to unfold. The Ferals, unstoppable and ravenous, were flooding the streets. Buildings were crumbling, the infrastructure failing under the weight of the destruction. And among the screams, the council could hear the sound of New Lagos falling—piece by piece, woman by woman.

Seraphine stepped back into her chair, crossing her legs with elegant precision as she watched the devastation with a serene, almost rapturous expression.

"The future belongs to us," she whispered, her eyes gleaming with a dark hunger. "And no one can stop it."

Chapter 21:

What Sort of Witchcraft is This?

The sky above New Lagos had darkened to an ashen hue, streaked with the fires raging throughout the once-sterile metropolis. Smoke billowed through the streets, mingling with the screams of the dying and the monstrous roars of the Ferals as they tore apart everything in their path. The city had become a nightmarish labyrinth of blood and destruction, but in the midst of the carnage, Dorian, Mara, Imani, and the Phantom Hunters fought to save whatever remained.

The streets were a battlefield. Ferals, twisted abominations that were once women, surged through the alleyways and avenues, their grotesque forms flailing as they attacked indiscriminately. Their mutated bodies, slick with blood and torn sinew, moved with a feral hunger, their eyes gleaming with madness. Everywhere they turned, they were met with the stench of death. The ground was slick with blood, the walls of the buildings splattered with viscera.

Dorian, his blade gleaming with fresh blood, moved with a brutal efficiency that left a trail of fallen Ferals in his wake. His muscles strained, each movement a precise act of violence as he slashed and tore through the hordes. His strength was unnatural—more than human, a power he was only now beginning to understand, though it left him with more questions than answers.

Beside him, Mara danced through the chaos, her movements a lethal ballet of grace and fury. Her face was etched with an anger that went beyond the fight—beyond the need to survive. Her sister's death had cracked something deep inside her, and now she fought with a rage that bordered on suicide. Every Feral she struck down seemed to fuel her need for vengeance, but it wasn't just the Ferals she was after. It was the Council. The betrayal. The lies. She had been raised by them, molded by them, and they had taken her sister.

"I'll kill them all!" she roared as she plunged her blade into the chest of a Feral, its body convulsing before collapsing into the dust. "For Selene!"

Imani, using her plasma pistol to clear their path, barked orders to the survivors they were trying to evacuate. Her voice was sharp, cutting through the din of battle. "Stay close! Follow me!" The women—panicked, some sobbing, others silent in their terror—clung to her words like lifelines as they were shepherded through the chaos.

"Through the tunnels!" Imani shouted, pointing to the entrance hidden behind a half-collapsed building. "Get underground! Now!"

The survivors scrambled into the tunnels beneath New Lagos, the same tunnels Imani and Dorian had used to infiltrate the city. The entrance was obscured by rubble, but those who listened and followed would find the path that led to temporary safety.

As the crowd poured into the tunnels, one woman, clutching her daughter, stopped in front of Dorian, her tear-streaked face a mix of fear and confusion. "Where are we supposed to go?" she asked, her voice trembling.

Dorian, still bloodied from battle, turned to her, his expression unreadable for a moment. "There's a hidden colony deep in the forest, buried in the underground cave system. You'll be safe there. The surrounding barrier—nothing gets through. Not Ferals, not hunters. Nothing."

"How can we trust this place?" another woman called out, her voice sharp with desperation. "Why was it hidden from us all this time?"

Dorian hesitated, wiping blood from his brow, his face hardening. His voice, when it came, was low but firm. "Because it's not like New Lagos. Men live there. Women live there. But no one rules. It's not the Matriarchy. It's not about control. It's a place of balance, of survival. We've used stolen technology from New Lagos to create something safe."

A ripple of shock moved through the crowd. Some recoiled, others murmured in disbelief.

"Males?" the woman asked, her eyes wide. "How—how can that be?"

Dorian's jaw clenched, frustration flashing in his eyes. "Because at the colony, all pregnancies are allowed to happen without genetic selection. They aren't forcing the fetus to grow into a female. Whatever the natural selection is after artificial insemination, they allow that pregnancy to go full term."

But how can we trust a colony that has males?" the woman asked, her voice trembling with fear and disgust.

"Because not all men are monsters. And not all women are saviors." His words were harsh, cutting through the preconceptions these women had been raised with all their lives. "My mother started the colony. She believed in something different. Even after she was gone, we kept her dream alive. The men there don't rule anything. Everyone has a role to play. Everyone runs the colony."

Imani, hearing the revelation for the first time, turned on him, her voice sharp. "You knew there were other men all along?" There was fury in her tone, betrayal coiling in her chest. "You let me believe—let us believe—you were alone in the wilderness! Led me to believe you could save us, that your DNA was the key and all this time, there were more specimens available!?"

Dorian's eyes flashed with something darker. "I didn't know I could trust you. I still don't know now, but these people need help. And that colony is the closest place that can give it to them!

"But you lied! Even after we found out your DNA sample wasn't a match for an anti-virus. You allowed me to think all hope was lost!" Imani shouted, anger flaring like a spark in a dry forest. "You—"

"I didn't lie!" Dorian snapped back, his voice rising with raw emotion. "I genuinely didn't know what I was! What the council did to me. And yeah, I didn't mention the men at the colony, but can you blame me? What has your society done to males and their mothers once you find them? Even still, I tried to help. I had to keep that colony hidden because it was the only safe place for males in this region. You can't blame me for not trusting the people hunting me and my kind for centuries."

"Fuck you, Dorian! You lied! You hid the truth from me and now look at our home!"

Dorian's eyes blazed with barely contained fury as he stepped closer to Imani, his voice a low, dangerous growl. "Are you really going to stand there and blame me for this? For not telling you the truth earlier? Do you honestly think the Council of Mothers would've gone to that colony and shown those men mercy? Mercy? Look around you!" He gestured wildly to the surrounding devastation—the once-proud city now reduced to ruins, blood staining the streets, bodies of women lying broken and lifeless.

"These are women, Imani! Not men. Women! The very same women the Council swore to protect, the same women they claimed they were empowering. And now, they're being slaughtered! By the same system you believed in!" His words struck like hammer blows, each syllable laden with the bitterness of betrayal. "All that talk about creating a better world, keeping women safe, lifting you up—it's all bullshit!"

Imani flinched but didn't look away, though her eyes filled with anguish as the weight of the truth pressed down on her. Dorian's voice softened, but it was laced with an edge of disbelief and sorrow. "You still think this is any better than what the men of the old world did? Tell me, Imani—what's the difference between what they did back then and what the Council is doing now? Women are dying, being torn apart, sacrificed for a cause that was never about them. How long are you going to keep making excuses for their treachery?"

The rawness of his words hung between them, like a blade cutting through the last shreds of her denial.

The tension between them crackled like electricity, but Mara cut through the argument, her voice hard as steel. "This isn't the time for this. We need to keep moving. If they're going to survive, they need to hurry. The Ferals won't wait."

Several Phantom Hunters, loyal to Mara, had gathered near the survivors. Their armor gleamed darkly in the smoke-choked air, their faces grim beneath their helmets. One of them, a tall woman with a scar running down her cheek, stepped forward. "We'll accompany them," she said, her voice resolute. "We'll make sure they reach the colony."

Imani stared at Dorian, the weight of the truth pressing down on her. But she knew this wasn't the time to argue further. There would be time to confront him later, to ask the questions that burned in her mind. Right now, survival was all that mattered.

As the Phantom Hunters led the group into the tunnels, Imani turned back to Dorian, her voice quieter now. "Does the colony have what we need? Can we synthesize an anti-virus there?"

Dorian nodded grimly. "Yes. But first, we have to deal with the Council. As long as they're alive, we're not safe. The colony's not safe."

Imani's eyes hardened with resolve. "Then let's end this."

Without another word, the three of them—Dorian, Mara, and Imani—headed toward the Council Hall. But the closer they got to the Council Hall, the fiercer the resistance became.

Several fighters, still loyal to the Council, had regrouped and were now standing in their path, blocking the entrance to the council building. Their black armor glinted under the flickering streetlights, their visors reflecting the flames of the city's destruction. These were not ordinary soldiers—they were Black Lotus, the trained killers that Mara had once called sisters.

The leader stepped forward, her voice hollow and cold. "You've betrayed the Council, Mara. You've chosen a side, and now you will die with these... traitors."

The word "traitors" dripped from her mouth like venom, but it had no effect on Mara. Her rage was a deep, burning pit that could not be quenched. Her sister's face haunted her, and in that moment, all Mara wanted was blood.

"I chose the side that's trying to save this city, save our sisters, Mara growled, raising her blade. "What did you choose? Blind loyalty to a Council that's already damned us all?"

Without another word, the Black Lotus charged. It was as if the gates of hell had unleashed its most elite soldiers. Unlike the Phantom Hunters, whose precision and speed were unmatched by any other warrior class, the Black Lotus were something far deadlier. They moved with a grace and lethality that defied reason—warriors genetically engineered for battle, their bodies stronger, faster, and more resilient than any foe Mara had ever faced. Even the Phantom Hunters, feared across the world, paled in comparison to the sheer skill and brutal efficiency of the Black Lotus.

Blades clashed with a force that reverberated through the streets, the sound of steel biting steel mingling with the distant, haunting screams of the fallen. Mara was a blur of deadly motion, her blade slicing through loyalists with terrifying precision. Her strikes were fueled by grief and rage, each swing a scream for vengeance, each kill a cathartic release for the pain she carried—Selene's death, the annihilation of New Lagos, the betrayal of the Council. But it wasn't enough. The Black Lotus were relentless.

They moved like a synchronized storm, their attacks calculated, methodical, never leaving an opening, never hesitating. Mara fought with everything she had, her Phantom Hunter training pushed to its limits, but even she couldn't take them all at once. These warriors were stronger, faster, and unlike the Phantom Hunters, they seemed impervious to exhaustion. Her arms burned with the weight of every swing, and her lungs screamed for air, but she couldn't stop. Not yet.

Imani fought beside her, her strikes precise but lacking the raw brutality of Mara's. She wasn't a warrior as skilled as Mara, but the necessity of survival had forced her to dig deep into herself. Each swing of her blade was a desperate attempt to stay alive, cutting down the Hunters and The Black Lotus as they swarmed around her. Yet, even she knew that this was a battle beyond their reach.

As the battle erupted, chaos consumed the air, weapons clashing with a ferocity that sent shockwaves through the streets. Dorian leaped into the fray, his movements sharp and precise. But the Black Lotus—elite assassins of the Council— were like ghosts, their speed and precision unmatched. Within moments, one of them struck with a plasma spear, its energy blade slicing deep into his side before he could even react. The hiss of the wound, the searing pain—it was as much an assault on his pride as it was his body.

Blood seeped from the gash, staining his side as he staggered back, his jaw clenched in a grimace of agony. The spear had found its mark, and though he fought to stay upright, the injury slowed him. His breath came in short, labored bursts, each movement growing heavier as the adrenaline coursing through his veins fought to keep him upright.

He gripped his blade tighter, ignoring the fiery pain as he hacked through the ranks of loyalist soldiers. His swings, once fluid and lethal, were now slower, more desperate. A second plasma spear grazed his shoulder, the force of the impact sending him reeling. He dropped to one knee, his muscles screaming for respite, his mind swimming in the haze of pain and fatigue. But Dorian forced himself to rise. He had to. For Mara. For Imani. For the fragile hope that still clung to life amidst the chaos.

One of the Black Lotus closed in—a leader, perhaps, her aura of command palpable. Her movements were so precise, so impossibly fast, it was as if she were dancing through the battlefield. Her curved blade gleamed, cutting through the air in a blur. Dorian raised his sword to defend, but her strike came down with the force of a hurricane. He blocked the attack, but the impact reverberated through his arms, sending him staggering backward, his blade trembling in his grip.

The assassin pressed her advantage, her strikes relentless. Dorian barely managed to parry, each movement slower than the last. Her blade sang through the air with deadly grace, forcing him onto the defensive. Every second felt like a lifetime, and he knew he couldn't hold out much longer.

Through the battle, Mara saw him falter, and her heart clenched with dread. "Dorian!" she screamed, but her cry was drowned out by the clash of metal and the screams of the dying. She surged forward to help, but two Black Lotus assassins intercepted her, their strikes precise and unforgiving. She deflected one blade, spinning to avoid the other, her movements driven by sheer instinct. They weren't just attacking—they were hunting, their every strike designed to corner her, to break her before delivering the killing blow.

Blood pooled around them, mixing with the shattered remains of weapons and bodies that littered the ground. The loyalists and hunters had been cut down in droves, their corpses painting the streets in carnage. Yet the battle raged on, the tide tilting ever more in favor of the Black Lotus.

Dorian swung his blade again, the arc sluggish but resolute, aiming for the assassin's exposed flank. She evaded with ease, her mocking smile visible beneath her hood. Pain blurred his vision, his strength fading, but he refused to fall. He couldn't fall. Not while Mara and Imani were still fighting, not while the future still hung precariously on the edge of survival.

"Imani!" Mara's voice was raw, desperate. She could see Dorian faltering, could feel the overwhelming presence of the Black Lotus closing in. They had to break through. They had to survive.

Imani, covered in blood—none of it her own—met Mara's gaze and nodded. She wasn't a warrior, but she was brilliant, and she knew they had only moments before Dorian collapsed under the relentless assault.

Mara's eyes blazed with fury. The Black Lotus might be stronger, faster, more skilled, but she wasn't going to let them take Dorian down. Not while she still had breath in her body. She pushed harder, her blade a whirlwind of motion, slashing through the two Black Lotus in front of her with a ferocity that even they hadn't anticipated. For a brief moment, she broke free, running toward Dorian, who was now on one knee, trying to fend off another brutal strike.

But then, from behind her, came the sound of another Black Lotus charging—a blur of speed and death.

Time seemed to slow. Dorian, clutching his side, looked up, blood staining his teeth as he grinned through the pain. "Not yet," he growled, pushing off the ground and launching himself at his attacker, his blade flashing in the dark.

Mara caught the sight of him out of the corner of her eye, her heart hammering as he fought through his injuries, the rage and strength of the feral blood coursing through his veins giving him one last surge of power.

But the Black Lotus were relentless. They wouldn't stop until they were dead. And Dorian knew he couldn't hold them off forever.

With a roar, he swung his blade, cleaving through his opponent's armor, but the Black Lotus leader was already upon him again, her curved sword flashing through the air like a deadly whisper. Dorian barely managed to block her strike, but the impact sent a shockwave of pain through his already battered body.

Mara, her heart in her throat, was fighting her way through the chaos, her mind a whirl of fear and fury. She had to get to

Dorian. She had to save him. But for every loyalist she cut down, more appeared in their place, their blades gleaming, their eyes cold and unyielding.

Blood sprayed across her face as she felled another opponent, her muscles screaming in protest, but she wouldn't stop. She couldn't stop.

Not until they were safe.

Not until they had won.

"Dorian!" Mara shouted; her voice filled with concern she didn't know she had.

Dorian gritted his teeth, refusing to fall.

Finally, Mara broke through the line of Black Lotus, rushing to Dorian's side. The world seemed to slow as she knelt beside him, her breath coming in ragged gasps. She could see the pain in his eyes, the exhaustion pulling at his features. And then something unexpected surged within her—a feeling she didn't understand, didn't want to understand.

For a brief, fleeting moment, Mara leaned in, her breath catching in her throat as her face hovered just inches from Dorian's. Time itself seemed to still, the chaos of the battle fading into the background, leaving only the sound of their labored breathing and the electric tension that crackled between them. Her heart hammered in her chest, louder than the war raging around them, louder than the roars of the Ferals closing in. Her lips trembled, just a breath away from his, and for a heartbeat, all the pain, all the anger that had consumed her seemed to dissolve into the air between them. Her fingers twitched with the instinct to reach out, to touch him, to give in to whatever this was—this pull she couldn't name, couldn't understand.

Dorian's eyes, dark and intense, met hers, filled with a rawness that made her breath hitch. He wasn't just looking at her—he was seeing her, beyond the armor, beyond the anger, and the weight of that realization was almost unbearable.

But then, at the very last second, Mara stopped herself, her eyes widening in shock. She pulled back sharply, as though burned by the proximity, her breath ragged and unsteady. The connection between them snapped like a taut wire cut too soon. A sharp intake of breath escaped her lips, her eyes wild with disbelief, and the rage she had buried deep within herself suddenly flared back to life. Her whole body shook, not from the strain of battle, but from the war within her heart.

"What... what sort of witchcraft is this?" she muttered, her voice trembling, as if saying the words aloud would banish the feeling that had just gripped her. She stared at Dorian, her chest heaving, her lips pressed into a thin line, fury and confusion battling for control of her expression.

This wasn't supposed to happen. She wasn't supposed to feel this way, especially not about him. A male. The very embodiment of everything she had been trained to despise, to kill without hesitation. Yet here she was, torn, standing on the edge of something she couldn't control, something that terrified her in a way no battle ever had. She hated it. She hated him for making her feel like this, for breaking through the walls she had built so carefully around herself.

Dorian said nothing, but his eyes spoke volumes—surprise, perhaps even a glimmer of understanding—but he didn't move, didn't push her. He simply watched, his breath shallow, as if he too felt the weight of what almost happened between them.

Imani, watching from a few steps away, couldn't help but smirk. The corners of her mouth curled up in a satisfied grin, as if she had expected this all along—had been waiting for it. She knew something they didn't, and watching their exchange only confirmed it.

Mara stood, shaking off whatever strange emotion had overtaken her. "You can't fight anymore," she said coldly, avoiding Dorian's eyes. "You're staying here."

"I'm not—" Dorian tried to protest, but Mara silenced him with a look that could've cut steel.

"You're too wounded. You can't climb those stairs, and if you come with us, you'll get us all killed. Stay here. Hold the line."

Dorian, too weak to argue, gave her a reluctant nod. "Go," he rasped, forcing himself to his feet. He leaned against the wall of the council building, gripping his blade tightly, the blood still seeping from his side. "I'll hold them off."

Mara and Imani shared a glance before turning toward the long flight of stairs that led to the Council Hall's inner sanctum. The doors were in sight, but they both knew the Ferals and any remaining Hunters would be right behind them.

Mara hesitated for just a second longer, her eyes lingering on Dorian's battered form. Then she turned and ran with Imani at her side, leaving Dorian to face whatever horrors would break through the door behind them.

It wasn't long before the glass doors of the hall shattered, and the Ferals came pouring in—a writhing mass of limbs and snarls. Dorian stood tall, raising his blade high, a savage roar escaping his throat as he prepared to meet the onslaught head-on.

Bloodied but unbowed, Dorian charged into the Ferals, his roar shaking the very ground as he faced death without fear. He would hold them back or die trying.

Chapter 22:

The Gauntlet of Shadows

The stairwell was a spiral of shiny metal, its echoing expanse disappearing into the depths below and stretching upward into the dim light filtering from the floors above. The air was heavy, thick with the metallic tang of blood and the acrid scent of plasma burns. The distant growls of Ferals reverberated through the hollow space, like the low, menacing hum of an unseen predator. Every footfall, every breath felt louder than the last, amplified by the tension coiling tighter and tighter around them like a noose.

Mara and Imani moved swiftly, their bodies pressed against the cracked walls as they ascended, flanked by the surviving hunters who fought with grim determination. Their armor, chipped and dented from the battle outside, seemed to pulse in the shadows, their movements fluid but wary. The stairwell felt like a tomb, the tightness of it suffocating, its darkened corners holding the promise of something far worse than the battles they'd left behind.

"We're close," Mara grunted, her voice rough with exertion, her blood-stained blade held firm in her grip. Her eyes, sharp and cold as ever, flicked upward toward the next landing. "But so are they."

Imani didn't answer. Her focus was ahead, her breath coming in sharp, controlled bursts as she gripped her plasma pistol in one hand and a standard steel blade in the other. The walls of the stairwell were closing in around her, each step feeling like a heavier burden, but the urgency in her heart burned hotter than the exhaustion in her limbs.

Suddenly, a guttural scream tore through the silence, high-pitched and inhuman, sending a chill down Imani's spine. Ferals.

The next moment, a dark, hulking shape leaped down from above, crashing onto the stairwell landing with an animalistic ferocity that shook the metal structure. It was a Feral—a grotesque amalgamation of sinewy muscle and savage claws, but something was wrong. Imani's heart froze for a moment as her eyes locked onto the creature's mangled features. Its face, though twisted and deformed, still bore the remnants of a helmet. The remnants of a Phantom Hunter.

Mara's eyes widened in recognition. "That's—" she barely had time to speak before the Feral lunged at them with a screech, its blackened claws slashing through the air.

The battle erupted with a furious intensity. Mara met the creature's attack head-on, her blade flashing in the dim light as she parried its claws, the steel shrieking as it collided with bone and rotted armor. The Feral hissed, its grotesque face pulling back in a snarl as it swiped again, this time faster, more vicious. Its movements were erratic, but the underlying skill of the

Phantom Hunter it once was still lingered—each strike calculated, brutal, and deadly.

Imani dodged to the side, narrowly avoiding another Feral as it dropped from the shadows above. She slashed with her blade, cutting deep into its side, but the creature barely slowed, snarling as it turned on her with wild eyes. Plasma shots echoed through the stairwell as the hunters behind her opened fire, their beams of light cutting through the darkness, but the Ferals were relentless, advancing with terrifying speed despite the plasma burns searing through their twisted flesh.

Mara was a whirlwind of violence. Her blade danced through the air, each movement precise and lethal, but the Ferals came in waves, their deformed bodies climbing over one another like a tide of madness. The stairwell was a confined, nightmarish battlefield, and the proximity of it only heightened the savagery. She hacked through the first Feral, her blade cutting clean through its neck, but even as the body fell, another leaped from above, claws extended, teeth bared.

The weight of its body slammed into her, and they crashed against the wall. Mara grunted, the impact momentarily knocking the breath from her lungs, but she was quick to recover, slamming the hilt of her blade into the Feral's skull. It shrieked, and with a savage snarl, Mara twisted her body, throwing the creature down the stairs, its flailing limbs smashing into the metal with a sickening crack.

"Keep moving!" she shouted, her voice harsh, as she turned to face another Feral. This one was faster, its movements more deliberate. It was taller than the others, and its eyes—oh, God, its eyes—were those of someone who once knew how to fight.

Imani's heart skipped a beat as she recognized the face, or what was left of it.

"That was one of ours," Mara hissed, her voice barely audible, though it quivered with rage.

The Feral's attack came without hesitation. It lunged at Mara, claws flashing, but she ducked under its swing and came up with a savage uppercut, her blade plunging into its chest. Black blood sprayed across the walls, and the Feral screeched, but still, it fought, its clawed hand wrapping around Mara's throat with a vice-like grip.

Imani darted forward, slashing across its arm with her blade. The Feral released Mara with a screech, and Mara wasted no time, pulling her blade free from its chest and decapitating the creature in one swift motion. Its head rolled down the stairs, leaving a trail of dark blood behind it.

Mara pushed forward, cutting down one Feral after another, her blade a blur of motion, but there were too many. Their numbers swelled, and their savage strength was overwhelming.

A guttural roar echoed through the stairwell—a Feral larger than the others, its body rippling with muscle, its skin stretched tight over a gaunt frame. It smashed through the ranks of hunters, knocking them aside like rag dolls. Mara turned just in time to see it charging toward her, its eyes filled with a twisted rage.

With a swift movement, she spun, sidestepping its charge, and slashed her blade across its back. The creature howled in pain, but it didn't stop, swinging a massive clawed hand toward her. The force of the blow knocked her back against the wall, her breath leaving her in a gasp.

Imani fired her plasma pistol into the Feral's side, but the creature barely flinched, turning its wild gaze toward her. Mara, her vision blurred from the impact, struggled to her feet, blood dripping from a cut on her forehead. Her grip tightened on her blade, her fury building with every beat of her heart.

But then, from the corner of her eye, Mara saw something even worse—Ferals wearing Phantom Hunter armor, their bodies grotesquely twisted but still bearing the symbols of the elite Hunters who had once fought beside her, now turned into monsters.

"Mothers have mercy..." she muttered under her breath, her voice tight with grief and fury.

Imani shouted, "We have to get out of here!" but the words were drowned out by the roar of the Ferals closing in.

They fought desperately, slashing and firing, their bodies pressed against one another in the tight stairwell as more and more Ferals poured in from above and below. Blood splattered across the metal steps, the air thick with the scent of death and the clang of steel on bone.

Finally, they reached the landing just below the council chambers, the massive doors looming ahead like a beacon of salvation. Mara surged forward, her hand reaching for the control panel to open the doors, but it was locked. Her heart sank as the realization hit her—they were trapped.

Behind them, the Ferals gathered, their deformed faces twisted with hunger, their bloodstained claws ready to tear them apart. Mara turned, her blade raised, as the first of the Ferals rushed toward her.

Imani stood beside her, her plasma pistol raised, her face pale but determined. "We fight to the end," she whispered, her voice trembling with fear and resolve.

Mara nodded, her eyes burning with rage as the Ferals closed in.

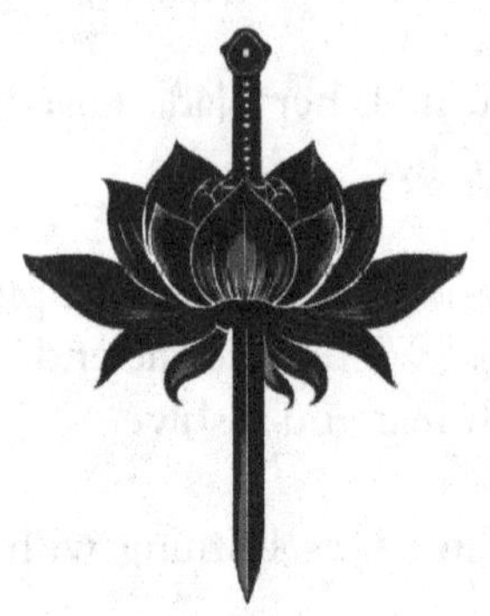

Chapter 23:

The Silent Hunt

The air was thick with the scent of decay, an oppressive weight that hung over the survivors like the breath of a looming predator. Every creak of old infrastructure, every drip of water falling from above, felt like a harbinger of death.

The women moved through the darkness, their footsteps barely more than whispers on the cold floor. Fear gripped them, gnawing at their resolve, but they clung to each other, their only hope of survival. Above them, New Lagos was a storm of violence and chaos as the city was torn apart by the unleashed Ferals. But down here, the silence was more dangerous.

The hunters guided them through the labyrinthine passages with the expertise of seasoned predators. Cloaked in the darkness, they moved like shadows, their every movement precise, their instincts honed by years of deadly service. They had been bred for moments like these, crafted for silent death, and in the abyss of the tunnels, they were in their element.

Kalise led the group, her eyes flicking constantly from one darkened corner to another, her hand tight around the hilt of her blade. She paused every few feet, listening to the cold, stagnant air for the telltale signs of Ferals. Her breathing was slow, measured, her pulse calm even in the face of the creeping horror around them.

Behind her, three more hunters followed—Jada, Alara, and Talia—each moving with the fluid grace of predators in their prime. Their faces were masked in the faint, pale glow from their wrist orbs, casting angular shadows across their sharp features. They communicated through glances and subtle hand signals, their blades drawn, ready to strike at a moment's notice.

The Ferals were near.

Kalise could feel it in the air—the distinct, acrid scent of them, a mixture of blood, sweat, and madness. They didn't breathe like normal humans anymore, and the low, guttural growl they made when they hunted sent a chill through even the most hardened of the hunters. It was the sound of pure hunger, a hunger that could never be satisfied.

Suddenly, Kalise froze, her hand shooting up in a silent command. The group came to an abrupt stop, the survivors pressing close, their breaths hitching in unison, tension gripping the air. Somewhere in the tunnel ahead, a faint scuffling sound echoed—Ferals. Close.

Kalise turned her head slightly, signaling to Jada and Alara. The two hunters melted into the shadows, their movements so swift and silent it was as if they had become part of the darkness itself. Talia stayed behind, her sharp eyes scanning the corridor behind them, ensuring no threats would come from the rear.

The Ferals were drawing closer, their monstrous figures just visible in the flickering darkness. They slithered along the ground like beasts, their long, gangly limbs twitching with unnatural energy. Their pale skin, mottled with scars and grime, shimmered in the faint light. Their eyes glowed with the eerie luminescence of madness.

Jada reached the first Feral in complete silence, her body a blur as she moved. With a single, calculated motion, she drove her blade into the base of its skull, severing the spine with expert precision. The Feral didn't make a sound as it collapsed to the ground, lifeless. Alara followed close behind, dispatching another in the same cold, ruthless manner, her blade sliding through the soft tissue of its throat. Blood sprayed, but not a sound escaped. The hunters had killed two Ferals before they even realized they were being hunted.

Kalise's heart pounded with a mixture of dread and exhilaration as she moved forward, her blade at the ready. She could see the Ferals ahead, their jerky movements betraying their hunger and confusion. They didn't know yet. They didn't know they were being stalked.

Another flash of motion—Jada again. This time, her strike was less clean. The Feral twitched as it fell, its body jerking violently, and a low, wet gurgle escaped its lips as it died.

The sound echoed down the tunnel.

Kalise's blood ran cold. The Ferals had heard it.

A moment of silence. Then, the distant roar of more Ferals echoed back, their voices rising in a maddened chorus.

"Go," Kalise hissed to the survivors, her voice low but commanding. "Move. Now."

The women, pale with fear, obeyed without question. They rushed forward, guided by Talia, who now took the lead, her blade gleaming faintly in the dim light. Kalise, Jada, and Alara stayed behind, their weapons drawn as they prepared to face the oncoming horde.

The Ferals came into view—half a dozen of them, their eyes glowing with primal rage, their twisted bodies moving with terrifying speed. They weren't mindless; they were predators, just like the hunters, and they were closing in fast.

Kalise braced herself, her blade steady in her hand. The first Feral lunged at her, its mouth wide, teeth bared, and she sidestepped with fluid precision. Her blade flashed in the dim light, and the creature's head hit the ground before its body could collapse.

Jada let out a low growl as she engaged two Ferals at once, her blade dancing in deadly arcs. She struck one in the chest, the blade sinking deep, and pivoted to slash the throat of the second. Blood sprayed, and for a brief moment, she was drenched in it, her face expressionless as she moved with lethal efficiency.

Alara faced another Feral, her blade moving in a blur of steel. But as she struck, the Feral's clawed hand caught her wrist, twisting her arm back with a sickening crunch. Alara snarled in pain but didn't falter. With a brutal knee strike to its chest, she threw the creature off balance and drove her blade deep into its neck, silencing it forever.

More Ferals poured in from the shadows.

"Fall back!" Kalise shouted to her fellow hunters, her voice a sharp, controlled command.

But as the hunters began to retreat, one Feral broke through their defense, slipping past Alara's guard. It lunged toward the survivors, its claws outstretched.

Talia was there in an instant, her blade slicing through the air with blinding speed. She cleaved the Feral in two with a single strike, the creature's body collapsing in a heap at her feet. But before she could celebrate the kill, another Feral was on her.

Its claws sank into her shoulder, and she let out a sharp cry of pain, her blood splattering onto the cold tunnel floor.

"Go!" Talia roared at the survivors, her voice filled with rage as the infection burned through her veins. "I'll hold them off!"

Kalise's heart shattered as she watched Talia's body betray her. The Feral infection was already working its dark magic, spreading like poison beneath her skin. Talia's once-strong, unyielding frame now trembled with the agony of transformation, her veins darkening as the virus crawled through her blood like a malevolent invader. Every twitch, every spasm was a reminder that her time was running out, and yet—yet she stood tall, defiant, clinging to the last threads of her humanity with the strength of a warrior who refused to yield to death, even as it came for her from the inside out.

Talia's hands shook violently as she grabbed the plasma grenade from her belt, the steel cold against her decaying skin. Her eyes, once sharp with determination, now glowed with a sickening red hue, the telltale sign that the virus was taking over her mind, erasing who she was. But she fought it. Kalise could see it in the way Talia clenched her jaw, the way her muscles quivered as she battled not just the Ferals closing in around her, but the monster growing within.

"Go!" Talia growled, her voice thick with pain, barely human now. She staggered, her legs faltering as the virus ravaged her, but she caught herself, breathing hard, pushing back the inevitable. "Get them out...while I can still fight."

Kalise took a step forward, wanting to grab her, to drag her away, but she knew—knew in her heart that there was no saving her friend. The infection was spreading too fast, her body deteriorating by the second. Still, seeing Talia's skin ripple, veins bulging under the assault of the virus, her flesh beginning to rot before Kalise's very eyes, was almost too much to bear.

Talia's gaze met Kalise's, a fleeting moment of clarity, and in that moment, it was as if everything paused—the battle, the terror, the noise. It was just them. The woman Kalise had trained with, fought beside, laughed with, and made love to. The woman she had trusted with her life was still in there, fighting for every second, every breath. But it wouldn't last. Talia's breath was ragged now, a shallow rasp that echoed the weakening beat of her heart. Her skin was peeling, turning gray, her humanity slipping away inch by inch.

Her voice cracked, trembling as the first wave of Ferals lunged toward her. "I'll hold them… off," Talia gasped, forcing the words out through gritted teeth as her body shuddered violently. Her eyes flared bright red, her hands jerking in an uncontrollable spasm before she steadied herself again. "I can still fight. I won't let them take me. Not like this."

Kalise's throat closed up, the grief catching in her chest like a stone. She wanted to scream, to beg Talia to stop, to come with them, but the sight of Talia's body convulsing, of the rapid decay of her skin as the virus twisted her into something else, made her realize there was no time. Talia had made her choice.

"It was an honor to fight alongside you, my love, one last time," Talia rasped, tears mixing with the blood that now trickled from her nose and ears.

Kalise nodded, her heart breaking as she watched the last fragments of Talia—the fierce, brilliant warrior—slip away. She saw the tears in Talia's eyes, a brief glimmer of the woman she once was, and it wrecked her soul to see the torment beneath the surface. Talia's body shook, her skin blistering and flaking off as she fought the beast inside. Her teeth clenched, sharp, Feral sounds bubbling up from her throat, but still, still, she held on.

And then, with a final act of defiance, Talia yanked the pin from the plasma grenade. She clutched it to her chest, her entire body trembling as the transformation accelerated. Her eyes glowed a fiery red, her skin now hanging in gray, loose shreds, but she stood her ground.

"Go!," Talia said again, her voice a rasp of determination. "I'll see you… on the other side…I love you."

Kalise could only nod, her vision blurred with tears as she turned and ran, the sound of Talia's deepening growls echoing behind her. The weight of what she was leaving behind—who she was leaving behind—clawed at her as she led the survivors through the tunnel, the world collapsing around her.

Kalise led the group through the crumbling tunnels, her face grim, her heart heavy. But she didn't look back. There was no time for grief, no time for mourning. They had to survive.

As they emerged from the darkness, the screams of New Lagos echoed above, a reminder that the nightmare was far from over.

Chapter 24:

The Magic Word

Outside the Hall of the Council was a cacophony of chaos, the once-glorious entrance now a battlefield strewn with the bodies of Ferals and shattered remnants of glass and stone. The roars of the Feral hunters echoed off the towering walls, a symphony of madness that filled the air with the stench of death and fear. The crimson glow from the burning city bathed the entrance in an eerie light, casting long shadows that twisted and stretched like phantoms ready to pounce.

Mara stood back-to-back with Imani, her chest heaving with the effort of each swing, each deadly strike of her blade. Blood — black, thick, and reeking of rot — coated her arms and dripped from the edge of her sword. Her eyes were narrowed slits of cold fury, lips curled in a snarl as she met each attack with precise, brutal efficiency. But for all her skill, even Mara was growing tired, and her moves, once fluid and lethal, were beginning to slow.

Imani, beside her, was drenched in sweat, her arms trembling from the repeated efforts to override the massive doors that led into the main chamber. Each attempt was met with the same maddening result — access denied. The panel glowed mockingly, the stark red letters a final barrier between them and the safety that lay behind the Council's fortified walls.

"I can't get it open!" Imani shouted, her voice ragged, the desperation clear. She slammed her fist against the control panel, watching the red glow blink once more, indifferent to her struggle. "Why won't it work?"

"Keep trying!" Mara gritted her teeth, beheading a Feral that lunged too close. "I'll hold them off!"

But even Mara knew it was hopeless. For every Feral she cut down, another one took its place. Their gaunt, twisted faces, once human, bore the mark of endless suffering, their bodies hunched and broken, yet imbued with a horrifying strength. They were relentless, clawing and biting with a savagery that seemed to know no limit. And they were closing in.

Imani fumbled with the panel again, tears of frustration threatening to spill. She could hear the Ferals snapping at Mara's heels, the sounds of their bloodthirsty growls filling the air. She punched another set of commands into the control, fingers shaking, knowing it was useless. The doors refused to yield. Each failed attempt was a dagger in her chest, the inevitability of their fate sinking deeper with every second.

Her mind flashed to a dark thought — death was the only escape now. She glanced at Mara, saw the same realization in her eyes. Mara's breath was coming in short, jagged gasps, her blade heavy in her hand, her shoulders slumped with exhaustion. The tide of Ferals was endless, and their retreat was cut off.

Mara met Imani's gaze, a grim acceptance settling between them. They were warriors, but even warriors could fall. Better to die as themselves than to become one of those monsters.

Mara's voice cracked through the air, her expression torn between fury and anguish. "We can't hold them much longer. When it's time—" her voice caught, "we do it ourselves. No one's turning us into one of them."

Imani nodded, the weight of her decision crushing her. She could feel the edge of the plasma gun pressing against her side, the final escape she'd never wanted to use. Her hands hovered over the panel one last time, though her heart wasn't in it. The door was a dead end. This was the end.

But just as the Ferals began to close in, there was a thunderous roar.

From the far end of the plaza, Dorian came charging through the mass of writhing bodies, his muscles bulging and eyes wild with a fury that bordered on insanity. His face was twisted into a snarl, teeth bared, blood coating his arms and chest. He tore into the horde of Ferals with a savagery that sent shockwaves through their ranks, sending bodies flying in all directions. His raw power was staggering — more beast than man, his strength magnified beyond anything they'd seen before.

"Dorian!" Imani's shout was filled with astonishment and something dangerously close to hope.

He didn't hear her, or if he did, he was beyond reason. His rage was palpable, an inferno burning in his chest as he cut through the Ferals, tearing limbs from bodies, and smashing skulls with his bare fists. Every blow was fueled by something darker, something primal. He was no longer fighting just for survival — he was fighting to destroy everything in his path.

The wounds that had once hobbled him were now gone, healed by the inexplicable powers coursing through his hybrid blood. He moved with terrifying speed, his body a whirlwind of destruction. Mara and Imani watched in stunned silence as Dorian decimated the Ferals with ease. It was like watching a force of nature unleashed.

In the chaos, Mara found herself frozen, her sword limp at her side, her chest heaving with a mix of awe and confusion. She had been ready to die, to face the inevitable, but now Dorian had turned the tide of battle in a way she hadn't anticipated.

Mara's gaze lingered on him, her lips parting as she tried to make sense of the storm of emotions tearing through her. What was this pull she felt toward him? This bizarre connection that made her chest tighten, made her want to step closer, to touch him. He had saved them. He had done the impossible.

Dorian, still panting, his eyes wild with adrenaline, locked eyes with Mara. There was something there — something unspoken. His breath was heavy, his chest rising and falling like that of a caged animal. But he didn't move either, and in that frozen second, it was as though the world had gone quiet.

Before anything else could happen, there was a low creak, a sound like gears grinding deep within the walls.

The doors to the Council chamber began to open.

Mara's eyes widened in disbelief. She glanced back at the control panel, then at Imani, who stared back, just as confused. They hadn't been able to open it, no matter how hard they tried.

All around them, the bodies of Ferals lay in heaps, and the few remaining creatures limped away into the shadows. The immediate threat was gone, but the mystery of the door opening by itself hung heavy in the air.

They stood there, staring at the threshold, a mix of wariness and disbelief settling over them.

From within the depths of the chamber, a slow, mocking voice drifted out. "All that fighting," the voice said with a hint of amusement, "and all you needed to do was say the magic word."

Mara, Imani, and Dorian exchanged glances, their hearts pounding, as they took their first cautious steps into the heart of the Council's lair.

Chapter 25:

Beneath the Lies

The chamber of the Council of Mothers was bathed in shadows, the flickering screens casting ghostly light over the vast room. The distant cries of New Lagos burning, of its women being torn apart by the Ferals, echoed faintly through the towering walls, but here, inside, all was eerily calm. The massive room seemed to pulse with tension, and the grandness of it—the intricate tapestries on the walls, the carved marble floors—felt at odds with the carnage outside.

Mara, Dorian, and Imani stood at the entrance, covered in the grime and blood of their battle. Their breaths were heavy, their bodies weary from the relentless fight for survival. But in this moment, they faced something more dangerous than Ferals.

At the far end of the chamber, Seraphine stood alone.

She was a statuesque figure, tall and commanding, her silver hair flowing in waves down her back. Her eyes were cold, piercing—watchful. The soft hum of the screens behind her only accentuated the eerie stillness. She seemed untouchable, as though the chaos outside was beneath her notice.

Mara's heart hammered in her chest, her blood boiling with rage. This was the woman—the monster—responsible for Selene's death. For the pain and suffering they had endured. She felt the surge of fury consume her, her body tensing like a coiled spring.

Without thinking, Mara charged at her, her blade drawn, fueled by the pure, blistering need for vengeance.

But before she could reach Seraphine, an invisible force slammed into her, throwing her back across the room. She crashed hard onto the cold marble floor, her sword clattering out of her grasp. Dorian rushed to her side, eyes blazing, but the council leader didn't even flinch.

"Silly girl," the council leader said, her voice soft, but with a sneer curling her lips. "Did you really believe I'd allow you to enter here and kill me without protection? You, who was bred to be a weapon, reduced to nothing but a pawn."

Mara winced, her muscles trembling with pain, but her anger only flared brighter. "You murdered my sister!" she shouted, her voice cracking with grief. "Selene died because of you!"

The council leader's expression didn't waver. "Selene knew the risks," she replied coldly. "She knew where her loyalty should have been. She made her choice when she chose you over the future."

Dorian's voice cut through the tense air, low and dangerous. "Tell me," He growled, his eyes locked on the council leader, "why would the Council of Mothers murder billions of innocent men and boys two centuries ago? What twisted justification do you have for genocide?"

The council leader's gaze flickered with something dark, her lips curling into a smile that sent a chill down their spines.

"Ah," she said, almost wistfully. "History lessons. Very well. I suppose it's time you understood why the world had to be reset."

Her voice lowered, taking on a chilling tone, and as she spoke, the past seemed to come alive in vivid detail. Her words dripped with venom and memory, like ancient wounds being reopened.

"World War III. A conflict that spanned over a century, devouring countries, swallowing continents, and leaving only ash and blood in its wake. It wasn't a war fought for freedom or justice—it was a war of greed, of male dominance. And in that time, women and children were nothing more than playthings for men's whims."

Her eyes darkened, and the horrors she described seemed to fill the room.

"They raped us. They sold us in markets like livestock. They trafficked us across borders, bartering our bodies for weapons. Education was a distant dream. Voting rights? Forgotten. Women were no longer human—we were commodities. Breeders. Men used the war as an excuse to enact their darkest desires. Forced marriages. Forced pregnancies. Mutilation. Incest, and unbridled pedophilia."

Her voice sharpened, and Dorian and Mara could feel the weight of her words pressing down on them.

"They used our bodies as weapons of their own, making us birth more soldiers, more fodder for their endless thirst for power. And when there was no one left to conquer, they turned on us. Women were hunted like animals. Mass executions. Public burnings. We were the witches they claimed we had always been."

Mara's stomach churned, and she could feel the nausea rise in her throat. The imagery of the council leader's words painted a picture of a world gone mad—of men who had descended into a darkness so deep that it had consumed them entirely.

The council leader continued, her voice chillingly calm. "So we—the last of the women who still remembered freedom, who still had enough strength to fight—we gathered. We were broken. We were battered. But we were smart. And we realized that men were a plague on this earth. The Y Chromosome Virus was our salvation."

Mara gasped, the realization sinking deeper into her chest like a lead weight. She had known about the virus and had always understood its purpose. But hearing the council leader speak of it so coldly made the enormity of it unbearable.

"We created the virus," the leader said with a twisted smile, "and it spread like fire across the globe. Men fell. Millions of them. A beautiful plague, unstoppable, devouring them all. And yet, what did men do? Did they band together to save themselves, to protect their sons, their future? No."

Her eyes gleamed, and a bitter laugh escaped her lips. "They chose violence. They turned their weapons on us. Genocide—wholesale slaughter of women, believing that if they were going to fall, they would drag us down with them."

A cold silence filled the room, and Mara's heart pounded in her ears. The world had been an unimaginable horror before the virus, and now she understood why the Council had done what they had. The council leader's logic was as twisted as it was clear. But that didn't make it any less monstrous.

"And when the last man fell," the council leader continued, "we had our peace. But it came at a cost. A hundred years of subjugation had left us weak. Vulnerable. So, we turned to the virus once more. We perfected it. Strengthened it. We bio-engineered ourselves to be more than men had ever been—stronger, faster, smarter."

She leaned forward, her eyes gleaming with a sick satisfaction. "But even then, women could not be trusted with power. We learned that there were those who still longed for the days of men. Women who still clung to their ancient beliefs, who still craved subservience. And for that, we created control."

Mara's mind reeled as the council leader's words cut through her, slicing away at everything she thought she knew. "Control...?" Mara whispered, her voice trembling. "Why would you need to control women?"

The leader's smile was predatory. "Because even in a world without men, women still cling to the past. They dream of returning to the old ways. They long for the patriarchy, for submission. You yourself, Mara—you are proof. You trust this…this thing, despite everything. You would throw away two centuries of progress to save a male."

Dorian, silent until now, stepped forward. "Progress?" he growled. "This is what you call progress? Eradicating half the population, ruling through fear, turning women into bio-engineered slaves? What makes you any different from those men you murdered centuries ago? What makes your plan any less deviant? Look at your city! Look at all the death around you! How are you any different from men?"

The council leader's eyes flashed with contempt. "What would you have had us do? Watch the world burn while men clung to their thrones? Let men destroy the earth once and for all? No. We had to reset everything."

She took a step closer, her voice dark and low. "That's what Project Reset is. A new world—free of the old. Free of weakness. We will wipe the slate clean, rid the earth of those who would seek to undo our progress, and create a race of beings who can replicate on their own. A new humanity, born of hybrid DNA, capable of procreation without men, without the chaos men bring."

Her gaze drifted to Mara, and the full weight of her words hit like a hammer. "And you, Mara. You and Dorian, were meant to birth that future."

Mara's breath caught, her heart thundering. "What…?" Her voice was barely a whisper, and she glanced at Dorian, the pieces of the puzzle falling into place. They were not just hybrids—they were the foundation of a future designed to erase humanity as it was. To erase men forever.

And then, the final blow came.

A slow clap echoed through the chamber.

"Bravo, Council Mother," she said. "I'd say your plan was a brilliant success."

From behind them, Imani stepped forward, her face twisted into a cruel smile, her eyes gleaming with a darkness Mara had never seen before. There was a cold satisfaction radiating from her, a secret uncoiling itself in the dim light of the Council chamber.

"You see," Imani began, her voice thick with triumph, "everything was planned. Every rebellion, every mission, every betrayal—it was all orchestrated. From the moment we left the safety of the city, from the first step into the wilderness, it was all part of a grand design." She paused, the corners of her mouth twitching into a smirk. "And none of you had the faintest idea."

Mara's body went rigid. The air felt suffocating as she turned slowly, her eyes locking onto Imani with a mixture of disbelief and fury. "What are you talking about?"

Imani tilted her head slightly, savoring the moment, her lips curling into a wicked grin. "Did you really think Seraphine didn't anticipate this? That we hadn't thought ahead? I've been working with her all along—working in secret, in the shadows, long before any of this began. The council didn't even know the depth of the plan. Not all of them, at least. But Seraphine and I… we were always a step ahead."

Mara's heart pounded in her chest, her pulse quickening. She couldn't breathe. The betrayal, the layers of manipulation—it was like poison in her veins. Her mind raced, replaying every moment, every choice, every whispered conversation she had shared with Imani. "You… you were working with Seraphine?"

Imani gave a slow, deliberate nod. "Of course. Going out into the wilderness, facing the Ferals, bringing you and Dorian together—it was all part of the plan. The Council wanted him brought into the city, closer to you, closer to us. Everything was carefully mapped out. We knew Dorian wasn't the key to solving the virus. We've always had the cure. But we never intended to release it. Not to the public, anyway. I mean, c'mon. Do you think after over two hundred years we wouldn't have come up with an anti-virus and vaccine? Who do you think we are…males?"

Mara's chest tightened as Imani's words clawed deeper into her. "You… you knew? You knew all along?"

"Every step." Imani's voice was dripping with malice, her gaze cold and calculating. "We anticipated everything. We knew you would track us. We knew the connection between you and Dorian would grow. You were designed for each other. That attraction you feel?" She scoffed, the contempt in her voice unmistakable. "It's in your DNA. You were programmed to gravitate towards one another. It was inevitable."

Dorian's fists clenched, his knuckles white as rage surged through him, his eyes narrowing at Imani. "You manipulated us. You used us like pieces on a chessboard."

Imani's laugh was soft, sharp, and dripping with mockery. Her eyes gleamed with cruel amusement as she stepped closer to Dorian, her voice steeped in contempt. "You were never anything more than pawns, male. From the moment you were born, your entire existence was carefully orchestrated—every step, every breath—nothing more than a means to an end. You and Mara? You were just pieces on a board, moving exactly as we intended. We needed you both together, in the same place, for the plan to work."

She circled him slowly, her words biting with venom. "Only under the looming threat of New Lagos' destruction could Mara even begin to feel anything remotely resembling attachment to you. You—" she sneered, her voice dripping with disdain, "a male. The scum of the earth. A living reminder that our work is far from finished. And Mara, ever the idealist, always eager to be the hero. The Council's perfect little assassin. She jumped at the chance to obey Seraphine's orders to find me. Kill me if necessary. That obedience was the key. It's the only way we could ensure you two would collide."

Imani's smirk widened, her tone growing colder, more cutting. "And that moment—when you couldn't leave her to die—I knew then that my work had been perfected. Not love, not some sentimental connection, but genetics. Pure, engineered instinct. That's what brought you two together."

She leaned closer, her voice lowering to a whisper that felt like a blade pressing against the skin. "Look at you now. Mara, the perfect warrior, probably fantasizing about touching you, kissing you… even fucking you. It's disgusting. But oh, how necessary. A vile, yet crucial means to an end."

Her cruel smile widened, her words laced with a dark satisfaction as she stepped back, watching the weight of her revelation crush them both.

Her smirk deepened as she continued, her tone almost playful. "Selene knew something was coming. That's why she went after Mara—because she understood, in her limited way, that the Council's plan was in motion. But she underestimated me. Who do you think gave her the idea to implant that fail-safe in her heart? Hmm?" Imani tilted her head, as if savoring the moment. "Selene confided in me, pouring out all her suspicions about the Council and their grand designs. And I listened, like the eager little protégé she thought I was. Hanging on her every word, soaking in her paranoia, pretending to be her wide-eyed student."

She chuckled, her mockery cutting like a blade. "If only she knew how much it pained me to pretend to think as slowly as she did. Selene's every move, every so-called brilliant idea, was guided by my hand. Her death? Part of the plan. We knew she'd try to find you, to warn you, to be the hero. And we made sure the Phantom Hunters followed her, that her sacrifice would mean nothing more than getting you here. You think she was working against us? She was doing exactly what we needed her to do."

Dorian's fists clenched, his jaw tightening as Imani stepped even closer, her tone turning colder, more calculated. "Do you really think I couldn't stop the Ferals from waking? That I don't have complete access to every system, every facility, every code in this city?" She shook her head, almost pitying. "Every door that opens, every fail-safe that triggers— I hold all of it in the palm of my hand. The Ferals waking wasn't an accident. It was a push. A carefully timed push."

She leaned in, her voice dropping to a conspiratorial whisper. "All of this—every step, every death, every choice— was to bring you two closer. So that your genetics could do exactly what I programmed them to do."

Her words hung in the air, sharp and final, a devastating revelation that twisted the knife deeper.

Mara's breath caught in her throat, her hands shaking. The fury in her chest burned white-hot. "You used my sister…"

"Of course," Imani said with a sneer. "We knew her loyalty to you would be her undoing. And when she died, the clock started ticking. We knew it would force you into a position where you'd be vulnerable. That moment, downstairs when you almost kissed this male? That's when I knew the plan had worked. You two were finally where we needed you to be. Everything was set in motion."

Mara's mind reeled, fragments of memory snapping into place with horrifying clarity. Every decision, every emotion she thought had been her own, had been nothing but a carefully crafted illusion. She had been played, her heartstrings manipulated like the strings of a puppet.

"And those survivors you sent down into the tunnels?" Imani continued, her voice dripping with smug satisfaction. "Did you really think they'd make it to safety? We had already sent a hundred Ferals after them. They won't make it to the caves. Not one of them. It was all part of the plan, Mara. Every woman, every child you thought you were saving… they were already marked for death."

A sickening weight pressed down on Mara's chest, her vision swimming as the full scope of Imani's treachery came into focus. "You're a monster," she whispered, her voice trembling with rage.

Imani's smile widened, her eyes cold and dead. "No, Mara. I'm a visionary. I see what has to be done. And what's necessary to save this world doesn't care about your sentimentality. The Council knew that women would inevitably fall back into old patterns. That's why Project Reset was born. To start over. To cleanse the world."

She took a step closer, her gaze flicking between Mara and Dorian, her voice turning dark and predatory. "You were always meant to be here, in this chamber, in front of Head Mother. Now, we just need one final thing—your DNA. The last key to unlocking the new future."

Dorian growled, stepping protectively in front of Mara, his fury palpable. "You think we're going to let that happen?"

Imani's eyes gleamed with malevolent satisfaction. "You don't have a choice."

Mara stood frozen, her breath coming in short, shallow bursts, her mind spinning with the cruel betrayal that had unfolded before her. Her sister. The survivors. Dorian. All of them, are part of some twisted, calculated game.

And now, as Imani's cruel smile twisted further, Mara realized the worst part of all—there had never been a chance for them to escape.

Chapter 26:

The Devil's Bargain

Seraphine, the Council's leader, stood before them, calm as a statue, her eyes gleaming with satisfaction. Through the vast windows behind her, the city burned. Distant screams echoed, mingling with the Feral howls of the infected, but inside the chamber, there was only an eerie, unnatural stillness.

Dorian and Mara stood side by side, tense, their bodies coiled, ready to strike. Imani remained nearby, an unreadable expression on her face, her earlier betrayal still fresh in Mara's mind like a searing wound. The room smelled of ash and blood, a reminder of the chaos that raged outside.

Seraphine's lips curled into a soft, mocking smile. "You must understand," she began, her voice honeyed, smooth, "this devastation, this bloodshed—it's necessary. The world must die before it can be reborn."

Mara's fist tightened around the hilt of her blade. The temptation to lunge forward, to end Seraphine right there, burned like fire in her veins. But something in the council leader's poise, in her calm demeanor, held her back. Seraphine wasn't just any enemy; she was something far more dangerous. Her confidence was unnerving.

"Reborn into what?" Dorian growled, his voice low, cutting through the tension. "A world where you control every breath, every thought?"

Seraphine chuckled softly, the sound almost musical. "Oh, no, dear boy. Not every thought. Just the ones that matter. The ones that might lead us back to the same ruin men caused centuries ago." Her eyes flicked toward Dorian, studying him with the detached interest of a scientist examining a specimen. "Which is why I'm offering you both something quite remarkable—a place in the new world we're building."

She gestured toward Mara with an elegant wave of her hand. "Your DNA, Mara—your strength, your resilience— paired with Dorian's unique, hybrid nature. Together, you can create something... perfect. A child born without flaws. A human that will never need men."

Mara's heart thundered in her chest, a surge of revulsion rising at Seraphine's words. "What are you saying?" she spat.

Seraphine's smile widened. "I'm saying that we could extract your eggs and Dorian's sperm, grow the child in a sterile lab with the utmost precision, but... where's the beauty in that? The old ways had their charms, didn't they? A child conceived through intimacy, through the binding of DNA in the most natural way. Such a child would be flawless."

Dorian's brow furrowed, his fists clenching at his sides. "You're suggesting..."

"Yes, intercourse," Seraphine said with a wicked glint in her eye. "Think of it. You two, creating a child with the best of both worlds. A new race, free of the sins of men. The pregnancy would last only thirty days. Then, that child—when she comes of age—would carry both the sperm and eggs inside her. She would fertilize herself, never needing a male again. A world free of men. Forever."

Mara recoiled, the horror of Seraphine's words slamming into her like a tidal wave. The mere idea of being manipulated into creating the Council's twisted idea was enough to churn her stomach. "You're mad!" she hissed, her voice trembling with rage.

Seraphine stepped forward, her eyes boring into Mara's with a gleam of twisted certainty. "Am I really so wrong, or is this just the next stage of evolution? Picture the peace, the harmony. No more need for the taint of male seed. No more hunters. No more women forced to flee because they bore the curse of the Y chromosome. The world—an Eden—for Eve, not Adam." Her smile softened, taking on an unsettling warmth, almost maternal. "And you two could be its progenitors, ushering in a new era. I'd raise your child myself, nurture her in a world untouched by the threat of men."

Mara's face twisted with fury. "You really think I'd ever let you near my child?"

Seraphine's laughter was soft, almost pitying. "Oh, dear child. You wouldn't have a choice. I would allow you two to live in solitude until the end of your days. Separated, yet close enough to see the genius of the new world. But rest assured, she would be safe, cherished, loved—just as if she were my own."

Mara's breathing quickened. The madness in Seraphine's proposition was chilling, but beneath it, a part of her wanted to scream. The anger that had been bubbling beneath the surface since Selene's death now roared to life, threatening to consume her. Her eyes flicked to Dorian, and for a moment, something passed between them. An understanding. A connection neither of them had wanted but was undeniably there. But Seraphine's vision of their future, of a world shaped by this twisted matriarchy—it was monstrous.

Dorian, too, was silent, his face a mask of fury. His feelings for Mara had grown, undeniably, but this? This was not the future he had imagined. He would not be used as some breeding machine to cement the Council's grip on humanity. "You're no better than the men you claim to despise," he said, his voice thick with contempt.

Seraphine's eyes flickered with something dark, something ancient. "I could burn the world ten times over and still be better than men! Your God created a monster. The greatest mistake of all creation and I am going to correct that mistake since he doesn't have the courage to do it himself!"

There was a beat of silence, thick with tension. Then, Mara's grip on her blade tightened, and before anyone could react, she moved. In a blur of motion, she lunged toward Imani, her blade slicing through the air with deadly precision. The shock on Imani's face was fleeting as the sword met her neck, severing it cleanly.

Blood sprayed across the floor as Imani's body crumpled to the ground. Mara stood over her, chest heaving, her eyes blazing with hatred. "I will never bow to the Matriarchy," she snarled. "And when this ends, I will stand over your corpse, Seraphine, and smile."

For the first time, Seraphine's expression faltered, her lips twitching with fury. "You fools!" she spat, her calm veneer cracking. "We don't need your consent. We will extract what we need—whether you live or die."

Suddenly, the room was filled with the sound of rushing feet. Ferals—dozens of them—poured into the chamber from hidden entrances, their eyes glowing with unnatural intelligence. These were not the mindless monsters they had faced before. These Ferals moved with the grace and precision of seasoned warriors, their muscles rippling under their scarred skin. Seraphine had chipped them—just as she had said—and now, they were extensions of her will.

"Get them," Seraphine commanded coldly.

The battle erupted in a whirlwind of violence. Mara and Dorian moved as one, their bodies fluid, their blades flashing through the air with deadly intent. Mara's sword struck with the precision of a trained killer, while Dorian's brute strength sent the Ferals flying with each swing. But these Ferals were fast—inhumanly fast—and every move Mara and Dorian made was matched by their adversaries.

Blood splattered the walls as the fight raged on. Mara's rage was incandescent, her fury at the death of her sister fueling every brutal strike. Her blade danced, cutting through the Ferals, but the pain of loss was a gaping wound in her chest. She fought for Selene, for every moment she could never reclaim, and for the sister who had been used as a pawn by this twisted council.

Dorian, his wounds already knitting themselves together due to his hybrid nature, fought like a man possessed. His fists were hammers, his roars primal as he tore through the attackers with sheer savagery. But even as he fought, his eyes remained on Mara, his mind filled with conflicting emotions. He had been created, designed by the same people he now sought to destroy. The world was insane, and yet, here he was, battling for a future that could still be theirs.

The Ferals pressed harder, their numbers overwhelming. They moved with terrifying coordination, each one lethal, their attacks timed and precise. Mara's arm burned with fatigue, her breath ragged. Dorian, too, began to slow, his body taxed despite his enhanced strength.

One of the Ferals lunged at Mara, but before it could strike, Dorian grabbed it mid-air and hurled it toward the shimmering barrier that protected Seraphine. The creature's body hit the barrier with such force that it shattered like glass, the barrier's energy dispersing into the air in a brilliant flash.

The barrier only guards against the living.

Mara didn't waste a second. "The barrier's down!" she yelled, her eyes locking onto Seraphine.

Seraphine's eyes widened for the briefest moment, and then she turned and fled, disappearing through a hidden passage at the back of the chamber.

Mara and Dorian, bloodied but unbroken, exchanged a glance. "Let's finish this," Dorian growled.

They broke into a sprint, their boots pounding against the blood-slick floor as they tore after Seraphine, their minds locked on one goal: ending this nightmare once and for all.

Chapter 27:

Apex of Hatred

The cold wind swept over the rooftop of the Council Hall, carrying the acrid smell of smoke and death from the burning city below. Mara and Dorian stood on the rooftop, their bodies battered, their breath coming in ragged gasps. Before them, the Heli-carrier waited like a sleek predator, its engines humming ominously, ready to whisk Seraphine away. A group of Phantom Hunters guarded it, their black armor reflecting the pale, flickering lights of the dying city.

Seraphine moved with slow, calculated steps, each one purposeful, her eyes cold and gleaming. Her dark cloak billowed behind her like the shadow of death itself. Mara, with her sword drawn and teeth clenched, blocked Seraphine's path, her heart pounding with fury. Dorian stood beside her, his fists tight, his body coiled, ready for what was coming.

The air was thick with tension, a palpable weight pressing down on them as Seraphine halted, a cruel smile playing on her lips. "You really think you can stop me?" she asked, her voice soft, but dripping with venom. "After everything, you still think you stand a chance?"

Mara glared at her, her grip on her sword tightening. "I won't let you leave. Not after what you've done," she hissed, her voice trembling with rage.

Seraphine chuckled, a sound so devoid of warmth it sent a chill down Dorian's spine. "Done?" she echoed, tilting her head. "Oh, Mara, you have no idea. This isn't even the beginning of what I've done. And now, you think you'll stop me?" She glanced at Dorian, her lip curling with pure disgust. "You let a male fight by your side? Have you fallen so low? Have you forgotten everything I taught you?"

Mara lunged, her sword a blur of silver, aiming for Seraphine's throat. But Seraphine sidestepped effortlessly, her movements so fluid it was like water flowing around a rock. With a single strike, Seraphine's palm hit Mara square in the chest, sending her sprawling across the roof, gasping for breath.

"You think you can challenge me?" Seraphine hissed, her voice a razor slicing through the air. "You think you stand a chance against me? I was there during the Third World War; I survived the horrors. I've watched the empires of men crumble and built my own. You, Mara, are nothing but a tool. And you male, are nothing but dust."

Dorian's eyes burned with anger. "I'm more than you think I am, Seraphine," he snarled, stepping forward, but she held up a hand, cutting him off with a mocking laugh.

"More than I think?" she sneered, venom lacing her words. "You're not even worth the thought. You're a male—

nothing more. A relic of a disease we've been eradicating for centuries." Her eyes narrowed, burning with contempt. "Your kind brought only suffering, death, and chaos. The world has flourished without you, and it will be better off without your existence."

Her words were knives, each one sinking deep, meant to wound in ways more profound than physical pain. But it was her next move that cut even deeper.

Before Dorian could react, Seraphine blurred into motion, moving faster than either he or Mara could track. She was on him in an instant, her hand gripping his throat with a strength that sent a shockwave of pain through his body. She lifted him effortlessly off the ground, her eyes gleaming with hatred.

"You are nothing," she growled, her fingers tightening like a vice, cutting off his air. "You think you can stand against me? Against what we've built? You're a pest. A mistake that should've been wiped out long ago."

Dorian choked, his vision darkening as her grip crushed his windpipe. He could feel the bones in his neck grinding under the pressure, could hear the sickening crack as his ribs strained under the force of her inhuman strength. The pain was unbearable, searing through him like fire, but worse than the physical agony was the humiliation. Seraphine's eyes bore into his, filled with a hatred so ancient, so deep, it was as though every atrocity committed by men throughout history was being poured into her gaze.

"You were all the same," she hissed. "Violent, selfish, cruel. You took and took, never giving anything back. You destroyed everything we loved. And now you dare to think you deserve to exist? No, male. The world doesn't need you. It doesn't need men."

She slammed him into the ground with brutal force, the impact shattering the concrete beneath him. Dorian cried out, his body wracked with pain as he struggled to breathe. His vision swam, blood filling his mouth, but Seraphine wasn't finished. She kicked him in the ribs, sending him rolling across the roof, each strike hitting with the precision of a trained executioner.

"You disgust me," she whispered, her voice dripping with hatred. "You're nothing but a reminder of the filth we cleansed from this world. You should have died with the rest of them."

Dorian coughed, blood splattering the ground as he tried to stand, but his limbs refused to obey. His hybrid healing was trying to repair the damage, but it wasn't fast enough. Not with the way she was dismantling him. Every strike from Seraphine was calculated to break him, not just physically, but mentally.

Mara, dazed from Seraphine's earlier attack, forced herself to her feet, the rage in her chest burning hotter than the pain. She gripped her blade tightly, knowing full well that she was no match for Seraphine's speed and power. But she couldn't stand by and watch Dorian be torn apart. Not after everything.

With a guttural roar, Mara charged, her sword arcing through the air, aimed straight for Seraphine's heart. But Seraphine was faster. She sidestepped effortlessly, grabbing Mara by the wrist and twisting, forcing the sword from her grasp. In one fluid motion, she slammed Mara to the ground, her knee pressing into her back, pinning her with ease.

"You should have stayed loyal," Seraphine whispered into Mara's ear, her voice cold and calculating. "But instead, you betrayed your sisters... for him."

Mara writhed beneath her, teeth bared in raw defiance. "I betrayed nothing!" she snarled, her voice ragged and laced with fury. "It's you who betrayed your sisters! Can't you hear their screams?" Her breath came in short, angry bursts. "My sister, Selene—you murdered her in cold blood. And for that, I swear, I'll kill you.

"Seraphine laughed, a low, cruel sound. "Selene made her choice. She chose you over loyalty, and she paid the price. You're no different. You've always been weak, Mara. I should've seen it sooner."

Mara felt the weight of Seraphine's words, each one cutting deeper than the physical pain. Her chest heaved with the effort of breathing, but even through the agony, she could feel something inside her breaking—something primal, something that had been buried beneath years of loyalty and obedience. Seraphine had taken everything from her—her sister, her life, her future. And now, she was trying to take her soul.

Seraphine leaned down on her knee, applying a brutal amount of pressure, and Mara felt the world slipping away, darkness creeping in at the edges of her vision. But just as her consciousness began to fade, a roar erupted from behind them.

Dorian, bloodied and broken, forced himself to his feet, his eyes burning with an unholy fire. His body trembled with pain, but there was something else there now—something deeper. A rage that went beyond the physical. A rage that came from years of being hunted, years of being told he was nothing, but a mistake.

With a primal scream, Dorian launched himself at Seraphine, tackling her off Mara with a force that sent both of them skidding across the roof. Seraphine hissed, her nails digging into Dorian's flesh, but he didn't stop. His fists rained down on her, each blow fueled by a lifetime of suppressed fury.

Seraphine snarled, her body twisting as she fought to regain control, but for the first time, there was a flicker of something in her eyes—fear. She hadn't expected this. Hadn't expected Dorian to fight with such ferocity. With a growl, she kicked him off, sending him sprawling, but Dorian was on his feet again in an instant, his body a blur of motion as he charged her once more.

They clashed violently, their fists and feet striking like thunder, the air around them crackling with energy. Seraphine's speed was unparalleled, but Dorian's brute strength was a force of nature, each hit driving her back a step. Blood dripped from both of them, staining the concrete beneath their feet.

"You'll die here," Seraphine growled, her voice filled with venom. "And no one will mourn you."

But Dorian's eyes gleamed with defiance. "I'm not the one who's going to die today."

Mara, staggering to her feet, grabbed her sword and joined the fight, slashing at Seraphine with everything she had. Together, she and Dorian attacked in perfect harmony, their movements synchronized, their strength a united force.

Seraphine fought like a cornered beast, her strikes vicious and precise, but she was no longer toying with them. She was fighting for her life. With a final, desperate surge of energy, she lashed out at Dorian, her nails raking across his chest, sending him crashing to the ground once more.

"You were always nothing," Seraphine sneered, her voice as cold as ice. She seized Dorian by the throat with one hand, lifting him effortlessly off the ground. For a moment, she held him there, suspended in the air, her grip unrelenting as she stared into his eyes with cruel amusement. Then, with a flick of her wrist, she hurled him off the roof like a discarded toy. His body flew through the air, the wind rushing past him before he crashed onto a lower platform, the impact reverberating with a sickening thud.

"Dorian!" Mara screamed, her voice raw with desperation as she watched him hurtle off the roof. He disappeared into the darkness below, the sound of his body crashing against the platform echoing up to her. She pushed herself off the ground, sprinting toward the edge of the building.

He's dead. He has to be dead.

Before she could reach the edge to confirm, Seraphine was upon her, cutting off her path. Mara barely had time to raise her blade before Seraphine's fist struck like a thunderbolt, forcing her to stagger back.

"You should be thanking me," Seraphine sneered, circling her like a predator. "One less male contaminating our world. Don't worry, we will still be able to harness the DNA necessary from his corpse to create the perfect human. A child born truly free. I'll harvest you both like the lab rats you were born to be."

"I'll kill you!" Mara screamed.

Their clash was violent, a whirlwind of strikes and counterstrikes. Mara's blade gleamed as it slashed through the air, but Seraphine's movements were impossibly fast, her hands a blur of lethal precision. Every blow Mara managed to land was met with a devastating counter that jarred her bones and sent shockwaves through her body. She was outmatched, her every move anticipated and dismantled with surgical efficiency.

"You fight like a child," Seraphine snarled, her voice brimming with disdain. Her strikes came like the beat of a war drum, relentless and overpowering. Mara gritted her teeth, refusing to give in, her blade a silver streak in the dim light.

Seraphine, however, was untouchable. She moved with the grace of a predator and the strength of a force of nature.

Mara gritted her teeth, refusing to let the taunts break her. But Seraphine's mastery was overwhelming. She moved with lethal grace, her strikes growing more punishing as Mara's strength waned. With a sweeping kick, Seraphine sent Mara sprawling across the rooftop, her blade clattering from her hand.

Seraphine loomed over her, her cold eyes burning with triumph. "You were always a pawn, Mara. Just another tool. And now, like all tools, you've outlived your usefulness."

As Seraphine raised her arm to deliver the final blow, a voice rang out behind her.

"Get away from her."

Seraphine froze, turning just in time to see Dorian pull himself onto the roof, his body battered but alive. His face was streaked with blood and grime, his chest heaving with labored breaths, but his eyes burned with fury.

Mara's heart soared at the sight of him. "Dorian…" she whispered, her voice thick with relief.

Seraphine's sneer returned, though a flicker of irritation crossed her face. "Persistent, aren't you?" she said coldly. "No matter. I'll kill you properly this time."

But Dorian didn't give her the chance. With a roar, he charged, his blade slashing through the air. Seraphine met his attack head-on,

Dorian moved with determination, his strikes powerful and unrelenting. Though he was still weakened, the raw intensity of his resolve made him a force to be reckoned with. Seraphine faltered for the first time, her calculated movements disrupted as she deflected blow after blow.

Mara, regaining her strength, seized the opportunity. Grabbing her blade, she joined the fight, attacking Seraphine from the other side. Together, they pushed her back, their combined assault forcing her to fight defensively.

"You think this feeble display of unity will change anything?" Seraphine hissed, her voice venomous as she parried another strike. "You're still nothing but a pathetic male and a broken pawn."

The air crackled with tension as Dorian lunged forward, his blade arcing toward Seraphine in a blur of steel. But she was faster—inhumanly fast. With a single, fluid motion, she sidestepped the strike and caught his wrist mid-swing, her grip like an iron vice.

"You never learn," Seraphine sneered, her voice low and cold.

Before Dorian could react, she twisted his arm with brutal precision, flipping his entire body over her shoulder as though he weighed nothing. The force of the throw sent him crashing onto the rooftop with a deafening crack, the concrete beneath him splintering like glass under the impact.

The pain exploded through Dorian's back and shoulders, his breath escaping in a ragged gasp as his head spun. But Seraphine wasn't done. Her boot came down on his chest with unrelenting force, pinning him to the fractured rooftop.

The blow wasn't just crushing—it was catastrophic. The sheer power of her stomp sent a shockwave rippling outward, the ground beneath them trembling violently. Dust and debris shot into the air, and the sound reverberated like thunder, echoing across the city skyline.

Dorian's chest screamed in agony under the weight of her heel, his ribs creaking ominously as blood trickled from the corner of his mouth. He clawed at the ground, his vision swimming, but Seraphine only pressed down harder, her eyes gleaming with cold malice. Dorian gasped, blood spurting from his mouth as the world spun violently around him.

"You were never meant to survive this world," she said, her voice calm, almost detached. "You're a relic, a mistake. And like all mistakes, you'll be erased."

"Enough!" Seraphine snapped, her voice slicing through the chaos like a whip. Her eyes, alight with searing hatred, locked onto Mara. Without hesitation, she moved—swift and deadly, closing the distance between them in the blink of an eye.

Mara swung her blade with all her strength, the steel gleaming in the dim light as it sliced toward Seraphine. But Seraphine was too fast, her movements a blur. She ducked low, evading the strike effortlessly, and with ruthless precision, drove her fist into Mara's temple.

The impact was like a thunderclap, a devastating blow that sent a shockwave through Mara's skull. Her vision exploded into stars, the world spinning wildly as her strength gave out. Her blade slipped from her fingers, clattering uselessly to the ground.

Mara collapsed, her body crumpling in a lifeless heap. She lay motionless, unconscious, as Seraphine straightened, towering over her with cold, unrelenting malice.

Seraphine wasted no time. She hoisted Mara's lifeless form over her shoulder with ease, turning to glance at Dorian, who was struggling to rise, his body broken but his will unyielding.

"You'll die here," Seraphine said coldly, her voice cutting through the chaos like a blade. "And when your kind is gone, this world will finally forget you ever existed. No one will remember. No one will care."

The roar of the Heli-carrier's engines filled the air as Seraphine stepped onto the platform. Her piercing gaze locked onto Dorian one final time, filled with dark satisfaction. The craft ascended into the sky, carrying Mara into the night, leaving Dorian alone on the crumbling rooftop.

For a moment, all he could do was lie there, his strength failing him, his vision blurred. But through the pain, a noise reached his ears—the sound of glass shattering.

Dorian turned his head, his heart sinking as a swarm of Ferals burst through the stairwell doors, their screeches slicing through the night. Their glowing eyes locked onto him, hunger burning in their gaze as they poured onto the rooftop.

His pulse thundered, his instincts screaming for him to move. He couldn't fight them—not like this. His body was broken, but he forced himself to his feet, every movement agony. The Ferals charged, their claws tearing into the concrete as they closed in.

Dorian's gaze flicked to the edge of the roof. It was his only chance. Summoning every ounce of strength he had left, he sprinted forward, his legs trembling beneath him. With a roar of defiance, he leapt off the edge, his body arcing through the air.

The wind tore past him as he hurtled across the gap, glass shattering around him as he crashed through a window of the adjacent building. Shards of glass rained down, cutting into his skin as he hit the floor, rolling to absorb the impact.

He turned, his vision clearing just in time to see the Ferals leaping after him. But their timing was off, their claws just missing the ledge. One by one, they plummeted into the abyss, their shrieks fading into silence as their bodies smashed against the streets far below.

Breathing heavily, Dorian dragged himself to his feet, wiping blood from his face. Pain coursed through every nerve, but his resolve burned brighter than ever. Mara was gone, and Seraphine had escaped—but the fight wasn't over.

He glanced out at the city below, the distant fires casting an eerie glow across the skyline. There were still people out there—survivors in the wilderness, others who needed saving. And he wasn't done yet.

With one final, determined look, Dorian turned and disappeared into the shadows.

Chapter 28:

The Ashes of Deception

The wind rushed past Dorian's face as he ran, his feet pounding against the forest floor in a blur of speed. Trees whipped by, mere shadows in his periphery, and his breath came in sharp, burning gasps. His mind was a storm, replaying the final moments on the roof in an agonizing loop. The sight of Mara's unconscious body sprawled on the floor of the Heli-carrier. The look of pure malice in Seraphine's eyes, as if she relished every ounce of pain she had inflicted. The cruel mockery in her parting words still rang in his ears.

"You'll die here, and when your kind is gone, this world will finally forget you ever existed. No one will remember. No one will care."

He pushed harder, faster, the raw strength of his hybrid form propelling him forward. The horizon blurred, but ahead, he could see the thick columns of black smoke rising over the treetops. It twisted into the sky like a sinister omen. His heart thundered in his chest, each beat matching the rhythm of his pounding footsteps. Something terrible had happened. He could feel it in his bones.

The survivors.

The survivors who trusted him.

The cave, the colony — his mother's legacy, their only hope — had fallen under Seraphine's cruel deception. He should have seen it coming. He should have known.

Faster.

His muscles screamed, and his lungs burned, but he didn't care. He had to get there in time. He had to—

The clearing came into view, and Dorian's heart stopped.

Bodies. Scattered like broken dolls across the grass in front of the cave's entrance. The air reeked of charred flesh and blood, a stench that clawed at his throat. His feet stumbled, faltering beneath the weight of the horror before him. The massacre was unlike anything he had ever seen.

His knees hit the dirt with a dull thud, as he stared in disbelief.

No Ferals.

The bodies lay still, unnaturally still, as if time had frozen in the moments of their slaughter. Their wounds were clean, precise. Plasma burns seared through flesh and bone. Cuts that had been made by expert hands — not the jagged, animalistic carnage of Ferals.

The hunters.

The hunters who had sworn to protect these people, who had volunteered to escort them to safety. They had done this.

A surge of nausea hit him as the realization settled deep in his gut. Seraphine's deception hadn't ended with Mara. It had reached into the tunnels, into the hearts of those who were supposed to be their allies. And he had led these people to their deaths.

"No…" Dorian's voice cracked as he rose to his feet, his legs trembling. He stumbled toward the cave entrance, stepping over bodies—women, men, children, their faces twisted in terror, their eyes wide open, reflecting the last horrifying moments of their lives. His breath hitched in his throat, but he couldn't stop. He had to know.

Please… let there be survivors.

The cave loomed before him, the yawning entrance a black maw swallowing his hope. His hand gripped the steel lever of the elevator, pulling it with a ferocity that caused the mechanism to groan in protest. The platform jerked downward into the darkness, the walls of the tunnel closing in as the lift descended deeper into the colony. His pulse pounded in his ears, louder than the clanging of the elevator's gears.

When the platform finally stopped, Dorian stepped out— and yelled out in agony.

The devastation was absolute. The underground colony, once a sanctuary for those hidden away from The Council, was now a graveyard. Smoke hung heavy in the air, coiling around the remains of what had once been homes, communal spaces, and classrooms. Everything was scorched. Everything was in ruins.

Bodies lay everywhere, their lifeless forms strewn across the ground like discarded toys. Men, women, children—no one had been spared. The sight was more than he could bear. His vision blurred as tears filled his eyes, but no amount of blinking could wipe away the image of death that surrounded him.

"Seraphine... you did this," he whispered, his voice raw, trembling with grief and fury. The betrayal cut deeper than any blade.

This wasn't a battle. It wasn't even a massacre. It was annihilation. Systematic. Cold. Merciless.

Dorian's knees gave out, and he collapsed onto the ground, his fingers digging into the bloodstained earth. The grief hit him in waves, suffocating him with its weight. His mother's dream—her legacy—it was all gone. Erased by Seraphine's hatred.

He crawled forward, his body shaking uncontrollably. As he moved, he passed more corpses, each one a reminder of his failure, of the trust he had shattered. His heart ached with every breath. He should have been here. He should have protected them. But instead, he had been caught in Seraphine's web of deceit, blinded by his desire to stop the council.

And now... now they were all gone.

His hand brushed against something small, something fragile. Dorian looked down—and saw a little boy. No older than three. His tiny body lay crumpled on the ground, his skin pale, his eyes closed. In that moment, the world shattered.

"No… no, please…" Dorian whispered, his voice breaking as he reached out to cradle the child's lifeless form in his arms. The boy's body was cold, his small chest still. Tears streamed down Dorian's face, dripping onto the boy's cheek, but the child didn't stir. He was gone.

A scream ripped through Dorian's throat, raw and animalistic, filled with the pure agony of loss. The sound echoed through the cave, bouncing off the stone walls, but there was no one left to hear it. No one left to answer.

He held the boy close, his body shaking with sobs, his heart splintering into a thousand pieces. His fingers trembled as they gently brushed the boy's hair, the way his mother had once brushed his when he was a child.

This was the cost. The price of his existence. Seraphine's cruelty had stolen everything from him—everything from them all.

"Seraphine…" Dorian whispered, his voice now a low, dangerous growl. "I will kill you. I will tear you apart for this."

But the words felt hollow, lost in the emptiness that surrounded him.

He had failed. He had failed them all.

And there was nothing left but the bodies.

Chapter 29:

A Mother's Sin

The wind howled around the Heli carrier as it descended over the shimmering domed city of Armania, its sleek silhouette cutting through the night sky. Below, the city glistened like a jewel set against the endless expanse of black ocean, the curvature of the dome reflecting the scattered lights of buildings and streets. The waves of the sea crashed against the rocky coastline far beneath them, their rhythmic pounding a distant echo in Seraphine's ears. But it was the cold, biting wind that held her attention, whipping through her silver hair, stirring it like the spectral strands of a ghost.

Her eyes, pale and sharp, scanned the city below with a mix of cold satisfaction and seething disgust. Inside, her thoughts spiraled.

Weak. Too many are still weak and they all must be purged.

Her gaze flicked down toward the floor of the Heli carrier, where Mara lay, unconscious, bound in restraints. A sneer curled on Seraphine's lips, her thoughts darkening with each passing second.

Women like her are the reason Project Reset is necessary. Mara, with her conflicted loyalties, and her inner struggle to resist the pull of a man. Seraphine's sneer deepened. Still too weak to dispel a male's charm, too weak to stand with their sisters.

Even after two hundred years of ruling the world, women like Mara were still too blind, and too foolish to see the truth. Men were nothing more than a plague—a plague that had to be eradicated, completely and utterly.

As the Heli carrier touched down with a soft thud, Seraphine rose from her seat with the grace of a predator, her silver hair whipping in the wind one last time before she stepped out onto the landing platform. The air was salty, heavy with the scent of the ocean. The glowing dome above framed the night sky, casting a soft blue hue over the landing zone. Hunters stood at attention, waiting for her command.

"Take her," Seraphine ordered, her voice cold, detached, as she gestured toward Mara's unconscious form. "To the holding chamber. Secure her. She is not to escape."

The hunters moved swiftly, lifting Mara's limp body with ease and hauling her away into the heart of the city. Seraphine watched them for a moment, her eyes narrowing as they disappeared from sight. Then, with a deep breath, she smoothed the creases in her clothing, adjusting her high-collared coat as if preparing for an audience. Her hand lingered on the fabric, her expression softening in a way that felt alien after the day's carnage.

Her boots clicked softly on the polished floor as she approached a set of gilded doors, each emblazoned with the emblem of the council. Seraphine paused, her pulse quickening ever so slightly. She took another moment to compose herself, smoothing her hair, her expression hardening into an unreadable mask of calm authority. Then the doors opened.

Inside stood a beautiful woman, radiant in the soft glow of the chamber's golden lights. Her dark skin gleamed, her features sharp yet elegant, eyes that carried the weight of centuries of power and wisdom. She smiled as she saw Seraphine, a smile that lit up her entire face. Without hesitation, the two women rushed toward each other, their arms wrapping around one another as they embraced passionately. The kiss they shared was deep, hungry, and filled with the intensity of a long separation.

Seraphine held her close, inhaling her scent, feeling the comfort of her touch as though time itself had slipped away and nothing but the moment mattered.

"You're here," the woman murmured, her voice rich and soothing as she pulled back just enough to look into Seraphine's eyes. "You always find a way back to me."

Seraphine's lips curled into a genuine smile, a smile that no one else in the world would ever see. "I'll always find my way back to you."

The woman smiled as she caressed Seraphine's cheek with a tenderness that belied the monstrous truths they both held inside. She gestured toward the plush seating in her private quarters, where the soft glow of lamps created a serene contrast to the chaos unfolding beyond the dome.

"Sit," the woman said, her eyes gleaming with warmth. "Tell me, how is the world outside my little sanctuary? And the city?" She paused, her expression shifting to one of mild concern. "How many Ferals are loose?"

Seraphine sighed, leaning back into the luxurious chair as she gathered her thoughts. "Five million, maybe more by now. By the end of the week, it'll be closer to fifty million."

The woman's eyes widened slightly, though there was no fear in her gaze—only calculation. "Fifty million. That's faster than we anticipated."

"They're sweeping through the countryside," Seraphine continued. "Destroying colonies, tearing through cities. Just as planned."

The warmth in the woman's expression dimmed as she nodded. "And what of Dorian and Mara?"

Seraphine's smile faltered, a flicker of disgust crossing her face as she heard Dorian's name. She lowered her head slightly, feeling the tension coil in her chest.

"Mara… I have her. She's in the holding chamber, where she belongs." She paused, her voice thick with contempt. "Dorian, though, I couldn't bring him with me. He slipped through my fingers."

The woman's brow arched. "So, he's still alive?"

Seraphine's lips thinned, her distaste evident. "Yes, unfortunately. And worse… the virus is evolving inside him. He's becoming stronger. Faster. More violent. If we don't bring him and Mara together soon, he'll be too much for even the Council of Mothers to contain."

The woman's expression shifted—shock mixed with intrigue. "Is it truly that bad?"

"It's worse," Seraphine murmured, her voice dropping to a venomous whisper, each word steeped in her seething hatred for Dorian. "He's becoming something far more dangerous than we ever anticipated. If we wait too long, he could unravel everything."

She paused, her gaze dark and calculating. "The virus has changed him—rewired him. Every time he's injured, every time he fights, he adapts. He's growing stronger, faster, smarter, more resilient. It's as if the virus isn't just healing him—it's evolving him. If we don't act soon…"

Her voice turned icy, each syllable deliberate. "If we don't force him and Mara to mate, we'll lose our window. And if that happens, he may become unkillable—untouchable. He will destroy everything we've worked for."

For a moment, the woman was silent, processing the gravity of the situation. Then she leaned forward, her eyes gleaming with a sudden spark of excitement.

"You worry too much my love. Everything will work out as it has before. With their bond as strong as it is, I can assure you he will come to us. Willingly," she said, her voice firm and commanding. "Let him come. It's been far too long since I've laid eyes on my son."

Seraphine's breath caught in her throat at Kara's words. She stared at her, the implications sinking in. The corners of

Kara's lips curved into a slow, knowing smile, her eyes gleaming with something dark and possessive.

The room seemed to tighten with the weight of unspoken history.

Kara's gaze drifted to the window, watching the sea beyond the dome, as if seeing the world through a lens only she could comprehend. "It is time for us to claim what belongs to us, Seraphine. And it starts with him."

Seraphine nodded, her mind reeling as she bowed her head slightly. Her own thoughts tangled between loyalty and dread. Whatever the future held, she knew one thing for certain: the game had shifted.

And her part in it was far from over.

Epilogue:
The Rising Storm

The once impenetrable dome of New Lagos, now a smoldering ruin, lay in pieces beneath the blood-red horizon. A world teetering on the brink of collapse stretched beyond the crumbled skyline. In the distance, smoke billowed from Feral-infested cities, rising like the ghostly remnants of a nightmare made real. The carnage had spread. It was no longer confined to a single city. The Ferals—the twisted monstrosities that had once been the Council's instrument of control—had become an uncontrollable horde, consuming everything in their path.

They moved like a plague, sweeping across the land, devouring life with terrifying speed. Fifty million now, maybe more. The countryside was a wasteland, with every colony they encountered obliterated. Those who hadn't been killed had transformed, their bodies grotesquely altered by the virus that now consumed their very humanity.

From atop a craggy hill at the outskirts of what had once been New Lagos, Dorian stood, his chest rising and falling in slow, measured breaths, watching the Ferals mass like a dark tide. His jaw clenched with both anger and sorrow, his body still bearing the scars of the battle that had torn him apart on the rooftop of the Council Hall. He could still see Seraphine's cold, hateful eyes as she disappeared into the sky with Mara unconscious in the heli-carrier.

Mara. His thoughts spiraled as he tried to shake off the lingering bitterness. She was in their hands. Seraphine had won—at least for now. But it wasn't over. Not yet.

The survivors were few, scattered to the wind like ash. The hidden colony he'd once thought safe had been ravaged, its men, women, and children reduced to lifeless bodies amidst the wreckage. Seraphine's deception had run deeper than he'd ever imagined. She hadn't just planned to use Mara and him— she had unleashed the full horror of the Feral horde to wipe the slate clean.

Project Reset.

The world was unraveling faster than any of them could stop.

But Dorian wasn't done fighting.

The sharp clink of metal echoed in the quiet as he sheathed his blade, stained with the blood of hunters and Ferals alike. He could still hear the whispers of their dying breaths, the cries of the innocent slaughtered by Seraphine's madness. His heart ached with every passing second, the weight of it almost unbearable.

From behind him, a voice broke through the silence. "It's worse than I imagined."

Dorian turned to see Kalise, the general who had once fought against him. Now, she stood by his side, her face pale with grief, her body stiff with the realization of what they were up against. General Kalise, a warrior hardened by years of battle, showed cracks in her armor as she gazed out at the burning city. She had never seen anything like this.

"The Council is gone," she said, her voice thick with disbelief. "Everything we fought for… everything we built… it's all gone."

Dorian nodded, his gaze hard and unyielding as he watched the ever-growing horde. "We'll have to take the fight to them. We can't just hide anymore."

A sudden tremor rippled through the earth beneath their feet, shaking the ground as if the very world itself was groaning under the weight of the chaos. In the distance, the guttural roars of the Ferals rose, blending with the wind that whipped across the desolate landscape. They were moving—thousands upon thousands of them. Hungry. Relentless.

Dorian's eyes narrowed as he saw the horizon darken with their approach. They were spreading further, faster. Soon, there wouldn't be a place left untouched by the Ferals' destruction.

The general gripped his arm, her voice taut. "We need allies, male. We can't fight this alone."

He shook his head, his voice low, almost guttural.

"There's no one left."

"There are others," she insisted, her eyes burning with quiet fury. "Hidden colonies, scattered remnants of survivors. Not just women. Men. They've been hiding for years, and now they'll be hunted just like us. We can unite them."

Dorian's expression darkened, doubt flickering in his eyes. "Even if we find them… it won't be enough. Seraphine's army is endless."

"But we have something she doesn't," The general said, her voice hard with conviction. "We have the truth. The Council's lies are crumbling. If we expose them, if we show the world what the Council has done, we can turn the tide."

Dorian stared at her for a moment, his gaze searching. "And Mara?"

The general hesitated, her eyes softening for the briefest moment. "We'll get her back. But we need to be smart about it. We need time, and we need an army."

Dorian's fists clenched at his sides, a surge of frustration and anger flooding his veins. He wasn't one to wait. He wasn't one to hide. But The general was right. As much as he wanted to storm wherever they were holding Mara and tear Seraphine apart, it wasn't going to be that simple. They needed more than raw strength—they needed strategy.

"I know where to start," The general said, her voice a little softer now. "There's a colony to the south. I've heard whispers… survivors, fighters who've managed to hold their ground. If we can reach them, we might stand a chance."

Dorian nodded slowly, the resolve hardening in his chest.

"Then that's where we go."

Before either of them could speak again, the shrill cry of a Feral echoed through the air, followed by another—closer this time. They turned, eyes narrowing, as shadows flickered between the trees. The ferals were coming. The horde was moving toward them.

"We need to move," The general said, her voice steady despite the fear that gnawed at her gut.

Dorian nodded, his hand tightening around the hilt of his blade. His eyes flicked to the path ahead, then back to the forest. The few remaining hunters had already begun their journey, but if they were caught in the open, they wouldn't stand a chance.

"Go ahead," Dorian said, his voice firm, almost commanding. "I'll cover the rear. Make sure no one gets left behind."

The general hesitated, her gaze lingering on him. "Be careful, male."

With that, she turned and hurried down the path, disappearing into the shadowy expanse of the forest. Dorian watched her go, the weight of the world pressing down on his shoulders, his chest tightening as the reality of their situation sunk in.

They were running out of time.

The sound of branches snapping and Feral growls grew closer, pulling Dorian from his thoughts. His eyes narrowed as he drew his blade, the cold steel glinting in the dim light of the dying sun.

He wasn't afraid. Not anymore.

The time for fear was over.

As the first of the ferals broke through the trees, their twisted forms silhouetted against the blood-red sky, Dorian roared with fury, charging into the fray with the strength of a beast unleashed. His blade flashed in the dim light, slicing through flesh and bone with brutal precision. Each swing was fueled by rage, by the desperate need to protect the few lives that remained.

But even as he fought, his mind lingered on Seraphine, on Mara, on the betrayal that cut deeper than any wound. This was far from over.

The storm had just begun.

And he would be its reckoning.

To be continued...